I0746979

the summer we kept secrets

THE DESTIN DIARIES

HOPE HOLLOWAY
AND
CECELIA SCOTT

The Summer We Kept Secrets

The Destin Diaries Book 4

Hope Holloway & Cecelia Scott

Copyright © 2025 Hope Holloway

This novel is a work of fiction. Any references to historical events, real people, or real locales are used fictitiously. Other names, characters, places, and incidents are the product of the author's imagination, and any resemblance to actual events or locales or persons, living or dead, is coincidental. All rights to reproduction of this work are reserved. No part of this publication may be reproduced, stored in or introduced into a retrieval system, or transmitted, in any form, or by any means (electronic, mechanical, photocopying, recording, or otherwise) without prior written permission from the copyright owner. Thank you for respecting the copyright. For permission or information on foreign, audio, or other rights, contact the author, hopehollowayauthor@gmail.com.

The Destin Diaries

Chapter One

Eli

The day dawned warm and salt-kissed, the kind of summer morning Eli Lawson once took for granted—until he was reminded that God could sure throw a curve ball when it was least expected.

Still reeling from the shock of his son's—and grandson's—arrival, Eli stood barefoot on the back deck of the Summer House, a mug of coffee cooling in his hand. As far as the eye could see, the Gulf slowly transformed from teal to turquoise, the light turning Destin's sand the sugary white that made this stretch of Florida famous.

A pair of pelicans soared past, riding the breeze along the beach, soundless but for the whoosh of their wings.

Eli let the beauty of the world settle over him, his heart sliding into a comforting morning prayer. He'd obviously skipped church this Sunday morning, but the Lord was present. So, Eli asked for peace, for wisdom, for all the right things to happen to these two families who, as they had thirty years ago, shared a home on this beach.

But in the 1990s, they'd been teenagers and thought they were immortal and invincible and that life was simple.

He could hear God laughing and winding up the next pitch.

He sensed there were more surprises in store, challenges and some clouds. None of what he'd expected when he decided to spend some time at the Summer House, hoping to develop a deeper relationship with Kate Wylie, the woman he'd rediscovered a few months ago.

From the kitchen just inside the beach house, he could hear her soft laughter right now. Kate was chuckling with his sister, Vivien.

The two of them—women who hadn't had babies in their arms for many years—were elbows deep into ChatGPT trying to figure out how to sterilize bottles and safely warm formula.

Eli closed his eyes for a moment, trying to process it all. His son, Jonah, had arrived on their doorstep like a wounded animal seeking shelter. Clutching Atlas, his newborn baby, Jonah looked as broken, ravaged, and wrecked as Eli had ever seen him.

And he'd seen that boy pretty far gone a few times in his life.

In halting words, Jonah had explained that Carly, the baby's mother and his on again-off again girlfriend, had gone out for diapers and never come home. She'd been killed in a collision with a truck when she'd run a red light—a sleep-deprived nursing mother who, Jonah insisted, should not have been driving.

Eli could practically feel the incalculable guilt, grief, isolation, and panic that ricocheted through Jonah's almost thirty-year-old body. The kid had suffered more pain than most old men had endured in a lifetime.

Which was no doubt why Jonah kept repeating the same thing over and over.

I'm cursed. I'm cursed.

Eli could still hear Jonah's dark pronouncement. He understood the sentiment, no matter how much he profoundly disagreed with it. Eli's wife had died in a private plane crash, and the loss of his mother had destroyed teenaged Jonah. Now the mother of Jonah's son was tragically killed fifteen years later.

Eli well remembered the sense that Melissa's death was somehow his fault, or that he should have been the one taken so Jonah and Meredith had a mother. Nothing made sense in the early days, and he could all too easily imagine the depth of his son's pain.

No, Jonah and Carly hadn't been married, but they had a child—three-week-old Atlas. And that baby, Eli knew, would be the reason Jonah would recover.

But it would take time.

It would also take something else that Eli had found in those dark days—the solace and comfort of knowing the Lord. Jonah had no faith, sadly. But he'd have to find *something* to help him handle this new and complicated life. In the meantime, Eli would do whatever he could for Jonah.

"Hey, Grandpa."

He turned, unable to keep from smiling despite the heaviness in his heart. How could he not at the sight of

Kate Wylie? She was the first woman in fifteen years of solitude to make him feel something that had to be love.

She was such a source of comfort. A beautiful, bespectacled, logical, lovely source of comfort and joy.

"Grandpa," he scoffed. "Yep, I guess that's what they call me now." He lifted his arms in invitation. "Come join me, Lady Katie."

Smiling at the name, she walked to him, sliding into his embrace, giving him a gentle whiff of lavender and... baby formula? He wasn't sure, but he adored it, and her.

He kissed the top of her head. "Have you checked on him—on them?"

"Both asleep at the moment." She eased back and reached for his coffee cup. "Is this hot?"

"Lukewarm at best."

She took it anyway, sipping and wrinkling her nose as she pushed her glasses up and over her dark hair, fluttering her bangs.

"Yeah, awful. We made a fresh pot but somehow it didn't last five minutes. Tessa and Lacey filled up and started a 'baby shopping list' they're taking to Target the minute it opens. Vivien and I are driving Matt and Emma to the airport, then she wants to do some nursery shopping. Crib, changing table, the works."

He studied her, processing it all. "I forgot your kids are leaving today."

She tipped her head. "You've been a little preoccupied. And, God knows, we need the space, even in this oversized monster built by my favorite architect." She grinned and leaned in, giving that favorite architect a light kiss.

"We'll give the smaller of the two bedrooms downstairs to the baby, and Jonah can go in the other one right across the hall," she said. "So Floor One will be baby central. I'll move in with Tessa now."

He frowned, thinking through the logistics, very happy he had designed such a spacious house when his mother had given him the assignment to build on this property well over a year ago.

"My mom and Jo Ellen are moving into the apartment above the garage," he reminded her. "Why wouldn't you take the other room upstairs? Lacey and Vivien are glued to each other in the main suite, so that leaves an empty bedroom up there."

She shook her head. "I'd rather be with Tessa. We should keep that room ready in case someone else from your family shows up. Crista might come back, or Meredith."

"My daughter leave work? Not only would my firm collapse, I don't think Meredith Lawson knows the meaning of a vacation."

"Does she know Jonah is here with Atlas? And what happened to Carly?"

He nodded. "I called her late last night to fill her in."

"And?"

He made a face, remembering the call. "She seemed really distracted. Sympathetic, of course, but something was on her mind. Knowing Meredith, she was face down in blueprints, reveling in the fact that she passed the ARE test and is now a licensed architect. Nothing will get in my little overachiever's way, even family tragedy."

"So she won't come here?"

He lifted a shoulder. "Unlikely, but by now she's probably ordered a two-month supply of diapers and vetted five nanny services on our behalf."

She laughed. "She sounds like a force, and I can't wait to meet her. But tell her to hold off on the nannies, please. We have two great-grandmothers, multiple aunts, and you, Grandpa. We don't need outside help for Jonah."

He sighed at that, cupping her cheek and looking into her dark eyes. "I'm sad about something," he admitted softly.

"Being a grandfather at fifty-three?"

"Are you kidding?" he laughed. "I'm thrilled about that, just not about what poor Jonah has to endure. No, I'm sad about this summer. It's going to turn into one big...babysitting gig. And I had...plans. A few fantasies. Some very romantic ideas." He leaned down and kissed her lightly.

"Plans?"

"To make you fall madly in love with me."

"Halfway there," she whispered, then lifted her brows playfully. "And the fantasies and romantic ideas?"

"Oh, you know. Long walks on the beach. Some champagne sunsets. Don't make me belt out the 'Piña Colada' song. I know it's on Tessa's oldies playlist."

She laughed. "We can squeeze in a few walks and sunsets, I promise."

"We will, but this isn't going to be the summer interlude I hoped it would be." He sighed. "But God always has different plans than we do, and they're always bigger and better."

A shadow crossed over her face, as it often did when he talked openly about his faith. She never questioned it, but she never wanted to hear more, either.

Instead, she snuggled closer and wrapped an arm around his waist, and they stood quietly in the sweet hush of morning.

"It's good Jonah had somewhere to go," she finally said.

"Family," Eli said. "It was the only place to go. But the poor kid believes he's cursed."

"Ridiculous," she said. "Do you really think Carly's parents will try to take Atlas?"

"They could try," he said. "He shouldn't have up and left without telling them where he was going."

"He has every legal right to take his child," she said matter-of-factly. "He said Carly put Lawson as Atlas's last name on the birth certificate. They *were* going to get married."

Eli nodded. "Yes, but Carly's parents' concern and involvement is inevitable. We need to handle it in a way that respects and helps everyone, including that tiny baby."

She turned to face him fully. "And we have to prove that Atlas is indisputably Jonah's baby. He should do a DNA test and hire a good lawyer right away."

Eli hesitated, uncertain of that path just yet. "I'd

hope we can reach an understanding with the Danes family without involving lawyers or DNA testing. We should talk to them first. Make sure they know that Atlas will be loved and safe. Here, he'll have a large family, stability, a routine. Jonah will go to culinary school and can give that child a good, loving home."

"Yes to all that, but we need the science and law on our side, too. Love isn't enough."

"It can be," he said, "if they're reasonable."

"Their daughter was killed three weeks after giving birth to their grandchild. Do you think they're thinking reasonably?" she challenged. "We may need to fight with everything we have."

While he loved the use of the corporate "we" in this regard, he wasn't a fan of fighting. "Well, a stable, loving family is definitely part of our arsenal. That's what Atlas —and Jonah—need the most. Routine. Stability. Faith."

Kate gave him a look, one he knew well—practical, skeptical, wildly logical. "And DNA tests along with a shark of a lawyer."

He met her gaze with one just as direct. "I assure you, I'll do whatever is necessary for Jonah to keep his son."

She nodded and eased back. "I have to get the kids off to the airport with Vivien. When Tessa and Lacey leave, you're on your own with two nearly eighty-year-old women, an infant, and one very shaky young man. Can you handle it?"

He just smiled. "What do you think?"

"I think..." She stood on her tiptoes and stole a kiss, her glasses plopping down on her nose when she backed up. "That you're the best-looking grandfather I've ever known."

He eased the glasses up to her eyes. "Long walks on the beach at sunset could be in your future, gorgeous."

"Mom! We have to leave soon!"

At the sound of her daughter's voice, Kate slipped out of his arms. "I have to go," she whispered.

Eli followed her into the house, reluctantly letting the intimate exchange come to an end.

There would be more loving moments this summer with Kate, he knew. Just not as many as he'd hoped.

AFTER SAYING goodbye to Matt and Emma, Eli armed himself with a fresh cup of coffee made the way Jonah liked it, and a bottle Vivien had prepared, then headed down to the lowest level of the three-story beach house.

When he'd designed what they called the Summer House, this was supposed to be where a family would congregate in a great room, flanked by two bedrooms, and a large bath, all leading out to the pool and boardwalk to the beach.

But now, it would be...what had Kate called it? Baby Central, reserved for Jonah and Atlas. Maybe he could add a small kitchen down here and they could really make it a home. There was certainly enough space and...

His thoughts trailed off as he reached the bottom of the stairs and heard...was that Jonah singing?

"You are my sunshine...my ray of sunshine. Those aren't the words, but you get the point..."

Smiling at the butchered lyrics and the love behind it, he walked into Jonah's room to find him lying on the bed with a tiny bundle next to him, so small he couldn't see a baby in the blankets.

"I bring baby breakfast and dad coffee," Eli said softly, interrupting the singing.

"Now that's a ray of sunshine," Jonah replied, very slowly rising, holding one hand on the baby. "Can I get up? I don't want him to roll off the bed."

"Pretty sure he can't roll," Eli said as he put the coffee cup on the nightstand. "Can I feed him?"

"Oh, yeah. Please do." Jonah blinked groggily, looking a thousand times better than he had when he'd arrived. "I slept for the first time in a month. I know this little guy didn't make it through the night."

"He did okay," Eli said, tipping his head toward the great room. "I took the sofa out there and did the midnight and two o'clock. Aunt Vivien came down and we switched places; she got him at five. And then he slept. Now, you come to your grandpa, little man."

"We can't keep up that schedule," Jonah said.

"We'll get a baby monitor and rotate a schedule." Eli gingerly lifted the tiny baby who was starting to feel familiar. "Remember me?"

Atlas opened his mouth and cried softly as Eli settled him in his arms, then mewed and turned his little bald head, making sucking sounds.

"He's rooting," Jonah said. "That's what they call looking for mom's breast."

Sitting on the bed, Eli nestled him closer and eased the bottle's nipple to Atlas's lips.

"Sorry, young man. This will have to do." Instinct took over, making Eli brush his fingertip along Atlas's cheek, somehow knowing—remembering—that it would make him suckle.

"He hadn't been doing so well breastfeeding anyway," Jonah said, dropping into the room's only chair with his coffee. "We'd started giving him some formula to augment." He took a sip and dropped his head back with a grunt of satisfaction as it hit. "Dad, thank you seems... basic. But let me say it anyway."

"For the night feedings?" Eli looked up from the tiny face. "It was fun."

"For taking me in." Jonah smiled for the first time in— well, maybe since he got there. "Both of us, really. Tough days ahead."

"There's an army of people who want to help," Eli said. "Please let us."

The smile grew. "There are more people in this house than when I left. And furniture down here—it was nothing but an air mattress when I was a resident."

"Jo Ellen was down here for a while, so Vivien furnished the room for her. But now she and Maggie are moving into the apartment you and I built over the garage. It's finished."

Jonah nodded, his sleepy eyes clearing with each ounce of caffeine. "Yeah, I picked up through the chatter that they're pals again. Artie wasn't the devil incarnate after all?"

Eli laughed softly, and as he got into the bottle groove with Atlas, he relayed the whole story that they'd learned just the day before.

"So your dad and Uncle Artie basically took down a Southern mob to protect their families?" Jonah asked when Eli finished.

"Pretty much. And that was why my mother and her best friend were separated for thirty years, so the two of them have a lot to catch up on. Now that they know the truth, they're just like they used to be—two peas in a pod."

"Moving into the apartment we built," Jonah mused. "Cute. I'm happy for Grandma Maggie. I know she can be difficult, but, man, did you see how she rose to the occasion last night? So protective."

"We all are," Eli said, snuggling his grandson. Now, he understood how and why his notoriously formidable mother turned a little mushy when it came to any of her grandchildren. "No one's taking this baby," he said.

Jonah snorted, the sound pure doubt.

"We won't let that happen, son," Eli said simply.

"Oh, it'll happen. Remember, I'm curs—"

"Stop it," Eli said, his sharp tone making the tiny baby startle. "Sorry," he whispered to Atlas. "But your father is wrong on so many levels, it hurts. He is *not* cursed."

Jonah finished the coffee, then put the cup down, closing his eyes.

"If not, then why did this happen, Dad? Why did she have to go get diapers when she was so tired? I told her if she'd give me just half an hour to finish making dinner—of course I put cooking above her needs, because I'm a fat jerk like that—but she insisted we only had one left in the apartment, and she wanted to get out. I knew she was exhausted. I knew I should have gone. I knew...things happen to mothers."

"Jonah." Eli's voice was stern, but not sharp this time. "You cannot blame yourself any more than I could blame myself for allowing your mom to get on a private plane."

Jonah winced. "She got on the plane for her *job*."

"It was Carly's job to get diapers—a parent's job. Bad things happen."

"I thought you believed in God and He's supposed to be so stinkin' good."

"He *is* good," Eli insisted. "But that doesn't mean bad things won't happen. It means that the bad thing should be the time when you lean on Him and get closer to Him."

Jonah rolled his eyes. "Whatever. The bottom line is I'm the dad and I should have gotten diapers and if I had, Atlas would have two parents."

Eli let out a sigh. "Grief tells lies, Jonah. Don't listen."

For a long time, neither of them spoke. Instead, Eli let little Atlas finish the bottle and pulled it out of his mouth, easing him up to rub his back for a burp.

"You're pretty good at that, old man," Jonah said softly.

"I'm not old and I had two kids." Atlas bubbled up a

little and out came...spit-up on Eli's T-shirt. "Whoa. Thanks, buddy."

"Bet Meredith never did that," Jonah teased. "Miss Perfect probably never spit up in her life. And if she did, she took your shirt and did the laundry." He blew out a breath. "Speaking of my flawless, disciplined, and successful sibling—does she know?"

Eli nodded, not wanting to push back on the low-key antagonism that Jonah always felt toward his younger sister. "I called her last night, and she is very worried. She loves you more than you can imagine."

Jonah looked suitably chastised. "Well, she's safe in the knowledge that she's still the architect superstar kid who never went astray, while I am the unemployed, cursed single father."

Eli's eyes shuttered. "Please don't say that, Jonah. You're about to start a fantastic culinary program and you are *not* cursed. You're just scared."

"Ya think?" Jonah choked. "Petrified is more like it. I'm terrified of Carly's parents and I'm sure I don't have a clue how to *raise a child*. And don't get me started on culinary school. How can I do all this, Dad? Maybe I should let them take Atlas."

Eli tightened his grip on the tiny body in his hands, the very words unthinkable to him. "First of all, no one knows how to raise a child. It's hit or miss, mistake after mistake, followed by failure and sleepless nights."

"Sounds fun."

"Actually, it is the most fun you'll ever have," Eli replied. "Second, they're Atlas's grandparents. I have no doubt they want what's best for him, and that is you, his father."

"Dad, I'm—"

"And *third*," he powered on, refusing to let Jonah argue with that, "you'll go to culinary school as planned. A million parents have gotten degrees and not very many of them had a house full of family all willing and able to help with the baby."

The speech made Jonah sink into the chair a little. "Yeah," he begrudgingly agreed. "I just wish I knew more than one song, but that *Sunshine* thing is all I remember Mom singing to me."

That made Eli smile. "You'll learn songs and tricks and patience and everything you need to know. We're here for you, every minute."

"I guess," he said. "But Carly's parents—"

"Are *not* taking this child," Eli insisted, punctuating that with a kiss on the baby's head, then looked up. "What are they like, anyway? What are we dealing with?"

"I don't know them that well," he admitted. "They live in Northern California. Carly has a sister, too, but she wasn't that close to her."

"You've met them all, I take it?"

He nodded, looking straight ahead, as though remembering. "They came to see us for a couple days after Atlas was born," he said. "It was cool, I guess. We were fine. I mean, they probably didn't think I was some kind of catch, but they thought culinary school was interesting. Then..." His voice faded and his whole expression changed...and crumbled.

"I assume they came again after the accident," Eli said gently.

He managed a nod. "It was so sad, man. Obviously, they were out of their minds with grief. The sister, her name's Rori, came, too. They all wanted to pack up Atlas and take him."

Eli sucked in a breath. "Three on one? How did you manage to not let them?"

"I told them I would call the cops. There was...kind of a scene. It was bad." His voice cracked.

"I'm sorry, Jonah."

He swallowed and dug for composure. "Anyway, they finally left and said they'd be back with a lawyer and court orders and blah blah *blah*. The minute they were gone, I packed what I could, and hightailed it to the airport, and here I am. The runaway unemployed father who kidnapped their grandchild."

Eli made a face, realizing it was a truly bad situation. "You didn't kidnap him. He's your son. They've never questioned *that*, have they?"

"No, no. Carly and I were solid before she got pregnant, and for most of her pregnancy. I was here for a couple of months when she booted me out because I didn't have a job." He gave a humorless smile. "That was the last problem of mine you solved. Do you sense a pattern here?"

"I sense parenthood," he said simply. "Parents help their kids out of binds no matter their age or how bad the bind. Have you called them to tell them Atlas is safe and sound?"

"I texted Rori and told her I took the baby to my family and he was fine. She never answered, but she saw the text."

"Can you reach her parents? What are their names?"

"Gary and Sally Danes," he said. "Gary's a tech dude with some computer company. Sally...I don't know. Investments? Law? Something lofty. But, yeah, I have all the phone numbers." He made a face. "The cops brought me Carly's phone after the accident, and I kept it. Was that wrong?"

"It was smart," Eli said. "Was Carly close to her family?"

He shrugged. "On and off. Her mom wanted her to get an advanced degree—I think she has one—but Carly wanted to stick with hospitality. Honestly? She might have talked to her mother more when she was pregnant and after I left."

"Are they nice people?" Eli asked. "I mean, could they be reasonable?"

"They're...grieving people," he said. "Broken, destroyed, and all they have left of their daughter is in your arms."

Eli's heart dropped. What would he do in that situation? Fight like a madman to raise this child. But Atlas belonged to Jonah, and they couldn't take that away.

Eli looked down at the sweet baby who was...red and filling his pants.

"Sure gave him the right name," Jonah said, pushing up. "He's got the weight of the world on his shoulders."

"Actually, it's in his diaper."

Jonah managed a laugh as he lifted the bag next to the dresser. "Here, I got it."

Eli stood and carefully handed the baby to his son. As he did, their gazes locked.

"You can do this, Jonah."

"The diaper change? I'm a pro now."

"Fatherhood," he clarified. "You can do it and do it well. You are not cursed. You are blessed."

Jonah just smiled, enough doubt in his eyes that Eli knew his words fell on deaf ears. It would take time.

The question was...did they have time before Carly's family swooped in and attempted to take this child?

Chapter Two
Meredith

ow? How in the name of all that was holy had she, Meredith Elena Lawson—the single most disciplined, organized, efficient, goal-oriented, five-year planner with no room for the slightest detour—*let this happen?*

Well, she knew *how* it happened, but didn't it happen to...*other* girls? Apparently, it could happen to smart ones, too.

Because she was looking at a faint, barely visible, but undeniable line that might as well spell out *you blew it, baby.*

Emphasis on *baby.*

She stared down at the pregnancy test in her hand—the fourth one she'd taken—as if sheer willpower could change the result, the stick quivering with every tremble in her body.

Very slowly, she lifted her gaze from the sink to the bathroom mirror, staring at her reflection, wishing someone else's face would appear.

Someone...dumb. Someone...foolish. Someone who made really absurd decisions and fell into bed with a man who was super hot and super temporary and all wrong except for that one moment when he was just right.

But no, it was her. Meredith.

"Who *are* you?" she whispered to the green eyes that looked back at her. "And what did you do?"

One arched brow rose in judgment as a random dark wave nearly fell out of the claw clip that held her hair off her neck and shoulders.

The expression reminded her of Grandma Maggie, the queen of the raised brow. And at the thought of the judgmental and opinionated woman who'd always had a soft heart for Meredith, tears sprang forward.

Maggie would be devastated by this.

And Dad?

She gulped, not really able to think about her father. Poor guy. He was currently up to his eyeballs taking care of the hot mess that was Jonah, the problem child. To Eli, she was the kid who had it all together—the conquering 4.6 magna cum laude superstar who'd just passed her boards and was ready to carry Acacia Architecture into the next generation.

She was also...*pregnant.*

With a groan, she dropped onto the closed toilet lid, looking around the pristine bathroom of her Buckhead apartment.

What was she going to do?

Absently, she clutched at the bathrobe that gaped open, glancing down at her tender breasts.

Their unexpected soreness had been her first sign that something wasn't right. She'd checked the calendar, realized she was late, then looked back on the brief and lopsided "relationship" she'd had this past spring.

Oh, Trevor Whitlock hated protection, and he *had* persuaded her to skip it once. Could it be that easy? She had at least three girlfriends who were "trying" and taking ovulation tests daily. And she...

Yeah, always the overachiever, that was Meredith Lawson.

Just after taking the first test last night—she was sure it had to be wrong—her father had called with the devastating news that Jonah's girlfriend had been killed.

After a sleepless and truly miserable night, she'd gone out at dawn, bought three more tests and now it could no longer be denied: the life she'd spent almost three decades meticulously building had just crumbled under the weight of this thin pink line.

And the only person who could help her was up to his eyeballs with his *other* dumb kid.

Closing her eyes, she stood and walked into the closet next to the bathroom, in a trance, unable to stop thinking about Dad.

Her dear, kind, deeply religious rock of a father who had raised her, loved her, trained her as an architect, and been both parents to her for fifteen years. Her closest confidante, her mentor, her hero.

What would Eli Lawson say when he found out?

She grunted and nearly folded to the hardwood floor. This would break him.

She took a few more breaths and tried to calm down,

staring at the color-coded clothes, arranged by season, then fabric, then sleeve length.

Was this the closet of a person who has a really questionable relationship with a guy who told her from Day One that he wouldn't be in town for long? Just a few months, Trevor had said. Then it's off to the next Beans & Buns franchise he was buying, courtesy of what she imagined were rich parents.

She didn't think Trevor was smart enough to build a business alone. He was certainly good-looking enough to catch her eye, though.

And his temporary situation was perfect, she'd decided on their first date. Meredith didn't want to get married, but she needed...other stuff. She needed an escape from the pressure of her architecture boards, a distraction from work, a little pleasure in a life that had nearly none.

All such sorry excuses.

"Dumb," she muttered as she grabbed a pair of jeans and a T-shirt to run an errand she so did not want to run. But she *had* to tell Trevor. And on a Sunday morning, she knew where to find the tall, charming, effortlessly sexy thirty-five-year-old entrepreneur.

And it sure wasn't church.

She had to tell him. She didn't want to tell him—she didn't really want to ever see him again, which was why she'd been strategically avoiding the coffee shop on the lobby level of her office building.

And now, what started as a casual hang after work, then a drink, then making out to the point of dizziness had led to...a painstakingly planned life brought to a screeching halt.

She stuffed her feet into sneakers and glanced at the clock. It was nearly nine, which was the worst possible time to try and talk to a man who owned a coffee shop, but telling him had to be her very first move.

The ten-minute walk through Buckhead to her office building didn't clear her head as she'd hoped it would.

Normally, the urban stroll made her feel invigorated for the day ahead, and so grateful to live and work in one of Atlanta's most upscale neighborhoods.

Today, it felt like she was walking through mud and about to fall into molasses, each step heavier than the one before, her thoughts much louder and more distracting than any traffic on Peachtree.

She often came in on a Sunday—what self-respecting workaholic wouldn't?—and knew that Beans & Buns was open and busy, with the franchise owner frequently working the front of the shop himself.

But today, as she rounded the atrium level to get to the street entrance, she didn't see his casual smile or tousled chestnut hair at the coffee bar. Inside, she took a whiff of espresso and fresh cinnamon rolls, the very smell of the stuff making her stomach roll.

Or maybe that was the conversation she was about to have.

She stepped up to the counter, where a barista she recognized was making up an order. The young woman looked up with a wide smile.

"Hi, Meredith. I haven't seen you in a while. Don't

tell me." She pointed. "Medium iced oat milk brown sugar shaken espresso?"

Meredith sighed, knowing her favorite drink wouldn't go down well. "Actually, I just need to see Trevor. Is he in?"

"Oh, yeah," the girl said. "He's in the back doing paperwork."

"Can you get him? I'd like to talk to him for a minute."

The barista nodded, finished her order, then disappeared into the back.

Meredith's heart thumped in her ears. She suddenly felt warm and exposed and vulnerable. Her gaze scanned the lobby, grateful she wasn't likely to run into anyone from Acacia Architecture on a Sunday.

Trevor appeared a moment later, wearing a backwards hat and his usual Beans & Buns shirt. Coming out from behind the bar, he gave her a surprised flicker of a look, which she'd expected.

They'd mutually decided their short relationship was going nowhere. His entrepreneurial spirit had attracted her and seemed like a great fit. Well, his looks and easy-breezy sex appeal had really attracted her, but it didn't take long for her to spot that he was cagey. Distant. Even secretive.

They'd gone out for about a month, but he refused to answer enough questions that she'd broken it off and got no pushback from him.

She knew it was a mistake to get involved with him. But her close girlfriends were married and moving into the next phase of life, and all Meredith had ever done was work.

She should have stuck with that strategy, she thought glumly.

Go off plan...and get knocked up.

"Hey, Mer," he said, giving her a quick once-over, probably because she never showed up in this building looking less than impeccable. "What's up? I'm kinda slammed."

"I'm sure you are," she said. "But I need to talk to you. Privately."

He raised an eyebrow, but nodded. "Okay. Outside?"

They stepped into the warm morning air, finding an empty table tucked next to a wall of hedges. A breeze rustled the shrubbery as Meredith sat, running damp palms over her jeans.

He perched on the other chair, looking like he might bolt at any second. "What's going on?" he asked.

She met his gaze, clearing her throat. "I have to tell you something."

Trevor's face paled in a way that was more guilty than worried. He always had that furtiveness about him, which she really didn't like.

"What? What is it?"

She swallowed what felt like a gulp of sand and stared down at the table, then back up at him. "I'm pregnant."

He blinked, the slight bit of color remaining in his face completely gone, his jaw slack. "Wait...what? Are you serious right now? Is this some kind of joke?"

She considered a sarcastic "just kidding" response, but he didn't deserve humor. He deserved to be smacked for pushing her to have unprotected sex because he liked it that way.

"It's not a joke and, trust me, it's not funny."

He cursed under his breath, looking unsteady. "Wait, are you sure? I mean—how, Meredith?"

She sliced him with a look. He knew exactly how it had happened.

He pushed back, then whipped off his baseball cap to stab his hair with shaky fingers. "Whoa. This is really, really bad. I...can't..."

Did he think she *could*? What did that mean? "Look, I don't know what I'm going to do, but I had to tell you first, so—"

"I don't care what you do."

She blinked at him, startled by the response. "You don't..."

"No, I don't. I don't know if it's mine."

She clenched her jaw, regret and shame rolling over her like tidal waves over the fact that she'd slept with a man who cared for her so little. What had she been thinking?

"Well, it is yours," she ground out. "And all I'm doing in this conversation is informing you—"

"It's your problem, Meredith," he spat back. "And you cannot tell anyone..."

As his voice faded out, she inched closer, not comprehending this despicable reaction.

"You're really saying that to me right now, Trevor? Are you serious?"

"I don't want a baby," he said. "And I don't want this turning into some huge thing. Look, do what you want, but leave me out of it. I need to be as far away from this as possible."

"What is *wrong* with you?" she hissed, her whole body clenching. "You don't even care? You're not even going to ask if I'm okay?"

He flinched. Then his jaw tensed. "Because I *can't* care."

"Why not?" she snapped back, pain and anger rising in her throat.

He looked at her plainly, dark eyes flashing as he swore under his breath.

"Trevor?" she pressed.

"I'm married."

The words hit like a punch to the stomach, stealing any breath and sanity she had left. "You're..." she drew in a ragged breath. "*What?*"

"I have a wife," he said, eyes darting around. "In Chicago."

She stared at him, mouth open. She slammed it closed as bile rose. "Tell me you're lying."

"I'm not."

She gripped the metal armrests. "You have a *wife?*"

He looked away. "Yes. And her family..." He glanced over his shoulder at the coffee shop.

"Funds your franchise," she guessed, puzzle pieces

suddenly falling into place. It wasn't his family money that kept his business growing. It was his *wife's*.

Meredith tried to breathe, but it felt like her lungs weren't working. Nothing was working—her brain was locked, her heart was cracking, and she was definitely on the verge of throwing up.

"I can't believe this," she managed to say. "You just *lied?* You told me you were single. You told me you bounced around different cities and could never commit to anyone because you were opening new shops and—"

"I didn't mean for this to happen," he said quickly. "It wasn't serious. It was just—it just got away from me, okay? And if you need anything—like money or—"

"Stop." She tried to swallow, but nausea choked her. "You've degraded me enough. I don't need anything except assurance that you'll stay out of my life and as far away from me as humanly possible."

"I'm, uh, actually out of here at the end of the week. Next store is in Portland and that's going to be a bear."

So was this pregnancy, but it was obvious he didn't care.

"Well, good luck with that." She stood, and he got to his feet, too.

"Meredith," he murmured. "You cannot bring my name into this. I'll give you what you need, but no paperwork, no tests, nothing. Ever. I'm out."

She flattened him with the most vile look she could muster, grabbed her purse, and took off.

She couldn't get home fast enough, where she fell on the sofa and wept.

SHE WASN'T sure how long she slept, but when Meredith opened her eyes an hour or so after collapsing there, she knew her crappy day wasn't over yet.

Her whole life, she'd trained herself to get the most annoying or difficult tasks out of the way first. She'd never understood the appeal of procrastination…until now.

She couldn't put this off any longer. She'd never made any major—or minor—decision in her life without consulting Eli Lawson. She'd probably talked to her mother a lot, too, but her memories of that woman grew dimmer every year.

She'd been thirteen when beautiful Mommy died, and sometimes she barely recalled much of life before the plane crash. Meredith remembered snippets, moments, snapshots of time, but mostly it was a blur.

Only one thing remained clear, calm, and stable—her father. From the day her mother passed away until this very minute, Meredith had leaned on Dad's strong and steady shoulders, and he'd never let her down.

"Oh, Dad. I wish I could say it went both ways." Because she was about to let him down, and hard.

It wasn't that he'd get mad—the man didn't have a temper. He'd be hurt and so deeply disappointed. He'd pray and beg her to do the right thing and never make her feel like the failure she was—which would only make it harder.

With a grunt, she fished out her phone, tapping Dad's name. That brought up a profile picture of him beaming at her on the day she graduated from college, so proud of his little girl.

The very same one who was about to break his heart.

Without giving herself time to think, she pressed the call button and speaker, taking a steadying breath as it rang two, then three times. *Please no voicemail. Please no—*

"Did you call to gloat?"

She drew back from the phone, the words and voice making no sense for a moment. "Jonah?"

"In the flesh," he said. "Dad's on baby duty, and he left his phone on the sofa."

Baby duty. The words pressed on her chest. "Well, that's fine. I want to talk to you. I'm so sorry, Jonah. I can't believe what happened."

He didn't answer, the silence stretching between them.

"Are you okay?" she ventured.

"I'm figuring it out," he said, as vague as Jonah always was with her.

It was maddening, to be honest. Before Mom died, she remembered being close to him—well, as close as a brother and sister born seventeen months apart could be when they were pre-teens and teenagers.

But they were cool—they played video games and watched movies and did hours of studying at the kitchen table, just two years apart in school.

After Mom died? No one was close to Jonah. No one.

"How's Atlas?" she asked, uncertain of where to take this unexpected conversation.

"He's...twenty-three days old." His voice cracked and it did something unthinkable to her heart. "And I don't know what the hell I'm gonna do."

At the sound of a strangled sob, she put her hand to her mouth so she didn't cry with him.

"Oh, Jonah. I'm so, so sorry. This is awful. But you have family."

"He's an orphan, Mer," he said gruffly. "Just like we were."

"We weren't orphans," she corrected. "We had Dad. And Atlas has you."

"For whatever that's worth," he said glumly, sounding completely different than the last time she'd talked to him, the day after Atlas was born. He'd been so upbeat and funny, ready to go back to Destin to get his culinary arts degree, then be a good father to his new baby.

He said Carly had been fierce during labor, and he loved her and believed they'd get married.

"It's worth a lot," she said, trying to reassure him. When he didn't answer, she rooted around for more information. "What does Dad say?"

"He says...we're going to do whatever we can to keep the baby, but I know Carly's parents want to raise him."

"No!" She was a little surprised at her vehement reaction, but it was genuine and sharp. "He's your son, Jonah."

"Yeah, I know. Dad seems to think we'll just tell them we want the baby and that'll be all it takes. He's, you know...praying."

She fought a smile at the thought. Her father was

alone in his deep faith, but it was one of a million things she loved about him. And another reason her news would gut him. And on top of a custody battle?

"Do you want me to have Dad call you?" Jonah asked. "Or give him a message?"

Not this message. It certainly wasn't something she wanted Jonah to tell him—in fact, she didn't want to drop this bomb over the phone.

Sitting up a little straighter, she stared ahead, her brain whirring through the open projects and client issues at Acacia Architecture. Did she have to handle all of them in person?

They had the world's most efficient office manager and several of the architects worked remotely. Dad was spending the summer in Destin—couldn't she? Suddenly, Meredith wanted that more than anything.

She needed family. She needed Dad. And from the sounds of it?

"You need me, Jonah," she whispered.

He snorted. "To come and wrap us all in spreadsheets and a to-do list?"

She ignored his sarcasm, forcing herself back a decade and a half, to a den where two kids played *Rock Band,* singing and laughing until they hurt. Everything about the Lawson family was different back then, and right this minute?

Meredith just wanted to capture that security and happiness and sense of home. She needed it more than she needed anything. And she could tell Dad her news in person.

That was so much better.

"Is there a place for me to sleep?" she asked.

He didn't answer and she braced herself for his rebuff, a snarky comment about how she didn't sleep because she was so busy conquering the world. And then she'd tell him how badly the world had beaten her up today.

"Yeah," he said, his voice gruff.

"Really?" She was more surprised by his response than the fact that the crowded house had room for her.

"I'd love you to be here, Mer."

She nearly folded in half. "Then I'm on my way, big brother."

June 12, 1992

We're officially BACK at the beach! It's been so much fun in the two weeks since we got here that I totally forgot to start a new notebook for this year. And let me tell you, this year I am THRIVING.

Well, sort of. Emotionally, yes. Spiritually, absolutely. Hygienically? TBD.

Because let me tell you what's NOT thriving: the main bathroom that is "just for the kids." Except...there are six of us, and that includes three fifteen-year-old girls (I'm one by the way) and two eighteen-year-old boys (I don't even want to know what they do in a bathroom). And of course, Crista, who's nine but still has to <u>bathe</u> like Cleopatra.

Six kids. One bathroom. One shower/tub combo. No rules. No boundaries. And one sad showerhead that dribbles instead of sprays, and exactly three inches of counter space.

This morning I had shampoo in my hair and one leg halfway shaved when the hot water cut out. Gone. Just ICE. I screamed so loud Eli knocked on the door and asked if I slipped and died.

Kate's already devised a sign-up sheet (which Tessa promptly ignored), and Eli thinks it's funny to say he's "training for the Navy" by taking cold showers, but really he just wants the bathroom first so he can hog the mirror and "perfect his hair swoop." Boys.

Tessa, though. TESSA. I love that girl to death, but she thinks every shower is full-blown beauty pageant prep that takes forty-five minutes. This morning she played Whitney Houston three times in a row on her waterproof cassette player and came out wearing a robe like she was getting ready to go on a talk show.

When I told her that FIVE of us use the bathroom, I got a hair flip and a reminder that beauty takes time.

Rude.

ANYWAY. Besides the bathroom horror, everything is amazing. The ocean is the perfect, Jo Ellen stocked the freezer with bomb pops (bless), and Peter carried my suitcase into the house without me even asking. I know, I know—he's probably just being nice. But also...maybe not??? I'm watching closely.

He and Eli found their "friends"—other eighteen-year-old big boys like Dustin "the Boogie Board Destroyer" Mathers. That kid got tall, but he's still a menace. My mom calls him a "wild child" and for once I actually agree with her.

He came over with Peter and Eli after their fishing thing last night and we made s'mores. He caught all his marshmallows on fire, which of course incited Tessa to swirl them around and do a fire dance. It was equal parts hilarious and terrifying, but also surprising because Dustin totally ignores her. Maybe he's blind.

So yeah. Summer is on.

Tessa just went back into the bathroom, so I have to sit outside the door for forty minutes to keep my place in line.

Love always,

Vivien

P.S. Peter called me "early bird" this morning because I was the first one up. It wasn't really a compliment. But still. Yeah, he's cuter than ever and ye olde crushe hasn't worn off, sadly.

Chapter Three
Tessa

"Whatcha reading?" Tessa stuck her head into the main bedroom, looking for Lacey but seeing Vivien on the king-sized bed, a notebook on her lap.

"If I told you, I'd never hear the end of it," Vivien said, closing the notebook and letting it fall on the floor next to her with a glimmer of guilt in her eye. "Come on in. I assume you're looking for your star employee. She's in the shower. She's got a date with Roman." Vivien added a grin. "Your son."

Tessa slowed her step, the words hitting deep. She was still getting used to the discovery that Roman Matteo wasn't merely a great-looking NFL wide receiver who'd stolen Lacey's heart—he was the baby boy she'd given up for adoption twenty-five years ago.

But his arrival did more than add a new person in her life to love. The secret Tessa had kept to herself for all those years was out now, and had somehow unlocked a stirring in her heart she didn't recognize or understand.

The sensation was real and made her restless, prowling around the house trying to nest in a place that really wasn't home.

"Come. Sit." Vivien waved her into the room. "Don't look too closely since I haven't finished this room or several others. I have another design client, and we've officially turned into the shoemaker's children."

Tessa came all the way in and headed for the only chair, plucking one of Lacey's tops off the seat before she got comfy. "Honestly, you two should have your own rooms."

Vivien laughed and gave a vague gesture toward the notebook she'd dropped. "Hey, it's Summer House rules—no matter how big Eli built this house, we still have a crowd. Every time Lacey's about to move into the spare room down the hall, we get another person. Meredith's coming, have you heard?"

"I did hear that from your mother, who is quite excited," Tessa said, tucking her feet under her to settle in for a chat. "It's very clear that Maggie's kryptonite is—*are*—her grandchildren. Did you see her rocking Atlas like he was the Second Coming?"

Vivien laughed softly. "My mother does seem happy, doesn't she? So rare."

Reconnecting with her lifelong best friend, finally understanding what happened in the past, and meeting her first great-grandchild all seemed to work like a charm on the usually formidable Maggie Lawson.

"So Roman's leaving this week, huh?" Tessa asked, glancing toward the closed bathroom door as the shower stopped and some humming started up.

Vivien nodded. "He has meetings with his agent and

coach in Jacksonville and then..." She made a face. "Has Lacey talked to you yet?"

"Talked to me about what?"

"Time off," Vivien whispered. "Roman's asked her to drive over later this week, spend some time in Jacksonville, then go down to meet his parents."

Tessa lifted her brows. "Goodness. Things are progressing. Of course she can have time off. We have two events this month and she's done all the legwork to get them ready. I love that he wants her to meet Faith and Bob." She smiled. "I'd like to someday, too."

"I'm sure you will, and they will thank you to the stars for giving them that amazing man."

"And I'll thank them right back for raising him so well when we meet at the rehearsal dinner."

"I can hear you two!" Lacey called from the other side of the bathroom door, making them both crack up. "Every word."

"Dry your hair so you can't eavesdrop!" Tessa exclaimed. "Or else I won't give you time off to go be an NFL girlfriend!"

They shared a look as the hair dryer started.

Vivien dropped back on the bed with a wistful smile. "That sound reminds me of what I was just reading." She reached down and picked up the notebook. "A Destin diary, this one when we were fifteen."

"We need to have another oral reading around the bonfire," Tessa said, reaching for the purple suede notebook she remembered Vivien scratching in late at night in the room all the girls shared. She smoothed her hand over the material, transported to a time when life was so easy and free and fun. "Fifteen, huh? What was happening that year?"

"The bathroom sitch."

Tessa snorted. "I know. I hogged." She flipped to a random page and saw the name "Peter" with a heart, then looked up at Vivien. "I see you still had your crush."

Vivien groaned. "I can't read them anymore. I miss him."

"He's coming back," Tessa reminded her. "Moving to Destin and taking a job with the PD. And not just for you, remember? Although, I'm sure his hope is eternal."

"He won't be here for a while," Vivien said on a sad sigh. "He has to sell his house and find something else, and close up a bunch of cases in Pensacola. He could change his mind, you know. And it would be my fault for breaking up with him."

"Are you sorry for that decision?" Tessa asked. "'Cause I'm pretty sure he'd take you back in a heartbeat."

"I'm...still wondering. Enough that I can't read those diaries."

"I'll read one," Tessa said, turning to the first page and skimming the words. "'Tessa, though. TESSA.'" She looked up. "All caps? Really?"

"Read the next sentence."

She did. "'I love that girl to death, but she thinks every shower is full-blown beauty pageant prep that takes forty-five minutes.'"

Tessa stared at the words, feeling a sharp pang of

guilt hit, and not for the bathroom hogging from the past. She closed the cover with a thud.

"Not much has changed," she said glumly.

Vivien frowned. "What do you mean?"

Looking up, she sighed and decided to share some of what had been on her heart. "I've been freeloading here for almost four months, Viv."

"Freeloading?" Vivien blinked. "Tessa! Don't say that. First of all, we all have our own bathrooms now."

She thumbed toward the ensuite. "You don't."

"I don't need a bathroom to myself," she insisted. "You belong here, Tessa Wylie. As much as anyone."

But the truth was…she *didn't* belong here. She didn't *belong* anywhere.

Tessa gave her a small smile but couldn't help the tightening in her chest. "Technically, this is your house. Yours and Eli's. And Crista's. I'm just…the add-on who never left. The squatter, remember?"

Vivien narrowed her eyes and pointed at her. "Don't do that. Don't minimize what you are to this family. You're not an add-on. You're a Wylie, and this house wouldn't be the same without you. Your very DNA is in this property."

Tessa nodded but said nothing, appreciating the sentiment. But these thoughts were definitely part of the feelings that had been nagging her.

As much as she loved this house—and she did, deeply —she was forty-nine years old and still sleeping in the guest room of a home owned by someone else. It was starting to feel like a comfortable pair of jeans that didn't quite fit right anymore.

Maybe that was the difference with having her secret out in the open. She didn't feel like she had to run all the time.

"Anyway," Vivien pointed at the diary, "if you're dying to dig through those, be my guest. I need a break from reliving my teenage obsession with Peter McCarthy."

Tessa grinned. "Are you sure? You might miss these painfully detailed entries about his jawline."

"Oh, I've memorized those," Vivien said dryly, rolling off the bed. "I'm going to transfer my new obsession to Atlas. I have a full workday tomorrow and want to get my Auntie Viv time in."

"You're done with Danny's house," Tessa said, thinking of Vivien's last rather complicated design client. "Who's your new client?"

"A couple who wants to remodel their guest house, I have more work for Fiona, and I do have to finish this place in case we sell in November."

"You guys haven't decided that yet?" Tessa asked, knowing that was her hard deadline. If the Lawsons sold, she had to leave. If they didn't sell...well, she couldn't sponge off their hospitality *forever*.

"Too much going on to make that decision," Vivien said. "But it's officially summer now, and Kate's here and Jonah, and Meredith's coming. We'll table the discussion for a while, I think. Oh, did you hear that?"

"Baby's crying."

"Yep." Vivien grinned and rubbed her hands together. "He needs Great-Aunt Viv. I'm off to spoil him. Happy reading. Please don't remind me about the hearts around Peter's name and, honestly, I never cared about the bathroom. I was just jealous because you came out more beautiful every time. Still do."

She blew a kiss and disappeared out the door.

Alone, Tessa leaned back, the purple notebook in one hand, her phone in the other. She flipped the notebook open again to the same entry.

Anyway, I gotta go. Tessa just went back into the bathroom, so I have to sit outside the door for forty minutes to keep my place in line.

The sense of déjà vu didn't feel good, not right then.

Maybe it was time to go. And honestly, maybe it was time to consider something she'd never had before—a place of her own.

Not a rental. Not a shared room. Not a free suite at the Ritz. A real home. She wanted to put down roots for the first time in her life, and she certainly could afford something modest. She'd saved a lot from her years at the Ritz—they'd covered her living expenses and paid well—and her new business was truly booming.

Not giving herself a chance to think too hard, she tapped the phone and got on the internet browser. With one fast thumb, she typed *Zillow* into the bar and waited for the house-hunting app to light up. When it did, she added the zip code, vaguely aware that the hair dryer had gone off.

She began to scroll through local listings. A stunner

near the water for over a million and a half. A very afford-able shack not far from the marina that looked like it had survived a hurricane and not much else. A townhouse that looked a little dark and dingy.

Tessa shook her head. "Good grief."

But then she spied a "charming coastal bungalow." The house had three bedrooms in 2,200 square feet, and was fifteen minutes away on the other side of Henderson Beach State Park.

She clicked through the photos of a house built in the 1990s but clearly remodeled and clean. A little yard—she could get a dog!—and not terribly far from the beach. Not *on* the beach, of course, but that would be asking too much.

An unexpected thrill danced over her as she scrolled through pictures, already in love with the seafoam green trim and the coastal vibe. The price? Okay, a tiny bit north of what she should pay, but maybe she could swing it.

A box highlighted on the listing got her attention. *Open House!*

And the date was…today. Now, in fact—well, 3:00 to 5:00 P.M.

She checked the time and got a little jolt that this might just be kismet.

"I have twenty-seven minutes," she muttered just as the bathroom door opened.

"To do what?" Lacey asked, tugging at a towel wrapped around her torso.

Tessa looked up, her mind going blank. Lacey would

not be happy if she left the Summer House—she'd join Vivien in a chorus of "you belong here" when everyone knew she most certainly did not.

"To get a proposal out for a new client," she said smoothly, pushing up and pointing at Lacey with the hand that held the phone. "Hair and makeup is a ten, Lace. Roman's going to swoon."

She smiled her thanks. "It's our last date for a while."

"Until you go on your East Coast jaunt," Tessa said. "And, yes, you should take time off, but only if you promise to tell me everything when you get back. When are you leaving?"

"I'm staying here an extra day because Meredith is coming, so I can go with you to meet with the retirement party client on Wednesday, have dinner with Meredith, and leave the next day," she said. "But after that, I'm off. Are you sure that's okay?"

"Yes," she said simply. "Follow your heart and go fall in love with the man of your dreams." She lifted a brow. "He is, isn't he?"

"Yep." Lacey beamed at her, clutching the towel with one hand and reaching toward Tessa with the other. "Thank you. I love you."

Tessa squeezed her tight, then leaned back, her mind on the open house she now had less than twenty-three minutes to make.

"Same, sweet girl. I gotta go." She planted a kiss on Lacey's head and took off. She only realized she still had the diary in her hand when she got in her car.

Oh, well. Maybe it would bring her good luck.

THE LONGER SHE drove through Destin and along the stunning coastline that was Henderson Beach State Park, the more Tessa had to ask herself a critical question.

Could she really give up living on—or at least near—the beach? Could she stand to know that the Gulf was right *there* and she couldn't see it?

Maybe, maybe not. But she had to start her house hunt somewhere, and this one was cute.

But it wasn't fifteen minutes, not in late Sunday afternoon beach traffic. She arrived at the address on Sunsail Circle at 5:20 and didn't see an "Open House" sign anywhere. There was no car in the driveway, and no happy Realtor named...

She squinted at her phone.

Lorna Gonzalez.

She took a moment to drink in the house, which was oozing with curb appeal and glimmering with a fresh coat of white paint and seafoam green trim that just grabbed her heart.

A swing hung from sturdy chains beneath the shaded front porch, creating a moment of welcome, as Vivien would say. The front yard was perfectly landscaped: neat shrubs, low palms, and a stone path edged with shell gravel.

Come in, it called to her. *Make me your home.*

Maybe Lorna was inside, cleaning up from the appetizers and drinks that any good agent would serve at her open house even though there was no other car in the driveway. Maybe someone was picking her up later.

Or maybe Tessa was late, and this wasn't meant to be.

Still, she optimistically added a little lip gloss and fluffed her hair. Looking down at her shorts and T-shirt, she hoped she looked like a legit buyer. If not, she'd call and make an appointment, because this house had potential with a capital *po*.

Walking up to the front door, she took a breath and hoped for the best. Then she knocked once, waited.

The door swung open to reveal the silhouette of a tall man, easily over six feet, with a silver beard and black-rimmed glasses.

"You are not Lorna," she said with a dry laugh.

"You just missed her," he replied, regarding her intently. "Potential buyer?"

"I hope to be. Are you..."

"The owner," he finished, rubbing a hand through salt-and-pepper hair. "I don't think I'm supposed to talk to you."

She laughed lightly. "The real estate gods will strike us down?"

He smiled. "Something like that."

"I understand," she said, unable to resist glancing behind him and seeing...homey beauty. "I guess I'll call Lorna and set something up...but..." She winced and caught the edge of kitchen perfection just past his arm. "I'm here right now and...we could just pretend we didn't talk." She lifted her chin and pinned her gaze on him.

"I'm a very serious buyer and I would love to see the place."

He studied her for a minute, the hint of a smile threatening under that beard. "Cash serious?"

"Not quite, but qualified for a fast mortgage." She hoped. Smiling, she reached out her hand. "My name is Tessa Wylie and I'm currently—"

"Wait. What? Who?" He drew back. "Tessa Wylie? Like from...the Lawson clan in the summers?"

Her jaw dropped. "Do I know you?"

"Knew," he corrected, inviting her in. "Dusty Mathers. You knew me as Dustin, but my wife decided I could not be Dr. Dustin from Destin."

She held up both hands, trying to catch her breath at this news. "Dustin Mathers? Are you *kidding* me?"

He laughed and reached out both arms for a friendly hug. "I should have recognized you, Tessa. Still a knockout."

"I'm stunned!" she said, giving his broad shoulders a squeeze. "What are the chances of running into you? This is your house?"

"The chances of running into me in Destin are pretty high, since I've lived here my entire life. And, yes, this is my house, unless you want to buy it. Come on in, Tessa. Would you like something to drink? Or look around first?"

"I'll look around in a minute," she said, studying him long enough to catch a shadow of the boy she remembered. She could see the twinkle in his brown eyes, and remembered he was tall, but beyond that? She'd have never recognized this man with distinguished hair and a silver close-cropped beard wearing a blue-checked button-down and khaki shorts as—

Wait. Did he say... "*Doctor* Dustin Mathers?"

He chuckled at the sound of disbelief in her voice. "Right? Somebody got his act together. I have a PhD in counseling psychology. Some might call me a shrink."

He guided her into the kitchen, which was beautiful and freshly remodeled. But her interest in the house waned at the unexpected reunion with an old friend.

"But I only shrink problems, not heads," he added, because Tessa was still struck speechless. "Iced tea or something stronger?"

"Tea's great." She sat on a barstool at a white quartz-covered island, watching him open the fridge and get out two glasses. "And color me surprised that the original wild child of our beach summers chose such a calm and nurturing profession."

He poured two tall glasses over ice and glanced up at her. "My wild days are over," he said, the tiniest note of sadness in his voice. "What brings you to Destin—and in the house market, no less? There's no way you've been around all these years and I didn't know it. Sooner or later, I meet everyone or hear about them in my office."

She took the glass he offered with a nod of thanks. "I came back a few months ago and ended up living temporarily in the same place, with the Lawsons, too."

"Seriously? That place was small."

"It's not anymore. Last year, Maggie—you remember her?"

"With fear and trembling," he said as he slipped onto the stool next to hers, lifting his glass for a toast. "To old friends."

"Careful how you use that word," she teased, tapping his glass with hers.

"Old or friends?"

She laughed at the quick comeback. "Nothing wrong with being friends, which we were."

"We were, and, good gracious, if you're old, Tessa, I'll take whatever magic pill you're popping."

She sipped and smiled at him over the rim of her glass. "Anyway, Maggie had the whole place razed. She rebuilt a breathtaking mansion on the beach. Eli's the architect who designed it, Vivien is staging it, and somehow we all ended up there." She shook her head, hoping he didn't want details of how *she'd* ended up there—the squatter story wasn't her proudest moment. "I'm sure you'd notice it if you go down Gulf Shore Drive."

"I'm never over there," he said. "You kind of have to know someone just to get on that street, right?"

"It is off the beaten path, but now it's quite crowded with Lawsons and Wylies. Like old times."

"Must be fun," he said. "And did you say Eli's an architect? I always admired that guy so much. Isn't his dad an architect?"

"Was. He's been gone many years. My dad, too."

He grunted and made a face. "Oh, I liked your father. Mr. Artie, I called him. Great guy. I'm sorry."

How sweet of him to say that, and to remember her

father's name. "We just had a celebration of life for him out on the Gulf."

"That'll do a lot to heal your hurt," he said.

She inched back, lifting an eyebrow. "Is it that obvious?"

"I do a lot of grief counseling," he explained.

"Ahh. Well, you definitely want to come and see us then," she said, thinking of Jonah but opting not to dive into that right then. Instead, she glanced around. "You mentioned your wife? Is she here? I'd love to meet her."

Once again, his expression softened. Saddened, even. "Not for two years," he said. "My wife Kelly passed away."

"Oh, Dusty." She reached out and put a sympathetic hand on his arm. "Now I'm the one who can see your hurt. I'm so sorry."

"Thanks. You'd think I'd know how to manage the grief, but it hasn't been easy. In fact, I couldn't even counsel people for a while. I took a hiatus and remodeled this place top to bottom." He glanced around. "Just me and a whole bunch of YouTube videos and the occasional expert when I screwed something up." With a soft laugh, he added, "I hope that doesn't make you not want to buy it because I really do want to sell. I thought I'd stay, but..." He shrugged. "I'm going to start over in a new place."

"Here? In Destin?" she asked.

"Most likely. I've lived here my whole life, have a practice here and a lot of friends. I also have a cousin in Vermont who wants me to move up there but..."

"You'd be cold," she finished.

"I think they call it skiing."

She smiled, but her heart ached for him as she looked around, seeing his home—and him—in a different light.

"You did an amazing job." She took in the quality of the finishings, the cozy breakfast nook, the shiplapped walls, the gleaming floor. "It's just perfect."

"Thanks." He took a sip of tea. "What about you, Tessa? Who was the lucky guy who finally reeled in the most popular girl on the beach? If it was Eli, I guess I understand."

She smiled at that, remembering she'd been frustrated by Dustin's refusal to pay any attention to her except for goofing off as friends.

"I never married," she said simply. "But Eli is just now embarking on a romance with my sister, Kate, so I guess what goes around really does come around."

His eyes widened. "Man, there's a lot to catch up on, so..." He picked up his phone as it chirped. "That's my reminder that I have a six-thirty appointment with a client. I'm sorry, I should have shown you the house. But we have so much to talk about."

"I totally understand." She stood and reached for her bag. "I'm so sorry for barging in late to the open house. I'll contact the Realtor and do this the official way, I promise."

He tapped the phone as he stood. "Trust me, I wish I could cancel, but it's too late. And you can come back anytime, Tessa, you don't need an appointment. Can't believe you want to leave a house on that beach, though."

"I don't want to leave the beach," she said. "But I am ready to buy and, sadly, waterfront is—"

He held up a hand. "Ridiculously expensive," he finished for her. "I was hoping to snag a piece of paradise myself, but Lorna has brought me down to Earth with a thud."

"I guess we'll have to play the lottery and hope."

Laughing, he walked with her back to the front door, bringing his phone. "You can call Lorna, but let me get your number so we can make plans. Even if you don't want this house, I have to catch up with everyone."

He tapped his phone and handed it to her to enter her number.

"Yes, you do. You definitely need to come and see us all. We should have a barbeque and get you to the house. They're not going to believe I ran into you." She typed in her number and looked up at him. "Oh. But can you keep a secret?"

"I'm a therapist," he reminded her. "I keep secrets for a living."

"Of course. Well, I don't want them to know I'm looking at houses," she said. "I think Vivien will put up a fight if I suggest I'm thinking about moving out."

"You got it, Tessa." He took the phone and made a face. "Vivien, huh? Has she forgiven me for breaking her boogie board?"

She laughed. "No. But she will."

Instead of laughing, the spark died in his eyes a little and he looked down. "Kids do dumb things," he said.

"Those weren't my, uh, glory days. I owe her an apology and a boogie board."

"All is forgiven," she assured him, reaching for the door. "I'll text you with a date to come to the house."

"I'd love that. And if you don't, I'll text you," he said. "Or I'll pretend it's thirty years ago and stalk the beach on Gulf Shore Drive."

She laughed. "Don't get lost. It doesn't look the same."

He gestured to his face and silver beard. "Who does?"

With a light and friendly hug, she walked out, smiling to herself.

Dustin Mathers. Well, Dusty. A doctor, a widower, a repentant former wild child.

"There is a lot more to that man than meets the eye," she mused, turning the ignition on.

And she couldn't deny...she kind of wanted to know what it was. Funny—she'd totally forgotten about the house.

Chapter Four
Maggie

"Maggie!"

"What?"

"Slow down!" Jo Ellen tightened her grip on the seatbelt and smashed her foot into the floorboard as though she had the brake pedal in front of her and not Maggie.

"I'm going thirty-five."

"In a twenty-five mile an hour zone."

Maggie shot her a look. "We told them three o'clock and it's five of," she said. "I don't *do* late."

"Do you *do* tickets? Because you're going to get one."

"In a neighborhood like this?" Maggie rolled her eyes. "Please. That speed limit is a suggestion for people who aren't sure. Plus, it's not my car. I can't help it if Vivien's SUV has a sensitive gas pedal."

Jo Ellen snorted. "Tell that to the judge, Mrs. Lawson."

Laughing, Maggie tapped the brake out of deference to her friend. "Honestly, I just can't wait to see Betty and Frank again," she said. "The last time we paid a visit, I feel like we left on a sour note and in a cloud of distrust. I was a little surprised Betty took my call and agreed to let us come over."

"We have a lot to tell them."

"We sure do," Maggie agreed. "They're going to be shocked."

"And relieved," Jo Ellen added. "I'm sure they've spent the last thirty years worrying about the sins of their past coming back to haunt them."

"Oh, there's the house," Maggie said, slowing as she drove down the residential street in Santa Rosa Beach she remembered from the last time they'd visited the Cavallaris. "I recognize that eyesore of a red front door."

"Betty never was subtle," Jo Ellen said. "But that's what we loved about her."

Pulling into the driveway, Maggie let out a sigh. "We did love her," she agreed. "I was so uptight and determined to find out the truth when we were here last month, I didn't take a minute to appreciate the, you know, Betty-ness of her. She's...bold."

"And hilarious."

"And drinks like a fish," Maggie added, turning to reach for the chianti and flowers they'd brought. "She'll like this."

As they climbed out, the door opened and Betty walked out slowly, as if she weren't sure what to expect. Like always, she wore a blindingly bright top—this time, the color of a tangerine—her white hair puffy, like she'd put a lot of effort in.

But she moved at a snail's pace, looking slightly unbalanced, and she seemed thinner.

Goodness, Maggie hoped their last unsettling visit didn't upset her that much. Good thing they'd come with wonderful news.

"We're back," Jo Ellen called brightly, rushing around the car. "And we have so much to tell you."

Of course Jo couldn't ease into it, Maggie thought with a wry smile.

"We also have wine and flowers." Maggie reached over to air-kiss Betty, noticing Frank standing behind her.

Had he looked quite that old the last time they were here? Quite that...well, yeah, old.

"These are beautiful," Betty said, putting her face in the bouquet to sniff it. "But no wine for me. Doctor's orders."

"Then you need a new doctor," Jo Ellen joked, stepping past Betty to hug Frank.

After the greeting and small talk, they ended up on the back porch this time, which was small but only because Frank apparently never met a plant he wouldn't pot and nurture to three times his size.

"Frank, can you get the tea, honey?" Betty asked as they settled around a glass-topped table for four. "And some pretzels or something." She turned to Maggie and Jo Ellen. "I'm sorry I didn't bake. I wanted to make more wedding cookies, but..."

"Are you feeling okay?" Jo Ellen asked.

Betty just gave a slight shake of her head and dismissed the question. "Now what's this news that has you two all hyped up? I assume it has to do with that... Cotton Ramsey business and the loan Roger took out."

Maggie waited until Frank was back, then leaned forward. "Cotton Ramsey is dead," she said.

"Did Roger kill him?" Frank asked, horror in his cloudy eyes.

Maggie had to laugh. "No, but Artie Wylie risked his life, wore a wire, and got that man arrested. He helped the FBI close down the whole Dixie Mafia Ramsey ran."

They both sucked in surprised breaths.

"Artie did that?" Frank asked, shaking his head. "Didn't know he had the, um, gumption."

"My husband had gumption and heart," Jo Ellen said proudly. "And Roger helped orchestrate the whole thing from prison. They negotiated for Maggie to secretly keep the Destin property—"

"And Artie made sure we had round-the-clock protection from the FBI," Maggie added. "We didn't even know we were in danger."

Across the table, the older couple wore matching open jaws as Maggie and Jo detailed the whole wonderful story they'd learned from the FBI agent who'd visited the Summer House.

"I'm shocked," Frank said when they finished. "We were protected, too?"

"And not indicted for your, uh, side business," Maggie said, pointing playfully at him but not actually saying the word "bookie." It seemed hurtful, and so long ago. "You're welcome."

He sighed as if he'd been carrying guilt and worry for all these years.

"It's great news," Betty agreed. "And you two"—she

pointed from one to the other—"are back. How did you make up?"

"Our husbands made us promise not to speak to each other," Maggie said. "For our own protection."

Jo Ellen nodded. "They thought if we were in contact, it might somehow lead Cotton's awful men to the other one. Then Roger died—far too soon—and Artie must have thought it was better for me not to talk to Maggie because her heart would break."

"And Roger died six weeks before the FBI was going to arrange for him to get out," Maggie said, the realization still a little tough to process. "I don't know if he'd have survived that heart attack if he'd been home, but I like to believe I'd have been able to save him."

"You might have," Jo Ellen said, putting a hand on Maggie's arm. "But it just wasn't meant to be."

"Anyway," Maggie continued, "we left here in a rush last time, because I was quite perturbed to learn that you'd led my husband straight into the clutches of mobsters, Frank—"

"Well, he—"

She stopped him with a raised hand. "He committed other crimes," she finished for him. "Taking a loan from a man who'd kill him and his family for non-payment was just another of them. I like to think he made up for it by helping the authorities. And Jo and I..." She smiled. "We *are* back, and it feels good."

"We're staying in Destin for the summer," Jo Ellen told them excitedly. "Living in the apartment above the garage in Maggie's gorgeous beach house."

"Oh?" Frank's eyes lit. "That's nice. So you're keeping the place?"

"The kids have to decide that," Maggie said, sliding a glance to Betty who...was falling asleep. "Are you all right?"

Betty shuddered softly and blinked. "Yes, yes. I'm taking some medication, and it just makes me so tired."

"Medication for what?" Maggie asked.

"Oh, nothing I want to talk about." She pushed up. "I'll go make some coffee to perk up."

"No, Betty." Frank put a gentle hand on her arm. "You should take your nap."

"When the girls are here?"

Maggie smiled at the term and pushed away from the table, giving Jo a quick look that she instantly read properly.

"We just wanted to tell you both the good news in person," Maggie said. "You can rest easy knowing that Cotton Ramsey's gang isn't going to rise up and kill you in your sleep."

"But something will," Betty muttered, stepping away and into the kitchen.

Maggie frowned. *What* did she say?

"Is something wrong with her?" Jo Ellen asked Frank on a hushed whisper. "She seems..."

He shook his head. "It's nothing for you two to worry about. But she does need that nap every day at three."

"Then she shouldn't have told us to come over," Maggie said, bristling a little.

"She'd never say no to you two." He pushed up, practically as wobbly as his wife. "And you know...life's short. She didn't know... Well, she wants to see all her friends before—"

"Frank!" Betty called. "Where did you put my pills, honey?"

Before *what?*

Once again, Maggie and Jo Ellen shared a look.

"We better go," Jo Ellen said, picking up her glass and Maggie's. "Just let us clean—"

"No, no," Frank insisted. "Give Betty a kiss goodbye and I'll get her pills. But don't leave. I want to talk to you privately. I need to ask you a favor."

"Anything," Jo Ellen gushed, worry contorting her features.

They gave Betty a kiss and Maggie could have sworn her old friend hugged her extra tight.

Was she *dying?*

The thought nearly made Maggie sway as she and Jo Ellen walked out into the bright afternoon sunshine to wait for Frank.

"Well, that didn't go quite as planned," Maggie said as they followed the walkway.

"She's not well," Jo Ellen agreed.

"I think we're about to get some very bad news." Maggie took Jo Ellen's hand. "And I don't want it."

"Neither do I, but we need to be strong for Frank. Whatever he wants as a favor, we say yes."

"Of course," Maggie agreed.

Frank stepped out of the front door, the sunshine highlighting the deep creases in his face and the lack of healthy color.

Were they both sick?

He made his way down the steps and met them in the driveway.

"Is she okay?" Jo Ellen demanded again.

"She's...got a dream."

Maggie tipped her head. "Excuse me?"

"Her whole life, she's had a dream," he continued. "A silly thing, maybe, but she wants a car."

"A *car*?" Jo Ellen asked, her voice echoing the disbelief in Maggie's head.

"I know, I know." He stuck his hand in his pocket and pulled out a folded piece of paper. "But I gotta do this for her, girls. All her life, she dreamed about a T-bird convertible—you know, like the song?"

What in the name of God was he talking about?

"I know," Jo Ellen said excitedly. "'And she'll have fun, fun, fun...'" she sang woefully off-key. "That one? The Beach Boys?"

"Yes, that one," Frank said with a sad smile. "You know how she loves The Beach Boys."

Maggie did remember that about Betty, always playing those songs on her record player.

"And look what I found." He showed them a computer printout with a color picture of a red convertible. "This one is 1957, the classic year for Thunderbird. Fully restored down in Miami Beach. I can wire the dealer the money, but I just can't go get it." He glanced toward the house. "I can't risk leaving her."

"You'd buy her a car?" Maggie practically sputtered. "Now? When she's—"

"If not now, then when, Mags?" Jo Ellen asked, obviously following Frank's insane logic.

"Exactly," he said. "What better time than when she's..." He looked over his shoulder to the house, letting his voice trail off.

Oh, no. Maggie's heart clenched. Should she ask how much time Betty had left? Was that appropriate or—

"Could you two go get it for me?" he asked.

What did he say?

"In Miami Beach?" Maggie scoffed. "No."

"Mags! We can do it," Jo Ellen insisted.

"Are you out of your mind?"

"You can take my old truck down and leave it there," Frank powered on, seeing an ally in Jo Ellen. "The car dealer agreed to take it as a trade-in for part of the payment. The T-bird isn't ready yet, but will be in about a week or so. Could you do it?"

Drive a truck from here to South Florida? And come back in a sports car? She could barely drive down Highway 98 in Vivien's high-end SUV.

"Frank?" Betty was at the door. "I think I need you."

Frank looked from one to the other. "Will you just think about it?"

"Non-stop," Jo Ellen blurted out.

"The answer is no," Maggie interjected. "We are not driving your bucket of bolts God knows how many days to Miami Beach and coming back in a Thunderbird!"

"Work on her, Jo," he whispered as he hugged them both, then shot back into the house, leaving them in the driveway alone.

"Maggie, we—"

"No, we're not doing it."

"She could be dying!"

"Then he'd tell us that, Jo Ellen. She could also have a headache from a hangover, which would be much more in character, if you ask me."

"She deserves joy," Jo Ellen insisted. "And if a car will bring her happiness in her final days, who are we to deny it?"

"We are seventy-eight-year-old ladies who can't see at night, are afraid of left turns, and don't know how to pass on the highway."

"Oh, Maggie, that's not true. You can do anything!"

Once, maybe. Not anymore. "Rope one of your daughters into this trip, Jo, but I won't risk my life for a car."

Jo Ellen looked glum as they opened their doors and climbed in, silent in the blazing heat of the SUV.

"We could find a route with only backroads, no left turns, and no night driving," Jo said softly.

"And you'll put a hole in that clunker's floor pressing a fake brake."

"You could pick all the music," she added.

Maggie rolled her eyes. "Beach Boys? No, thank you."

"You could get an audiobook of *Gone With The Wind*

and listen to it the whole way." She reached over. "I'd let you recite the parts you know by heart."

Maggie almost smiled, but she had to stand firm. "Frankly, my dear..." She gave a smile. "I am still saying no."

Jo Ellen huffed out a breath.

"Can't you just see the headlines?" Maggie asked as she backed out. "'Two seventy-eight-year-olds killed on I-95.' And people think, 'What were those two old bags doing behind the wheel on the interstate?'"

Jo looked at the house and her shoulders sank. "Oh, Betty. The world won't be as bright without you."

Maggie stared at the road ahead and remembered the last time she'd been on an interstate highway. One heart attack after another. She had too much to live for now—including a great-grandson.

"Come on, Mags." Jo Ellen actually whined. "It would be so much fun. We'd be like Thelma and Louise."

She gasped. "Have you seen that movie?"

"No, but the ads always looked like so much fun."

She slid a withering look at her poor, deluded, always optimistic friend. "They die in the end."

"Oh." She shifted under her seatbelt. "I thought they just, you know, got friendly with a young Brad Pitt."

Maggie snorted. "We can watch the movie together, Jo," she said, trying to make her voice a little gentler to ease the disappointment. "But that's the closest we're going to get to a road trip."

Jo Ellen turned and looked out the window, clearly

sad about the decision. She didn't even use her pretend brake when Maggie got too close to a truck.

Her silence was unfortunate, but Maggie was certain this was the safe and sane decision, and she wasn't going to change her mind no matter how hard Jo tried.

And she *would* try, so Maggie had to have resolve.

Chapter Five

Jonah

Jonah opened his eyes, deeply disoriented. Where was he? What time was it? Who had the baby?

Pushing up, he blinked in the dimly lit bedroom, then peered at the empty bassinet next to his bed.

There was a time, not so very long ago, when he didn't know what a "bassinet" was, let alone had one in his room. But then, life changed.

With a grunt, he rolled over and patted the bed to find his phone and check the time. Eleven-fifteen? Crap. He needed to get up.

For the last few days—he'd seriously lost count of how many—the family had fallen into a rhythm. They slept while Jonah handled waking up in the middle of the night to feed and change his son.

Some nights—the rare, good ones—that was once at midnight, and again at five. After that, Aunt Vivien or his dad or Lacey—*some* loving soul—came down the next time they heard Atlas cry on the baby monitor some other loving soul had bought him.

Other nights—like last night—Atlas woke on the hour, purely miserable.

Did he miss his mother? Of course he did. And that had to hurt at a month old the same way it hurt at fifteen years old. Jonah understood that longing, that emptiness, that bone-deep misery.

And he hated for his sweet, helpless, utterly innocent son to feel it already. The only thing he hated more? Feeling responsible for Atlas's pain.

No, he hadn't been behind the wheel, but he should have gone to get the diapers. Why didn't he?

Because he lived under a black cloud of death that was probably a ticking time bomb until the next person he loved and needed was met with tragedy.

Grabbing a T-shirt that yet another angel of mercy had washed, dried, folded, and left on the dresser for him, he stopped in the bathroom then marched upstairs to find Atlas and coffee.

Maybe not in that order.

It was quiet up here, bathed in late-morning sunshine. But he heard the soft hum of a woman, murmuring sweetly, high-pitched and babyish. That was Kate, he knew. And Atlas was undoubtedly in her arms.

He stopped for the coffee, which was miraculously brewed and warmed already. How did they run this house with military precision and heavenly peace, satisfying the needs of what felt like dozens of occupants ranging in age from a month to nearly eighty?

Jonah had no idea—maybe it was his dad, maybe it was Aunt Vivien, maybe the strong hand of Grandma Maggie, or maybe it was...her.

He stood at the open sliding glass doors and looked

out at the brand-new rattan rocker that Aunt Vivien had purchased for the sole purpose of "Atlas feedings." Whoever was on duty got to sit on the second-story deck, looking out at the horizon and turquoise water, enjoying the salt-infused air of Destin.

Kate was out there alone—not counting a blissfully quiet Atlas in her arms—an empty baby bottle on the table next to her. Atlas was conked against her chest, his teddy bear blanket spilling onto Kate's lap.

Her eyes were closed, too, her head back, her glasses...somewhere. On the table, probably. She hummed a soft, sweet tune that would put anyone to sleep—even Atlas, who decided sometime around four A.M. that he was never sleeping again.

Kate had conquered him.

But then, Kate won a lot of battles, Jonah thought with a smile. She quietly fought them with logic and love, and conquered whatever was in the way.

This past spring, Jonah had been a mess, and Kate—a stranger to him, but not his father and aunts—blew into his life and somehow achieved the impossible.

She'd stepped into the role of mother for him and his whole life changed. She'd seen something in him. Encouraged him. Fussed over him. Let him cry. Essentially treated him like they were all treating Atlas.

And somehow, without even trying, she'd started to fill a space in him that had been empty since his mother died when he was fifteen.

Could Kate ever know how grateful he was?

"Oh, hello." She opened her eyes and whispered the greeting. "I didn't know you were here, Jonah."

"I didn't want to wake him," he said, just as softly.

"Nothing will wake him." She patted Atlas's back. "He's conked."

"Thank you." He walked out and settled on the sofa near her, putting his coffee on the table.

"It was my pleasure," she assured him. "I had to kick all other takers to the curb to get my time. The great-grandmothers went back to their apartment arguing about something quite secretively. Your father had to take a work call, but he's in the back office. Tessa and Lacey went to see a client, and I don't know where Vivien is, but I assume she's working, too. Anyway, no need to thank me. The line to love Atlas is long."

He took a sip of coffee as she chattered about all the help. That wasn't what he wanted to thank her for, but he hadn't had enough caffeine to get mushy yet.

"Have you eaten?" she asked after a beat.

He shook his head. "I'm on the all-coffee diet. It's working wonders."

Kate gave him a dubious look. "There's leftover quiche in the fridge. I can—"

"I'll eat, Kate. I promise." He ran a hand through his hair and exhaled. "It's just...a lot. I feel like I'm failing at everything except changing diapers."

"You're not," she said simply.

"You don't know that."

"I do." She shifted Atlas very gently to the other

shoulder, earning a tiny whimper and angelic sigh as he nestled closer into her neck and chest.

Kate gave a soft laugh, the breath fluttering the dark bangs that fringed her eyes. "He's too perfect!" she mouthed, rubbing his tiny back.

"I don't deserve him," Jonah whispered.

"Yes, you do. And please don't say you're a failure. You're not even in the zip code. You're showing up. You're loving him. That's ninety percent of it right there."

He looked at the baby. His son. His everything. "You're good with him."

Kate smiled, her eyes softening. "I love babies. Always have. I wish I'd had more, but I also wanted to research everything Cornell could throw my way." She looked down at the baby. "Goodness, he's special."

Jonah nodded, then shifted on the sofa, wanting to take advantage of this quiet and intimate moment.

"Listen, Kate. Thank you. For everything."

She regarded him, her expression softening. "I don't need thanks."

"But you should get them. If it weren't for you, we both know I'd have never even thought about being a chef, let alone apply to that program. But more than that, you showed up and made things feel...better. Safe. I don't know—just good."

"Oh, honey." Her shoulders dropped as if she actually felt the weight of his words. "You don't have to thank me."

"Yeah, I do." He paused. "I know you and my dad are, you know, getting serious, so..."

She gave a short laugh. "Jonah, I'm not applying to be your stepmother."

"I know." He smiled, then looked at his cup. "But I'm not weird about it, if that's what you were wondering. I get it. My dad hasn't looked this...alive in a long time. I don't think I ever saw him this way, even when I was a kid."

Kate didn't respond right away. Then, softly, she said, "From what I've heard, your mom was wonderful."

He nodded. "She was...everything. I know she'd want Dad to be happy—she wanted everyone to be happy. Honestly, I think he finally is."

"I'm not trying to replace her," Kate said gently. "No one ever could. I understand. But I'm here. And I'm glad to be in your life. You and your whole family."

He nodded again, unspoken words catching in his throat.

"Now," she added, tone shifting to bright and practical, "let's talk about this culinary program."

He groaned. "Do we have to?"

"Yes. Because it starts soon, and you haven't really mentioned it or gone out to buy the knives you need or done anything in the way of preparation."

"I'm not really a 'preparer.' That's my sister's job. Speaking of Meredith, didn't she leave Atlanta at the crack of dawn today? She should be—"

"Don't change the subject, Jonah."

He shuttered his eyes and fell back on the sofa cushions. "I haven't decided yet," he said.

"Decided?" Kate blinked. "What's to decide? You got

accepted into the program, it starts next week, and you need chef's knives and some good aprons."

He shook his head. "I have a baby. And a pile of emotions that hit me like a train every morning. And I don't sleep. And I keep thinking..." He hesitated and looked away.

"What?"

"I'm cursed."

Kate straightened, pressing Atlas into her chest. "Jonah."

"I'm serious."

"I know you are, and that's what worries me. Cursed! Please. The concept is so supernatural, it hurts me to think anyone as intelligent as you would even consider it."

He looked up, defensive. "I'm not talking about voodoo dolls and hexes. But how do you explain it? My mom dies in a freak plane accident when I'm a kid. I flail through high school. I fall in love with someone who makes me feel like I can build a life—and she dies three weeks after having our baby. What else am I supposed to think?"

Kate repositioned Atlas with the grace and ease of a practiced mother, cradling him as she seemed to gather her thoughts before answering.

"Here's what that means," she finally said. "Life is random. Tragedies don't follow a logic pattern or moral code. Your situation doesn't mean you're cursed. It means you're human, and bad things happen sometimes."

"Twice? To the same person?"

Kate fixed him with her no-nonsense stare. "You know how many times the same person is struck by lightning in their lifetime? Statistically? It happens. But it's not fate. It's math. If you stand on a hilltop during every thunderstorm, it increases your odds. But it doesn't make you cursed."

He huffed a laugh. "I stayed in the kitchen so my béarnaise sauce didn't break, and let my girlfriend, who was walking dead exhausted, get in a car and drive to Target for diapers. I didn't stand on any hills."

"I'm comparing your logic to superstition," she countered. "Which is what curses are. There's no scientific basis for them. None. The very idea is a baseless crutch that you're allowing to scare you."

He looked away, silent for a long moment. "My dad doesn't want me to say it out loud. He acts like if I say the word 'curse,' I'm invoking it."

Kate leaned forward. "Eli believes in blessings and curses because his faith has room for that. I...get that. Can't say I truly understand it, like it, or even respect it, but he does. On the other hand, I deal in facts, figures, and formulas. You are not cursed, Jonah. You're just in pain. That's not the same thing."

He stared out at the water, wondering how she and his father could reconcile that difference in philosophy, but the thought was fleeting. His own problems seemed bigger right then.

"It's hard not to feel like something's stacked against me."

"I get it. I really do." She lowered her voice and

rocked forward. "But if Carly were here—if she could see you now—what do you think she'd want?"

He didn't hesitate. "She'd want me to go to the program. She was pretty excited about it. She even said..." He swallowed, remembering the conversation and how happy it made him. "She was thinking she'd move out here for the year I'm in the program. We were going to get married and..." He couldn't finish. It hurt too much.

"She believed in you, Jonah. She loved you. And you have to go to school and labs and internships and whatever they ask of you. We'll all help with Atlas. You don't have to do it alone."

His throat grew thick with emotion. "I don't know how I got this lucky. To have you. And Aunt Vivien. And Dad. All of you."

"You deserve it." She looked down at the baby, then back at Jonah. "You both do. And, Jonah, can I give some practical advice?"

"Don't believe in curses?"

"Much simpler. Get out of the house. Go get your knives and aprons. Get your life together. This place is teeming with people who want to love and care for your baby—take advantage of that. Please?"

He didn't answer because a door banged, followed by a young woman's voice he knew very, very well.

"Hello? Anyone home? I'm here!"

"Meredith," he said with a humorless smile. "Let the comparisons begin."

"Jonah, stop." Kate stood and offered the baby to him. "Introduce him—and me—to his aunt, please."

"You've never met my sister?" he asked, just realizing that.

She shook her head. "No. And I understand she's quite protective of your father, so have my six, will you?"

"Forever," he said, a little surprised at the syrupy response, but not willing to change it. He loved Kate Wylie, and would defend her to anyone.

As he took Atlas in his arms, he heard his dad's voice and Aunt Vivien greeting Meredith. He tipped his head for Kate to come with him as he walked inside.

They stood in a cluster, hugging, showing off the house. Meredith turned and her whole face lit up.

"Hey, stranger," she said with a grin.

"Hey," Jonah replied, walking toward her giving Atlas a little *Lion King* lift.

"Oh, my gosh! Let me see him!" She reached out both hands and he gave the sleeping baby to his sister. "Hello, Atlas." Her voice cracked and she looked up, unexpected tears in her eyes. "Jonah, he's perfect."

Was she really crying? Meredith? She was the strongest, most stoic person he knew, a trait he both envied and adored about her.

"Yeah, he's...cool. Except when he's not, which is usually somewhere around three in the morning."

She laughed and traced his little face with her finger. "Oh, my goodness." Her voice caught again. "I'm just overwhelmed."

The reaction touched him, and he turned to the

woman next to him to cover his reaction. "Oh, this is Kate," he added, putting a hand on her shoulder to ease her closer. "Dr. Kate Wylie."

Meredith's gaze shifted to Kate and her green eyes widened. "Hi, Kate. I've heard so much about you."

"As have I about you," she said. The two of them exchanged a light hug without squeezing little Atlas. "We're so happy you've come down."

Meredith sighed, looking from the baby to Jonah. "I had to step in and be an auntie," she said, her voice unusually soft. "And keep an eye on my big brother."

"I have many eyes on me down here," he said, gesturing around the room.

After they all chatted some more, put Atlas down for a nap, and showed Meredith around, she made her way back to Jonah and put an arm around him.

"You okay?" she asked softly.

He studied her for a moment, noticing the slightest darkness under her eyes, which were normally bright and painfully healthy. Not that she looked unhealthy, but she did look tired.

Well, she'd just taken the architecture boards, so she probably was.

"Define 'okay,'" Jonah replied with a shrug. "And how's your perfect life?"

She rolled her eyes. "Woefully flawed," she whispered.

Something in her voice touched him—she so rarely admitted a weakness.

"Then I'm glad you're here," he said.

"Of course I'm here. What do you need? Anything at all, I'm your girl."

He remembered the conversation with Kate, and decided to take her advice. "I need someone to go with me to get chef's knives, a couple of aprons, and maybe a beer in the sunshine."

"Done and done!" She smiled, then it faded. "No beer for me."

"No?"

"No, I...am...perfect, remember?" she quipped with a wink.

"Oh, yes, I recall that about you, Mer."

Still, he was happy she was here. This was his sister, who knew every ugly chapter in his life and hadn't walked away.

And he needed her now. Whether he wanted to or not.

Chapter Six
Meredith

Meredith shifted her purse to her left arm and glanced sideways at her brother, who was carrying a shopping bag from a high-end kitchen store in one hand and a matte-black box of Henckels knives in the other.

"You look like a man launching a Michelin career," she teased as they wormed their way through the crowds of HarborWalk Village.

"Or one who will very swiftly lose a thumb in my first week in the culinary school kitchen."

"Are you in the kitchen from Day One?" she asked. "Or is it classes and presentations?"

He snorted. "I have no idea. I'm not even sure I'm going."

She came to a sudden halt. "Jonah!"

"I know, I know. I'm getting the, 'You can't give up now, kid,' lectures left and right." He threw her a look. "First of all, I'm not you."

She jabbed him with her elbow. "Stop it."

"Second, I have a baby and, yes, the free world wants to help me take care of him, but he is my responsibility, first and foremost. That changes everything."

Taking a breath, she considered that comment and how it cut through her as if he'd used one of those expensive knives. She had a baby, too, only it was barely a poppy seed now, and no one knew about it, let alone had lined up to take care of it.

Pushing the thought out of her mind, she tried to sink into the vibe of the sun-drenched tourist mecca of this boardwalk shopping area directly on the harbor. The breeze fluttered her hair, carrying the scents of salt, sunscreen, and seafood. Families wandered in and out of boutiques. Music from a street performer floated past them, and kids ran squealing around a bubble machine near the water's edge.

Meredith inhaled, willing herself to breathe it all in. Anything but the turmoil lodged in her throat. And the low-key nausea from that shrimp place they just passed.

"Well," she finally said, choosing her words carefully, "I just bought you a set of knives, so you're committed to the program now."

"I could sell them and pay you back."

She glared at him. "You could use them and make a fortune and pay me back. Also, keep them sharp and someday you can leave them to your son." She gave a dry laugh as the words tumbled out of her mouth. "Shoot, Jonah Lawson, you have *a son*."

"I know." He huffed out a breath. "Proof that the universe has a sense of humor."

She wasn't sure about that. "So, what's the culinary school workload like?" she asked. "Can I help you study? It's my specialty."

"Don't I know it," he said on a chuckle. "It's a new program just launching at this school, so there isn't any curriculum or buzz on Reddit. As far as I can tell, they'll start us with a mix of culinary foundations—which means everything from knife skills to basic *mise en place*."

"Sounds...French."

"It's just..." He smiled. "Let's just put it this way—you'd get an A."

"Well, I always get A's but I'm not a great cook. What is *mise en place*? How do you spell that?" She fished for her phone, but he put a hand over hers to stop her.

"It's about making the kitchen organized, clean, and ready for action. No chaos, all order."

"Ahh. Sounds like my wheelhouse." She eyed him as he pulled out his phone. "You just stopped me from screen time."

"I know but..." He slid his thumb over the device. "I want to make sure everything's okay with Atlas."

"He's fine. He's not even a month old. He didn't run off the boardwalk into the water."

He shot her a look. "You don't understand, Mer. A baby is...huge. It's a whole life. A whole stinking life. And I'm responsible for it."

She swallowed. "I understand," she managed. "I personally think it's been good for you. Not losing Carly, obviously. That's the worst thing imaginable. But you're handling it better than I expected."

"You weren't there during the snot-riddled breakdown when I arrived. Next-level ugly."

Her heart shifted thinking of him in so much pain.

He'd cried a lot when Mom died, and it had been one of the hardest parts of the whole grieving experience. Watching her big, beautiful, popular, handsome football player of a brother shrivel into a sobbing mess who wouldn't get off the sofa was one of the darkest things in her young life.

"Well, you seem pretty strong," she said. "I mean, you're the same old wry and sarcastic self-hating pain in the backside, but grounded now."

He just smiled. "A tiny human will do that. Honestly, Mer, it's like he rearranged my whole heart and life."

Oh. The words slammed her in the solar plexus. Did she *want* her life rearranged? She wasn't sure.

She glanced at her brother again. Was there any better person on Earth to share her secret? Who could possibly understand the weight and worry of it like Jonah? And he might be able to help her figure out how to tell Dad, who was, of course, over the moon to see her.

He wouldn't be so over the moon when she broke the news.

"I have to tell you something," she said before she could stop herself.

Jonah glanced at her. "Yeah?"

No. *No, no, no, no.* She nearly stumbled on the walkway at the force of that voice in her head. She knew telling him was right—but not now. Not here. Not yet.

She waved it off. "Nothing. Just...you're doing great. I'm proud of you."

He gave her a sideways smirk. "You're not just saying

that because you're out a couple of Benjamins for these knives?"

"No, but that is a factor."

He laughed and they walked in comfortable silence for a minute, while she convinced herself that not telling him her secret was best right now.

They passed a cutesy art gallery with blown-glass dolphins in the window, then stopped to admire a booth selling hand-carved wooden spoons and cutting boards.

"You need a good cutting board," she said.

"I think the school supplies them." Jonah studied one shaped like a sea turtle, flipped it over, then winced at the price tag. "Also, I need to be a celebrity chef before I buy artisanal kitchen supplies."

Meredith nudged him forward, her eyes scanning the crowd for something—anything—that might distract her from blurting out her secret.

What would it even sound like?

Hey, b-t-dub, I'm pregnant by a man I knew was all wrong for me and real temporary and guess what? He forgot to mention his wife, so...what do you think of that and the fact that I have a baby inside me and no idea what to do with my life?

But Jonah didn't need that. Or maybe he did. Maybe learning that even the mighty Miss Perfect could topple from her pedestal would make him feel better.

Still, she couldn't do it.

"So," she said instead, fishing for safer conversation, "I'm having dinner with Lacey tonight. I wanted to meet her new boyfriend, but I guess he's left town for a while and she's doing the same. Roman, right? An NFL player? I hear there's quite a backstory."

"I've heard bits and pieces but have been in a baby fog since I got here," he said. "But I guess Tessa secretly had a son in her twenties and gave him up for adoption, and now he's dating Lacey. Pretty sure there's more to it, but honestly, I haven't absorbed the details."

"I'm sure I'll get that all tonight. Have you met him?"

"My first night here, but that was chaos. Atlas threw up and I didn't get to spend much time with Roman." He looked skyward. "Yes, the first time I ever get to meet a professional ballplayer, and my kid decides to Barf-nado all over me. A Cat 5 of puke, honestly."

She cracked up, feeling that old sibling love for her hilarious brother.

"It's humbling, this parenting thing, I'm telling you."

She smiled, but the hearty laugh made her feel unexpectedly lightheaded, so she ushered him to an empty bench in the shade.

"I need a break," she whispered.

"You? The original Energizer Bunny? Dad says you never stop buzzing around Acacia Architecture like its future owner on a mission."

There it was. That little bit of...competition. Envy, maybe. It had developed in the years when Jonah wanted to give up on everything, and Meredith's coping mechanism was to work until she couldn't see straight, then work some more. During those years, they'd drifted completely apart.

Could this time in Destin bring them back together? She hoped so.

"Well, this bunny is stopping," she said. "Humor me. Also...can you go get me water? This Florida heat and humidity has me parched."

"Sure. Watch my overpriced knives and use them on anyone who looks dangerous. BRB." He set off to a small booth vendor selling water and snacks, leaving her to let the dizziness pass. And reconfirm her decision that this was not the time or place to share her secret.

When he came back with two cold waters, they sat in companionable silence—except for his latest phone check to make sure Atlas hadn't stopped breathing—and sipped water.

"So speaking of unexpected relationships," she said, "you and Kate seem close."

Jonah cracked one eye open. "Fishing for Summer House gossip, Mer?"

"Not gossip. Intel. I mean, she's been amazing for Dad, I can tell," she said, and meant it. "He talked about her non-stop after he got back to Atlanta, and he kind of looks like he's aging backwards. But what is she really like?"

He tilted his head and smiled. "She's smart. Like, scary smart. And no-nonsense. But kind. She's helped me a lot. Even today, she tried to talk me out of believing I'm cursed."

"You think you're cursed?" Meredith blinked. "What is that all about?"

"It's about my crap luck and bad history," he said. "I am cursed."

She drew back at his matter-of-factness. "That's crazy."

"So I've heard. Kate gave me a full lecture on superstition and statistics. She's very...logical. There is no such thing as supernatural to Kate Wylie."

Meredith nodded slowly, not giving much credence to his curse, but the subtext was very interesting, and not something she'd heard from Dad.

"So she's...not into faith."

"Nope," Jonah said. "All science, all the time. Meanwhile..." He threw her a look that said he was following her train of thought. "Dad'll want to put a prayer bench on the beach before the house is completely finished."

That probably wasn't even that much of an exaggeration.

"How does that work with them?" she asked.

He shrugged. "I guess they sort of orbit each other on that one. I don't really know."

"It seems pretty fundamental to a relationship," she mused. "Dad can't love someone who doesn't believe."

"Yeah, he can. Kate's smart. Maybe she'll make him see that there isn't much to that stuff."

She bristled, because she might not be a church-going, Bible-reading believer like her father, but over the years she had grown to understand his faith and had never met anyone from his church she didn't like.

She went with him on enough Sundays to appreciate the whole thing, and to know Dad *couldn't* love someone who didn't share his beliefs or at least deeply respect them.

"If that's true, then she isn't right for Dad."

Jonah shot her a look. "Don't try to break them up, Mer," he said, all humor gone from his voice. "She's the best thing that ever happened to him."

"I wouldn't," she said. "I just want him to have his eyes wide open." But as soon as she said the words, she realized what a hypocrite that made her. Talk about going blind into a relationship. She'd kind of forgot to ask Trevor if *he was married.*

"And how about you?" Jonah asked, pulling her back to the moment.

"Me? What about me? I go to church with Dad sometimes but…"

"No, I mean…you look kind of, I don't know, different."

Pregnant, she thought, biting her lip. "I'm just tired," she said. "It's been crazy at work. In fact, I'm the one who should be checking my phone endlessly."

"You're right," he said, standing up. "Let's go back. I miss Atlas."

Jonah proved that by talking endlessly about the baby, and when they got back to the Summer House, he practically sprinted into the entryway.

"Where's my kid?" he called.

Kate responded from upstairs. "He's on the deck! With your dad!"

Jonah disappeared around the corner, bolting through the kitchen to the open sliding glass doors.

Meredith wandered after him, in time to see him scoop up Atlas with a reverent kind of joy. He held him close, whispered to him, kissed his fuzzy little head. Meredith could feel the reunion ripple off him like heat from the sun.

Wow. Would she feel like that about her baby?

She stood in the doorway and watched her brother with his son, feeling the sting of tears for the four billionth time this week.

"You look tired from all that shopping," her father said, walking up to her.

"I am, Dad," she admitted. "I'm going to lay down until I go out with Lacey tonight."

He inched back, a frown threatening. "I don't think I've ever known you to nap."

She managed a casual shrug. "Well, you always talk about the magic of Destin. Maybe the magic is that it slows me down."

THE SUN HAD JUST DIPPED beneath the Gulf, streaking the horizon with apricot and gold, when Meredith reached across the table at Pompano Joe's to steal a hush puppy from Lacey's plate.

"And you *both* thought faking a relationship would be a great idea?" Meredith asked, eyes wide.

Her cousin grinned, unbothered by the hush puppy theft. "It was his idea, technically. I just...couldn't say no."

They sat in the corner of the deck under an umbrella they didn't need at sunset. Around them, the beach-front restaurant thrummed with a busy dinner hour, the sound of the surf competing with laughter, chatter, and some steel-drum music on the speakers.

Meredith shook her head with a bemused smile. "Lace. It's not like you to lie to your mother. You tell Aunt Vivien everything."

"Well, I couldn't. I wasn't supposed to tell anyone that Tessa had a baby. She confided in me and I...did some sleuthing, used the info I had, called the hospital, and boom..."

"There he is," Meredith finished. "All six-foot-whatever of him, wanting to be your fake boyfriend. Ack, it's so rom-com!"

"I know, right?" Lacey picked up her half-empty wine glass, then put it down again. "But it's real," she added on a whisper. "And I don't even know how I feel about that."

Meredith gazed across the table, feeling a surge of affection for her younger cousin. Blond, blue-eyed, and full of life, she was the closest thing Meredith would ever have to a sister.

However, dear Lacey had just admitted she was terrible at keeping secrets or promises, so Meredith knew this wasn't going to be a spill-all dinner. But Lacey did know something about another topic that intrigued Meredith very much—adoption from the child's standpoint.

She didn't want to drag the conversation there yet.

Lacey's totally unconventional romance was too tempting to change the subject.

"So you decided pretending he was your boyfriend was a safe and smart way for him to meet Tessa without her knowing you did this." Meredith raised an eyebrow. "Really?"

"All him," she said. "He wanted to protect me and get to know Tessa without dropping a bomb. It was supposed to be a few days, tops. Then..."

"You caught feelings."

"Hard," Lacey confessed with a laugh. "Somewhere between pretending and pretending-not-to-be-pretending."

Meredith slid her fingers up and down the condensation on her water glass, smiling at her cousin. "So what's next? He's in Jacksonville for a few weeks?"

She nodded. "He has to meet with his agent, do some medical stuff, some training video classes, sessions with the coaches."

"Sounds...NFL-y."

She laughed and shook her head. "I still can't believe that, but anyway, I'm leaving tomorrow to meet him there. He wants me to see his house, the town, meet some of the players, check out the stadium—"

"Where you will sit in the VIP box with the other players' wives, all Taylor Swift-like."

"Puh-lease."

"That's where it's going," Meredith insisted.

Lacey lifted the glass to drink. "I don't know where

it's going, but after that, we're going down to Satellite Beach, which is a few hours south, to meet his parents."

Meredith launched a brow. "Please don't make me wear sage in your wedding. It's my least favorite color."

Lacey nearly choked on her sip. "Stop."

"Why? You're meeting the parents, Lace. That's... big."

"It's a little more awkward than usual," she said. "You know—I love and work for his birth mother."

Meredith's stomach gave a small, unexpected flutter. "What's the dynamic there?" she asked, taking a sip of water and wondering if Lacey noticed she hadn't touched the wine she'd ordered.

"The dynamic with Roman and his parents?" Lacey asked. "It's pure love. He adores them. Could not be happier he landed in their arms and is deeply grateful to Tessa for making that decision."

The water lodged in her throat, but she managed to swallow, looking across the table. "How does he...feel about being adopted?"

She shrugged like it was kind of a dumb question. "He has no issues. He's just glad he got Faith and Bob Matteo for parents. He really had a charmed childhood—lived on the water, in a small town, superstar in high school and college."

And what child wouldn't want that?

"How did...Tessa find them?" Was that a weirdly direct and stupid question? She didn't know, but again, Lacey didn't seem to think much of it.

"I think Tessa's father—you've heard them talk about

Artie? I think he handled it for her. Apparently, he was awesome and gave Roman the fishing gene. But as far as being adopted, it was the best thing that ever happened to him."

The words settled like a stone in Meredith's chest.

"And Tessa?"

"Oh." Lacey leaned back. "There was drama. She was upset that I'd broken my promise to her and that she'd spent weeks getting to know him under false pretenses, but she forgave us, and all is well."

"How did she feel about...giving up a child for adoption?"

"It must have left a hole in her heart because I actually guessed," Lacey said.

"How?"

"I could see her expression change to wistful sadness whenever the subject of her not ever having children came up."

Meredith shifted, eyed the untouched wine, and took another drink of water.

"Do you think," she said carefully, "that Roman ever felt like...something was missing?"

Lacey considered that. "We've talked about that, obviously. He said no. That he always felt chosen, not abandoned. And now that he's met Tessa, it just added to the good in his life. It didn't replace anything, but he says it made his world bigger."

"And his parents agree?"

"They're grateful to her, too. She was twenty-five, you know, so not a scared teenager. She could have had a baby and, knowing Tessa, who is smart and accomplished like you? She'd have slayed motherhood. But she made what everyone thinks is a very unselfish decision, and so many people benefited from it."

Meredith blinked against the sudden sting in her eyes. "Sounds like he got lucky."

"He got loved," Lacey said. "And he's the kind of guy who makes the most of what he's given."

Meredith's chest tightened. Her fingers moved to her stomach without thinking. Still flat. Still secret. Still hers...for now.

Lacey leaned across the table, reaching toward her. "You okay, Mer?"

"Oh, yeah," she said quickly. "It's just...quite a story. And, hey, I'm a little jealous of that NFL box."

"You? Jealous of me?" she scoffed. "I've looked up to you for so long my neck hurts. You've always had it together more than anyone I've ever known. To hear your father talk about how you run Acacia Architecture for him? Nothing's changed."

Oh, but everything had changed. One mistake and—poof—all changed.

"I mean, Meredith, you've been the gold standard forever—school, career, style, ambition..."

Meredith gave a soft laugh to cover the ache inside. She sure wasn't going to be the gold standard when they all found out how dumb she was.

Maybe she could go somewhere, take a long trip, give the baby up for adoption, and come back and be like Tessa.

Meredith swallowed hard and looked away.

"Are you sure you're okay?" Lacey pressed, a frown pulling over her big blue eyes. "'Cause you seem...off."

"I am off," she admitted. "Probably because I haven't had a vacation in, well, ever, and this place feels like I'm living on vacation." She rooted around for a good and safe subject as she picked at what was left of her dinner. "So, Aunt Vivien. Your mom juggling two men? Now that's something I never thought I'd see."

The two of them had spent endless hours discussing Lacey's parents' divorce, her father's classic mid-life crisis, and her mother's incredible strength through the trauma of it all.

"She's come a long way," Lacey said with unabashed pride. "As far as Danny and Peter? I think she realized she was so fresh out of marriage, it was too soon with either one. She's been hard at work on herself, and I just love her for it."

"Did you have a favorite of the two?" Meredith asked.

"Oh, I'm fully on Team Peter and he's supposedly moving to Destin, so..." She held up crossed fingers. "Maybe I'll be the one in an ugly sage-colored dress."

Meredith laughed, not hating the idea of someone wonderful for Aunt Vivien. They talked about Peter for a while, then the conversation moved to Grandma Maggie and the big revelation about the criminal grandfather they never knew.

It was easy to sit and gossip about the fam as the two of them had done for years, staying at the table until well after sunset.

They walked out to the car, the air sticky and warm with the coming night. Meredith paused before getting in.

"How long will you be away?" she asked Lacey.

"I'm not sure. A few days in Jax, and then he said we could stay at his parents' house for a while. How long are you going to be in Destin? I don't want to miss the chance to hang with you."

"I don't know," Meredith said. "A few weeks, I think. I'd like to be here if and when Atlas's grandparents show up. If Jonah needs a show of family solidarity, I'm here. I can work remote and...you know, take a...gulp, vacation."

Lacey laughed. "Now you sound like the Meredith I know and love."

But would she be that woman when Lacey found out the truth? Or would the news push her right off the pedestal her little cousin had put her on?

As they pulled out of the parking lot and turned toward home, Meredith's gaze lingered on the quiet sky, and the road ahead that seemed to stretch forever.

She had no idea what she was going to do about this baby, but with each passing day, she knew she had to figure it out.

July 11, 1992

1:47 a.m. (I can't sleep, I'm still sandy, and I have the obnoxious voice of Dustin Mathers stuck in my head.)

Today was... wow. Something happened that just stuck with me and will definitely become a "remember when" story next summer. Maybe even sooner. Possibly by breakfast.

We were all just being normal, okay? Me, Tessa, and Kate. Our three matching striped towels lined up on the beach. We brought snacks and books and dragged out the big turquoise umbrellas to make what Tessa insists on calling "her cabana." (She also wore her snow-white bikini on her ridiculously tanned skin which makes all the boys do that cartoon eyeball bulging thing and I am NOT exaggerating.)

It was sunny and perfect, and really peaceful. Tessa was flipping through Seventeen, and Kate was doing that thing where she eats Goldfish crackers one by one and looks like she's solving math problems in her head, and I was just soaking up the sun.

Enter: Dustin "Who Invited Him?" Mathers.

We heard him before we saw him.

Well—technically, we heard the sound of a beer can cracking open and someone singing what I think was supposed to be "Thunderstruck" by AC/DC, but it was so off-key I thought it was a dying seagull.

He stumbled down the boardwalk with two other guys I vaguely recognized from around town—maybe locals? Dustin was definitely the leader of the idiot parade (so named by Tessa), shirtless, barefoot, and <u>drunk</u>. I've seen him like this before at some beach parties, but this was the middle of the afternoon!

And of course he spotted us.

"WYLIE TWINS! LITTLE LAWSON!" He literally shouted across the dunes like we were contestants.

(For the record: <u>I am not little</u>. I am 5'4". That is average.)

We all groaned in unison. Except Tessa, who waved, because of course she did.

We knew Dustin was drunk right away when he tripped over absolutely nothing and landed in a sprawl in the sand in front of us.

He smelled like beer and Nacho Doritos. His eyes were bloodshot but sparkly, and he literally slurred his words like a cliché.

We complained about him wrecking our peace, but Tessa pronounced him "harmless" which got her a very drunk grin from him. He said he wasn't harmless. He was wild. Actually he said, "I am untameable. I am the storm." (Picture my eyes rolling.) He was barely coherent, that's what.

And he kept calling me "Little Lawson" which irks. Crista is little. I am fifteen, but he was in no shape for an argument. The thing about Dustin is he's got this way of saying things where you're not sure if he's teasing or being genuine, and that smile is annoying because it makes it harder to stay annoyed.

Then it got weird.

Tessa kicked him—playfully, of course—and told him he should probably get home before his parents freak.

He was really quiet. Weirdly quiet for a long time. Then all he said was: "Nah, there are too many ghosts at home."

I had to write it down so I didn't forget. Ghosts?

Even Kate looked up from her Goldfish math.

But right away, he snapped back into Dustin Mode and yelled "I'M GONNA SWIM TO THE BAHAMAS!" and took off running down the beach like a maniac.

Tessa shouted that it wasn't the ocean. Actually she yelled, "It's the Gulf of Mexico, you idiot!"

He didn't even turn around. Just dove into the water fully clothed and started doing a sloppy backstroke while singing "Bohemian Rhapsody." Kate said we should leave him and let the sea deal with him. But I sat up and watched him, making sure he kept moving.

Tessa sighed and called Dustin a "loveable mess." She's kinda right.

What did he mean about the <u>ghosts</u>? It kind of sent chills up my spine.

Maybe there's more to him than chaos and beer cans.

Maybe not.

Okay. Shutting this down before I get too philosophical and accidentally become Kate.

Viv

Chapter Seven

Tessa

It had rained the morning of their barbeque, which left behind a fresh, summery scent that mixed beautifully with the lingering aroma of grilled ribs and charred corn. Tessa picked up the last of the dinner plates and discarded napkins, listening to Vivien and Kate's chatter in the kitchen. More masculine voices echoed up from the pool level where Eli and Dusty had gone to clean up a well-used grill.

Tessa took a moment to breathe it all in, letting snippets from the long afternoon and lazy family-style dinner float over her. Inviting Dusty had been a stroke of genius, she decided. He was just the blast from the past they needed to fill the house with laughter, conversation, and memories.

This past week, things had been a little more tense than usual—mostly with Jonah, and the stress of having an infant in the house. Dusty had honored her request to keep the specifics about how they'd bumped into each other to himself. Everyone—including Jo Ellen and Maggie—had been happy to see someone they remembered from the past.

Maybe they didn't remember him as well as Tessa

did, though. She had the benefit of Vivien's old diary, which she'd kept. This morning, knowing Dusty was coming over, she'd skimmed the pages looking for his name, and boy, had she found it.

The words fifteen-year-old Viv had written only served to make Tessa notice that more than just his name had changed. Dustin—now Dusty—Mathers was nothing like the wild, out-of-control, smart-mouthed teenager he'd been that day.

Life had seriously changed him.

Vivien appeared in the doorway with another dessert tray.

"Oh." Tessa inched back. "I just put out cookies."

"This is strawberry shortcake," she said. "Maggie insisted."

"People are going to roll out of here," Tessa said on a laugh.

Vivien shrugged. "Sorry, but if you have barbeque, you're required to have something with whipped cream after. It's a Southern law."

Tessa snorted and eyed the platter of yummy short-cakes and clouds of cream. "Well, I guess I'm not in Upstate New York anymore. We just do decaf and the occasional chocolate chip cookie."

"Decaf is being brewed." Vivien waved her toward the house and the kitchen. "Come gossip with Kate. We must talk about Dustin—er, Dusty now."

She glanced toward the spiral stairs, confident that he'd be downstairs with Eli for a bit. "I'm down for some coffee and gossip."

She followed Vivien into the kitchen, where Kate was humming away, wiping down the counters and smiling.

"You look happy," Tessa noted, sliding onto a barstool to face her sister.

"I am, Tess." Kate leaned over the counter, bartender-style. "Whatcha havin', little lady?"

"I heard there's decaf and gossip."

"Plenty of both," she said, turning to fill the order while Vivien sat next to her, glancing around.

"What happened to Jonah?" she asked. "He was just here."

Kate sighed. "Atlas cried, so he went downstairs. Meredith went to find the Baby Bjorn to take the little nugget to the beach."

"That always calms him," Vivien said. "Nothing like a pink-tinged sky and lapping waves. Kid lives the life, I tell you."

"Funny how we know that little man already," Kate mused. "He's lived here, what, a week or so?"

"Lived here?" Tessa scoffed. "He runs the place."

The others laughed, but no one argued. Life had been turned upside down by the nine-pound screamer, but they all loved him so.

"Still, I worry about Jonah," Kate said.

Vivien nodded. "He was so quiet during dinner and barely ate. I remember barbeques when he was a kid, able to put away three ears of corn."

"Well, we were talking about things that happened in the last century, long before he was around," Tessa said. "Maybe he was bored."

"Maybe." Kate poured three cups of decaf. "He's supposed to start classes later this week. He might be preoccupied with how he's going to balance school and fatherhood. And we haven't heard from Carly's parents yet, so that's on his mind."

Tessa nodded and glanced around, noticing that her mother and Maggie had also disappeared. "And the sorority sisters?"

"They went up to the apartment to rest." Kate slid a cup of coffee toward her and the bottled creamer she liked.

A beat of silence passed as Tessa fixed her coffee.

"Sooo..." Vivien dragged the word out with a playful song in her voice.

"Dusty Mathers!" Kate and Tessa replied in perfect unison, making all three of them laugh.

"Seriously," Kate said, leaning over the counter like she'd been dying to start the conversation. "It's like he's not the same kid. Well, obviously he's a fifty-two-year old man, but he's so grounded and sensible and warm. Nice-looking, too."

"And he brought me a purple Boogie board!" Vivien exclaimed, making a face. "How sweet of him to remember he broke mine."

"That was too cute," Kate said. "He's just awesome."

"He's been through a lot," Tessa said. "His wife died, and I get the impression she was sick for a while."

"Oh, that's so sad," Vivien said. "But he seems so... stable. Knowing him as a teenager, I would have expected..."

"Jail time," Tessa finished with a snort. "And I say that as the current owner of one of your diaries."

They both gave her questioning looks.

"I flipped through it looking for his name today," she confessed. "Do you remember the time he showed up on the beach drunk in the middle of the day?"

"He barely had one beer today," Kate noted.

"He said there were ghosts," Vivien said softly, sitting up as she remembered.

"Yes! That's what you wrote in your diary. What did he mean?"

"I don't know, but I never forgot it," Vivien said. "I remember the hairs on the back of my neck standing. I was a kid. I thought he meant real ghosts."

"Maybe he did," Tessa said.

"Please." Kate tapped the counter. "He lived around here, right? He was a local, not a summer kid, as I recall."

"He's definitely a local," Tessa confirmed.

"Well, I'll tell you something else that changed," Vivien said, leaning in playfully. "He looked at you like you were made of gold-dipped bacon all day today, Miss Tessa Wylie."

"Oh, come on."

"It was adorable," Vivien added. "And weird. He used to be the only boy in town who wasn't in love with you."

"We were always buddies," Tessa said. "And as I recall, we got into enough trouble being friends."

"Hmm." Kate nodded as she sipped. "One word: bonfire."

Tessa cringed. "It was his fault the fire department had to come."

"Well, you could call them tonight," Vivien teased. "He burned you with every look."

"Will you stop?" Tessa rolled her eyes. "I think he was just grateful I invited him. And with all the reminiscing, no one brought up how frequently he was kind of a wreck."

"All in the past," Kate said. "And, for the record, Vivien's right. Any chance that attraction is reciprocated?"

She was saved by the sound of male voices and footsteps coming across the deck, answering with a noncommittal smile.

"Grates need a soak," Eli announced, heading toward the sink carrying a big black iron...thing.

"We attempted to do it the old-fashioned manly way," Dusty said, holding up his filthy hands. "But we're not old-fashioned or manly."

Tessa would disagree, but she just smiled. "Make that shine and there's a strawberry shortcake in your future."

"Yes, ma'am."

Jonah walked in from the front door, his posture tight, jaw set.

"Oh, I thought you were on the beach with Meredith," Vivien said.

"And Atlas," Eli noted. "Is he with her?"

"No, Dad. I left my month-old baby on the beach alone," he retorted, no humor in the snark.

"Whoa," Tessa muttered. "There's strawberry short-cake on the deck if you need some sugar to get sweeter."

His eyes shuttered and he started to respond, then stopped.

"Are you okay?" Eli asked, stepping forward.

Jonah took a breath, then held out his phone to his dad. Tessa couldn't see the screen, but she had a good idea what the picture might be.

"This came up in my memories," Jonah said. "I miss her, that's all. I still can't believe she's...gone."

He looked around, wearing that ravaged and lost expression that made less frequent appearances but still could be evident.

"Sorry," he murmured, looking at their guest. "Didn't mean to ruin the party." He looked at the photo, then shook his head and turned. "I'm going to lie down. God knows that kid won't let me sleep tonight."

He walked out and down the stairs, leaving a wake of silence and discomfort.

"I'm going out on a limb and guessing he's referring to his son's mother?" Dusty said.

Eli nodded. "She was killed less than two weeks ago in a head-on collision."

"Oof." He gave his chest a punch. "That's...wow. I hear a lot of tragic stories, but with a newborn? He's actually handling it remarkably well."

Eli nodded. "Most of the time, but Atlas's grandparents have threatened to try and take the baby, although we haven't heard anything from them. And while he's got all of us to help him, he's supposed to be starting an intensive program at a local college."

The frown on Dusty's face deepened, showing some creases...and plenty of empathy.

"Hey, I don't want to overstep, so tell me to shut up and go home, but..." He put his hands in the pockets of his khaki shorts and settled his gaze on Eli. "Could I talk to him? As you know, I'm a therapist, but grief is kind of my specialty. I don't want to push, but maybe I could help."

Eli considered that, then nodded. "That would mean a lot and, honestly, as his father? I feel like I should have the words. Nothing prepares you for this."

He put a hand on Eli's shoulder and gave a warm look. "You're doing amazing, my friend."

Tessa watched the exchange, vaguely aware of pressure on her chest. How kind he was, and how...cool. He had something—emotional intelligence, she presumed—that was sorely lacking in most men. Most men in her life to this point, anyway.

Just then, he turned to her, almost as if he sensed her gaze on him. He started to say something, but caught himself.

"I'll be downstairs," he said, giving a nod as he walked out.

She watched him go, utterly caught off guard by... something.

Vivien leaned in and inhaled softly, sliding Tessa a look that said she knew exactly what that something was. Attraction.

"Shut up," Tessa whispered as Kate and Eli started talking to each other.

"I'm just sayin'..."

Tessa smiled, but then it faded.

"He has ghosts," she whispered, meaning his late wife. But maybe those ghosts went back further than that. She didn't know, but she wanted to.

AN HOUR LATER, conversation was hushed on the deck, though some laughter had resumed when Meredith returned from the beach with baby Atlas snuggled into sleep again. Everyone had started to relax, but Tessa's mind kept wandering down to the first floor.

Dusty had been with Jonah for an hour.

Finally, she shared a look with Eli, who tipped his head and gave a questioning glance.

"I'll go check," she said, pushing up. "I invited him and he's my responsibility."

Eli smiled and nodded, obviously grateful.

She padded down the stairs to the lower level and paused without popping around the wall that hid her. She could hear them talking in Jonah's bedroom, so the door must be open.

Just as she was about to clear her throat and make her presence known, she heard Jonah laugh quietly, the sound melting her heart.

"I get that," he said. "But..." The smile left his voice. "It's that sledgehammer feeling again. Some mornings I wake up and I don't remember she's gone. Just for a split second. And then—boom. It knocks the snot out of me, and I feel like I can't breathe for the rest of the day."

"That's the thing about grief," Dusty replied. "It doesn't walk through the front door—it crashes through the ceiling. And it doesn't ask for permission."

Tessa hesitated, one hand on the banister. She should go back upstairs. This wasn't her moment to eavesdrop. But something about Dusty's voice—so gentle, so knowing, so strong and steady—rooted her to the step.

"It's not like I expected this," Jonah continued, quieter. "I mean, no one does. But Carly was strong. Like... mountain-climber strong. She knew if she kicked me out—and that wasn't easy—that I'd finally get my act together, and I did. Yes, everyone in this house helped me, including my dad and Kate, but it was Carly who forced me. And when I came back, she believed in me. She was my whole world."

"And now you have Atlas," Dusty reminded him. "To Atlas, you are *his* whole world."

"I know, man. And I can't...I have to..." He swore under his breath.

"You can and you will, son," Dusty said softly.

"I just want to be happy to have a kid, you know? But I can't. I feel like it's wrong. Like somehow I'm betraying her if I laugh or have fun or take a picture of Atlas. I feel like it's wrong that I'm alive and she's not. I don't want to feel any joy, but I do. And I know it's wrong."

"It's not wrong, not at all," Dusty assured him. "Time will allow you to let go of that feeling, I promise you.

Right now, you have classic survivor's guilt. I have a brief program to help you through that, if you want it. A couple books, a lecture I give that I'll share with you."

"I don't...yeah, I guess."

"I'm here for you," Dusty said. "No charge, any time, day or night."

Tessa felt something crack in her chest.

"And in the meantime," he continued, "remember that grief and joy can live in the same heart. You don't have to wait for the grief to be gone to start letting some joy back in. You have a newborn son and he's amazing. You should let yourself feel the thrill—and absolute sleeplessness—of that."

As Jonah chuckled, she turned to slip back up the steps—she'd heard too much, this was private—but her footstep betrayed her.

Inside, the voices stopped.

Then Jonah's familiar snort floated through the door. "Whoever's out there better be a spy with strawberry shortcake or else."

Tessa laughed and came down the rest of the stairs, walking to Jonah's open door.

"I swear I wasn't eavesdropping," she said, stepping inside.

The room was dimly lit by one standing lamp, casting a soft golden glow over the messy unmade bed where Jonah sat. A box of tissues, five of them used and balled up, balanced on Jonah's pillow.

Dusty was in the chair, leaning back, looking remarkably comfortable.

Even with the evidence of tears, Jonah looked like a different man. His shoulders weren't quite so high, his eyes not so shadowed. Whatever "therapy" had gone on down here, it had worked.

Dusty glanced at her, amused. "What? No shortcake?"

"We saved some," she said. "I did not mean to interrupt."

"We were just wrapping up," Jonah said, pushing off the bed and stretching. "I should go check on Atlas anyway."

"He's conked out and being traded from loving arm to loving arm."

Jonah smiled and looked at Dusty. "See?"

The other man shrugged. "All part of the process."

She had no idea what they had talked about, but clearly the connection was strong.

Jonah reached out and clasped Dusty's hand. "Thank you, man. For real. That... helped more than I thought it would."

Dusty rose, too, pulling Jonah in for a quick guy-hug. "Anytime."

Jonah turned to Tessa. "He's better than a bourbon." Then he grinned. "Okay, maybe not better. But close."

With that, he ducked out and climbed the stairs, leaving them alone in the quiet room.

Tessa perched on the bed, arms crossed, eyes on Dusty. "So who stole the bad boy of the beach and replaced him with...a kind, sensitive, remarkably good therapist?"

He chuckled but then his smile faded. "Life did the dirty work, Tessa. But it's nice of you to notice the improvements."

"They're kind of hard to miss, unless you break into a chorus of AC/DC—then I'll know it's you."

He regarded her for a moment, looking just a tiny bit exhausted, which was understandable after an hour of grief counseling.

"So, have I done my due diligence yet?"

She lifted a questioning brow. "Free therapy?"

"Nah, that's actually fun for me. I mean...I did the reunion, re-met the family, picked up where we all left off." He reached for her hand and guided her to her feet.

She frowned, still not following. "Was that an effort for you?"

"Oh, no. It was awesome. I love being here, same vibe from thirty years ago, just more gray hair. What I meant was I know that was the proper thing to do before..."

"Before what?" she asked, vaguely aware of his strong hand holding hers.

"Can I ask you out on a proper date now?"

Oh. She literally felt a little tilt in her world. "A... date?"

He laughed softly. "It's a thing single, unmarried, and mutually attracted people do. Usually includes dinner, maybe some awkward eye contact, a few confessions, and, if we're lucky, a kiss goodnight. And to be honest, you'd be my first in a long time, so it might also involve some patience on your part."

And the world tilted some more, making her wonder if she might fall off.

"I always thought you...well, that I wasn't your type."

"You're everyone's type, Tessa," he said on a chuckle. "But mostly, Eli put a wall of protective ownership around you, and he was one of the few decent guys here who could stand me. Most of my friends were losers, as you might recall."

She did, but didn't say anything, letting him continue.

"So I kept it friendly out of deference to a kid I really respected. I still do," he added quickly. "But he seems to be into Kate, so I take it the coast is clear and I can ask you out. Yes?"

She hated that the little speech left her breathless. She was almost fifty years old, for heaven's sake. She shouldn't be breathless. But there was something so real and so different and so wonderful about this man.

Drunk, bad, wild Dustin Mathers...who was none of those things anymore.

When she didn't answer, he stepped closer, close enough that she could smell the faint salt from the sea in his shirt, feel the steadiness in his posture.

"So is that a yes?"

Tessa tipped up her head. "Yes," she said on a whisper.

He exhaled in mock relief. "Thank God. I was terrified of rejection."

"Oh, Dusty," she joked as they walked out of the room. "I don't think you're terrified of anything."

"Then you'd be wrong," he said, walking with her to the bottom of the stairs. She placed her hand on the rail, paused, then turned back to him.

"And by the way? That thing you said to Jonah? About not needing the grief to go away to feel joy? I'm going to write that one down. I've struggled with that since my dad died."

He smiled. "You don't have to write it down. You're already living it."

She gave him a grateful look, then climbed the stairs with a heart that felt lighter than it had in months.

Chapter Eight
Maggie

The interior of the Toyota SUV smelled faintly of Vivien's perfume mixed with Jo Ellen's drugstore hand sanitizer and...fear. That last one was all on Maggie, who tried not to grip the wheel and say very unladylike things at the horrific traffic and really stupid drivers.

"It's like maneuvering a school bus," she muttered to Jo Ellen, who, of course, was clutching that bar above her window like they were chasing tornadoes instead of looking for a decent place to have lunch after a shopping excursion at TJ Maxx.

"I still don't understand why you didn't drive here from Atlanta. You'd have your own car," Jo Ellen said. "It's a pain to borrow Vivien's every time we want to go anywhere."

"I had my reasons," she said, although chief among them was Maggie's bone-deep terror of interstates. "I had to rush down here to get to the event where my granddaughter was the star. Flying made more sense."

"Yes, the wedding fashion show," Jo Ellen recalled. "But then you stayed. Couldn't someone have gotten your car here? Meredith or Eli? Maybe Crista could drive it down and fly back?"

"Crista's pregnant and everyone wants their own car and I'm fine borrowing this one."

"But Vivien's so busy and we so rarely get out." Jo Ellen leaned forward and pointed. "By the way, that was the turn the GPS said to take."

"It's left," Maggie replied. "Without a light. Not a fan."

She felt Jo Ellen's piercing gaze and knew Maggie's fears were about to be discussed—no doubt in the context of that inane road trip she still wanted to take.

"But you skipped the last turn, and it was a right."

"I didn't like it." What she didn't like was the truck in the other lane that looked...big. She could have side-swiped the thing.

"I'm happy to drive, you know."

"That's worse," Maggie muttered.

"Worse than you, who never met a turn signal she could use or a yield sign she...yielded?"

Maggie tsked. "No one pays attention to turn signals, and I had the right of way on that last merge. Trust me, you want me to drive. I'm not a good passenger."

"Oh, but you're a *great* driver." Jo Ellen rolled her eyes, then inched closer. "It's why you won't go on our road trip, isn't it?"

Maggie hated that this woman could still read her mind—even after a thirty-year hiatus.

"Please, a road trip with you?"

"You love me!" she exclaimed defensively.

"I do," Maggie assured her. "But you are a very nervous passenger and that puts me on edge."

"Well, your driving puts me on edge."

"And, Jo, you know our kids would be furious if we pulled a stunt like that. And that...vehicle—if you can call Frank's truck by so lofty a name—looks like it's held together with rust and spit."

Jo Ellen just shrugged. "Betty's Thunderbird'll be ready soon. Frank's called me twice, and I just don't know what to say to him."

"The word is 'no,' Jo Ellen. *No*. It rhymes with...slow and *whoa!*" She pressed the heel of her hand on the horn. "Stay in your own lane, buddy."

"He was. You were the one swerving."

Maggie sliced her with a side-eye.

"And it also rhymes with go," Jo Ellen said. "Which is what I think we should do. In fact"—Jo Ellen pulled a stack of neatly printed pages from her oversized straw tote like a magician producing a rabbit—"I made this. Just a little itinerary. With help."

"You told someone? Kate? Tessa?" Maggie tapped the brakes as they neared an intersection. "We agreed that we'd—"

"First of all, does it matter if you won't go?"

"No, but I like secrecy."

"You always have," Jo Ellen agreed. "But I only told Oscar."

"Who is Oscar?"

"What I call my ChatGPT. He's so smart." She

sighed heavily. "And he just knows me like no man except Artie."

"Wait...*what?* You chatted with Oscar? What are you talking about?"

"ChatGPT. It's a robot. Actually, artificial intelligence. Very high-brow stuff, Maggie. I'm surprised you haven't heard of it."

"I've heard of it," she snapped. "I just...I thought you needed a big IBM computer or something."

"Honey, it's on your phone." She waved hers. "You type in stuff—or, if you get really good like I have, you can dictate—and it helps solve all your problems. I mean, the ones that have answers. Oscar'll never bring Artie back, but he makes a mean itinerary. Do you want to hear it?"

Maggie continued driving, glancing side to side for a suitable restaurant but everything looked like a greasy spoon to her or a treacherous left turn without a light. "I don't trust robots or that fake stuff," Maggie said. "I don't like computers."

"Well, then you'll die in the dark, my friend. This is the way of the future. All I did was ask Oscar to write me up a plan for two old ladies driving from Destin to Miami Beach."

"We're not—"

"Yes, we are. I told him no highways, if possible, and no more than three to four hours a day on the road with plenty of stops at tourist places and gardens. You like gardens, I know."

Maggie just narrowed her eyes and shook her head. "I

don't trust robots. They don't know anything. They don't know how hot the pavement gets in August."

"Oh, but they do, and Oscar will tell you in Fahrenheit, Centigrade, and what are the best shoes to wear."

"I don't need—"

"Just listen to this." Jo Ellen flipped through the pages. "Day One—depart Destin on scenic highway 30-A. Very famous, as you know. We'll drive through Grayton Beach, Seaside—which looks like a postcard—and lunch in Rosemary Beach."

"Fake town," Maggie said. "They just lifted it up out of nowhere, I heard."

Jo Ellen flipped her hand. "After all that, we'll take an easy drive to Panama City Beach."

"Great. Spring breakers. We can enter a wet T-shirt contest and chug beer."

Laughing, Jo flipped the page. "Actually, we can stay at the Driftwood Lodge, which Oscar says is a classic—"

"Travel agent-speak for 'it has bugs and mold.' No, thank you."

"Mags!" She gave a playful slap on Maggie's arm with the paper. "It's two and a half hours in the car on Day One."

"At that rate, we'll get to Miami in September." She gave a soft look to her friend. "I appreciate your—and Oscar's—work and enthusiasm, but I'm not going."

"But we can stay at a waterfront inn in Apalachicola," she said, undaunted. "It has a wraparound porch and rocking chairs. The owner's got a one-eyed cat named

Crabcake and serves key lime pie for breakfast. I mean, come on, Mags. Let's live."

"Or die...in Frank's bucket of bolts we take to a town named after a soft drink."

Jo Ellen dropped back with a sigh of resignation. "You're doing it again."

"What? Being reasonable, sensible, and wise? I can't help it."

"Covering your deep fears with sarcasm and dry wit." Jo Ellen folded the papers and slid them back in her purse. "You did it the day I met you, in the dorm at the University of Georgia. You decided my name was Sue Ellen, not Jo Ellen."

"A nod to Scarlett O'Hara's sister."

"The plain one," Jo said. "But what you were doing was covering your fear that you wouldn't like sharing a room with a stranger. A Yankee, no less." She fake fanned herself. "I do declare, Captain Butler!"

"Will you stop?"

"Will you?" Jo countered. "Don't think I can't see what you're doing, Maggie Lawson, when you use your intelligence and rapier wit to get what you want."

"Look, there's a little diner that doesn't look too bad. Should we try it? I'm very hungry." She gave Jo a side-eye. "Don't make me pull out my rapier wit, whatever that is."

"It cuts to the core and, yes, let's go there."

Maggie pulled into the parking lot of a strip center, finding a spot close to the restaurant. Parked, she turned off the engine and looked at Jo Ellen.

"All kidding aside, I'm not going, Jo, even if it is by way of Apa-coca-cola. I'm not risking my life—or yours—on some highway adventure in a rolling death trap with more miles than the space shuttle—"

"Speaking of, we can make a day trip to the Kennedy Space Center."

"I'm not..." Maggie swallowed, knowing she just had to speak the truth. "I'm not...I'm not a good driver."

How was that for an understatement?

Maggie hadn't driven more than an hour alone in nearly a decade. Highways made her palms sweat and that was the reason she wanted to live with Crista—so her daughter could do the majority of the driving.

She merged like a mouse coming out of hiding and any distance made her feel disoriented and panicked and like something terrible was going to happen the second she hit sixty-five miles per hour.

She wasn't a good driver. She *knew* that. Admitting it out loud, though? That would be like admitting she was one step from assisted living.

Jo Ellen was clearly undaunted by Maggie's confession, shaking her head like she had all the arguments covered by her stupid computer with a name.

"We'll take it slow, Mags. No more than three or four hours each day. We'll stop at flea markets and antique stores. We'll eat pie. We'll talk and listen to playlists—Oscar can make us one from our college years—and laugh and maybe scream a little when we miss an exit."

"I already scream when I *don't* miss an exit," Maggie muttered.

"We need this. *You* need this."

"I need…" She turned away, looking out the window and rooting for the words that would make this argument end.

But something bright orange coming out from one of the stores or offices in the strip mall caught her eye. She hadn't seen a color quite that hideous since…the last time they were with Betty and she had that same top on.

"What is she doing all the way out here?"

Jo Ellen followed her gaze and sucked in a breath. "Is that Betty?"

"Yes, and we're a long way from Santa Rosa Beach." She watched her friend, deep in conversation with another woman who had a scarf on her head, then the two of them hugged.

"People can drive places, you know," Jo Ellen said, her voice barely above a whisper as they watched Betty wipe beneath her eyes with the back of her hand as they parted.

"Is she crying?" Maggie murmured.

Betty waved to the other woman, then walked off in the other direction, dabbing her eyes again.

A familiar dented truck rumbled into the frame. "Oh, no," Maggie groaned. "It's Frank and the clunker."

The truck squealed slightly as it stopped beside Betty. Frank got out slowly—like his knees were catching up with the rest of him—and came around to open the passenger door.

Betty stepped in with care. He reached for her hand,

held it. Then, without saying anything, he leaned in and pulled her close.

It wasn't a casual hug. It was the kind of hug you gave someone when you didn't want to let them go.

Maggie felt something inside her go still as the truck drove away.

Neither of them said a word about it, but they hefted their purses and got out of the SUV with almost as much care as Betty had used getting in that truck. They walked toward the restaurant, which took them right past the door of wherever Betty had been.

Slowing their steps, they read the small sign: *Emerald Coast Infectious Diseases Medical Group/Chemo patients please check in next door.*

"Oh." The sound slipped out from Maggie's lips. Without thinking, she reached for Jo's hand, and they held onto each other as the truth hit them.

"It *is* her dying wish," Maggie whispered.

Jo Ellen could only nod, her eyes filling with tears. "Let's go back home, Mags. I'm not hungry."

Maggie almost agreed. Almost. But her head was spinning, and her heart was pounding, and a big black ball of guilt was pressing on her chest.

Guilt and fear. Was there any worse combination?

"Well, I want to go in that restaurant," Maggie said, tugging her along.

"How can you eat?"

"I don't want to eat," she replied, bringing Jo with her into the upscale diner.

She hadn't understood. Not really. Not until now.

Betty wasn't just sick. She was *dying*.

That trip in the Thunderbird was more than some nostalgic lark. It was the thing Betty had clung to while she still could. One more ride. One more beautiful dream. And Maggie—stubborn, scared, prideful Maggie —had nearly stolen it from her by saying no.

The fear didn't go away. It sat in Maggie's chest like an anchor, pressing down on every bone.

But something else had shifted. Maybe not courage— at least not yet—but clarity.

They slid into a booth and instantly Jo picked up the paper napkin to wipe tears from under her eyes.

"Give it to me," Maggie said.

With a question in her expression, Jo Ellen held out the napkin.

"No! The itinerary from Roscoe or Oswald. Whatever you call him."

Her eyes flickered, a hint of brightness returning. "Oscar." She fished in her tote. "It's here. Right here." She shoved it across the table. "He made a printable version with cute little clip art and—"

"Hush. I can't read and talk at the same time."

Jo Ellen instantly closed her mouth, staying silent while a waitress brought them water and menus as Maggie skimmed the ridiculously detailed itinerary. Oscar was clearly an over-thinker.

But it looked...doable.

Apalachicola. Cedar Key. The Villages? She'd skip

that one or Jo Ellen would have them condo shopping. But mostly it was tiny towns, back roads, ice cream shops, antiquing, and pie.

It wasn't the trip that scared her. It was what it meant: letting go of control. Admitting fear. Being vulnerable enough to say *yes* to life, even when it terrified her.

Because Betty Cavallari was dying.

She blinked away tears as she put the stack of papers next to her. "We'll do it."

Jo Ellen gasped. "You mean it?"

"For Betty," Maggie said, her voice rough. Then, quieter, "And maybe for me."

Jo Ellen reached across the table and took Maggie's hand. "It's the right thing to do, Mags. And we'll have fun."

Maggie took a shaky breath. "God help us," she muttered.

Jo Ellen smiled. "He already has. He gave us Crab-cake the cat and a robot travel assistant. What more do we need?"

"A miracle," Maggie said. "And good weather. I hate to drive in rain."

"Of course you do."

"And we will not tell anyone where we're going," she added.

"Do you think that's smart?"

"They'll never let us leave," Maggie told her. "And we have to get that car. For Betty."

Jo Ellen picked up her water glass. "For Betty," she said.

They toasted with water—which was probably bad luck—and decided they were hungry after all.

Chapter Nine

Eli

With Tessa having officially taken over the only legitimate office space in the Summer House, Eli had moved his workspace to the dining area. As much as he wanted to blow off every minute of this summer, it was somewhat overcast today, and the house was unusually quiet.

Maggie and Jo Ellen had surprised them all with an announcement that they were going to spend a week or so at Betty and Frank's house, helping Frank garden and learning some new recipes with Betty.

He supposed that after thirty years, the old friends had a lot of catching up to do. His mother was a bad enough driver that she certainly couldn't spend an evening with a couple of heavy wine drinkers like Frank and Betty and drive home, so he fully supported their visit.

Vivien had gone to a networking breakfast with some other local designers, and Kate said she'd be on baby duty while Jonah got dressed and ready for his first day of classes.

It was really the perfect time for work, so Eli had persuaded Meredith to review a packet of early concepts one of the architects in the firm had sent for a massive renovation project. This was normally right in her wheelhouse, but today, she didn't seem as into the process as she usually was.

Eli zoomed in on the outdoor elevation plan, trying to figure out what was wrong—with the sketch *and* his daughter.

"I don't like that arch," he muttered, glancing at Meredith.

Like she had a million times since she'd learned what a plumb line was, Meredith sat next to him, her sketch pad open, her gaze flicking from the rendering to some notes and drawings in front of her.

But this time, her gaze looked...off. Her pencil wasn't moving, her questions lacked their usual crispness. Normally, Meredith was all bite and brilliance—sharp as a tack and twice as fast at spotting an error on a design than Eli had ever been.

A third-generation architect, Meredith was gifted and driven. But today, she was...distant and lost. Her fingers idly tapped the rim of her mug, a tea bag dangling from the side. Since when did she fuel with herbal tea and not her usual gallon of caffeine?

"You okay?" he asked casually as he used the mouse to highlight the offending arch.

"Yeah. Just tired, I guess."

He nodded but didn't press. She'd tell him if she wanted to. Or not.

Behind them, they heard footsteps coming up the stairs, a little light to be Jonah's. Eli turned to see who it was, spotting Kate, barefoot in cutoff jeans and a V-neck tee, holding a squirming Atlas in her arms.

"Sorry to interrupt, but...we have a problem."

Eli turned completely. "Atlas blow a diaper?"

"No. Jonah." She pushed her glasses up and took a few steps closer. "He's still in bed," she said in a hushed tone.

"You're kidding." Eli abandoned his laptop and checked his watch. "His class starts in an hour."

She nodded. "I've been knocking and calling through the door, but he told me to take Atlas and leave him alone."

Eli's stomach dropped. Jonah's mood had improved since he'd had that long conversation with Dusty last weekend, but he was erratic at best, and somehow this news didn't completely surprise him.

Not bothering with questions, Eli rose and headed straight for the stairs, vaguely aware that both Meredith and Kate followed him.

On the first floor, the morning light was completely different. It filtered through shades and bounced off the pool, giving the gathering room a soft, inviting glow. But there was nothing soft or inviting about Jonah's closed bedroom door.

Eli knocked on it anyway, silently sending up a prayer for help that he sensed he would need. "Jonah? It's Dad. Open up."

No answer but a faint grunt.

"Jonah," he said more firmly, keeping his voice level. "Talk to me, son."

Another grunt. Then a muffled, "Go away."

Meredith stepped next to him. "Let me try." She crouched near the door. "Jonah. It's me. Just open the door, okay? You don't have to explain anything. We're just worried."

Nothing.

Atlas, fussy and wriggling, let out a piercing wail. They heard the sheets rustle. Footsteps. The click of the lock. Then, slowly, the door opened a crack.

Jonah's eyes were red, his hair matted to his forehead, and his shirt twisted from a night spent curled on top of his covers. He looked like he hadn't slept, eaten, or moved since yesterday.

"I'm not going," he said thickly. "I'm not going to class. Ever."

Kate started toward him, but Jonah reached for Atlas instead. The baby calmed almost instantly as Jonah pulled him close and stepped back into the dim room.

Eli didn't hesitate to make his move. "Mind if I come in?" he asked. "Just to sit with you and Atlas?"

Jonah didn't answer, but he didn't say no.

Eli stepped inside, his heart aching. The shades were drawn, casting the room in shadows. The air was stale. A tray with a half-eaten sandwich sat on the desk.

Atlas had already rolled against his father's chest, his tiny mouth slack, one hand curled in the collar of Jonah's T-shirt.

Another beat of silence, and something cracked in Eli's heart, creating a deep longing. Only one thing could fill that hole. Only one place to go. Pausing, he turned to the doorway where Meredith and Kate stood side by side, their expressions drawn in concern.

"Meredith, can you do me a favor? Run upstairs to my room and grab the Bible by my bed."

He caught the flicker in Kate's eyes—he'd seen that look before. A tightening. A step back. But she said nothing.

"Gimme a sec." Meredith disappeared and Kate sighed, looking as if she had no idea what to do.

"Can we all stay?" Eli asked Jonah. "Kate and Meredith, too?"

Jonah closed his eyes on a sigh as he rested on his back, still holding Atlas against his chest. "I don't care. I'm not talking. And I'm not going."

Eli gestured for Kate to sit in the chair as he dropped on the corner of the bed, silent until Meredith returned. She handed over a blue leather-bound Bible, worn from Eli's constant use.

"This was your mother's," he said, running a reverent hand over the binding.

"Mom had a Bible?" Meredith asked.

"She had started reading it a few months before..." His voice faded out. "Yeah, she had a Bible."

From the bed, Jonah nodded—almost as if to say he knew that—and baby Atlas let out a sigh. His little head rose and fell with his father's breaths, tiny fingers splayed like starfish.

"She wrote in it sometimes," Eli said, fluttering a few pages before spying her handwriting in a margin and some underlined words. "And she liked the Psalms."

He flipped there. The pages, now well read, almost opened by themselves to one of his favorites.

"Mind if I read it?" he asked the small audience of three...and a half.

Jonah grunted. Meredith nodded. Kate arched a dubious brow, but then lifted a hand.

"Please do," she whispered.

"I like this one," he said. "Psalm 34. It's one of the few that give us backstory—when David pretended to be insane."

Jonah opened one eye. "I'm not pretending."

"You're not insane," Eli countered, skimming the words and notes to get to the section near the end that he wanted to read. "'The Lord is close to the brokenhearted and saves those who are crushed in spirit. The righteous person may have many troubles, but the Lord delivers him from them all...'"

His voice was steady, reading with great awareness of who was hearing this—his broken son, his curious daughter, his deeply non-believing...whatever Kate was to him. And his grandson, who he hoped would listen to hours of Eli's Bible reading in the course of his life.

"How can there be a God who'd let this happen?" Jonah asked, his voice thick and jagged. "To me? To Carly? To Atlas? What kind of God does that?"

Eli paused and looked up, gathering his thoughts. "He's not the God who *does* it, son. He's the God who walks with you *through* it."

"But why me? Why do some people get normal lives,

and I get this? I get a..." He closed his eyes. "I know, I know. Not a curse. Just really bad luck."

"Because you can carry it," Eli said, his voice firm as he let the Holy Spirit give him wisdom that he certainly didn't have on his own. "Not alone. But with Him. With us. You're not cursed, Jonah. You're in a season of growth and preparation. You've been chosen for that."

Jonah gave a bitter, disbelieving laugh. "Chosen?"

Eli nodded. "To love this child. To survive the loss. To rise up stronger. You think Jesus didn't suffer? His people betrayed Him. He was mocked. Whipped. Crucified. That pain wasn't pointless—it was part of the plan. Your pain doesn't mean God's forgotten you. It means He's ready to shape you, prepare you for fatherhood, and soften your heart."

Silence stretched as he let the words settle.

Kate still hadn't said a word. Meredith wiped a tear she clearly did not want to shed.

Very slowly, Jonah sat upright, holding tight to Atlas as he peered at the open book on Eli's lap. "Can I see it?"

"Of course." Eli slid the Bible closer, turning it so his son could read without putting the baby down. As he did so, pressure squeezed his chest. Would Jonah throw it across the room? Rip out the page? Or...read?

His gaze skimmed the scripture. "Who did all this doodling? Mom?"

"Yep. I don't write that much in the Bible. I'm more of a reader."

"What's this?" He pointed to a verse earlier in the psalm, where Melissa had drawn a heart and a star, highlighting some verses and writing something Eli couldn't remember. He leaned over and squinted at the small words.

"'Taste and see that the Lord is good,'" Jonah read out loud. "Look. She wrote JFL next to it. My initials." He glanced at Kate, who might not know that. "Jonah Fredericks Lawson," he told her. "Why would she put my initials there?"

"Something about that reminded her of you," Eli said.

"Taste and see? Like..." He stared at the note like it was a lifeline. Then he looked down at Atlas, asleep and safe in his arms. "Like...a chef would."

No one said a word as they all looked at him and collectively held their breaths.

Jonah sat stone still for three, four, five heartbeats. Then, with slow deliberation, he slid off the bed and placed the sleeping infant in the bassinet.

"I need to take a shower and get dressed," Jonah said, voice shaky but stronger. "Oh, and I need to borrow a car."

"You can have mine," Meredith and Eli answered in perfect unison, making Jonah smile.

"I'll take your truck, Dad." He notched his head to the Bible. "Can you leave that here? I didn't realize that was Mom's and, well, do you need it?"

He needed it more than his next breath, but he just smiled. "Got one on my phone. You keep it."

"Thanks."

As they all walked to the door, Kate turned and

looked at Jonah. "I'll be with Atlas today," she said softly. "Everything will be fine."

"I know. Thanks."

They slipped out quietly, closing Jonah's door and standing in the great room together.

Meredith broke first. She turned to Eli and hugged him fiercely, dropping her head on his shoulder. "Good work, Dad."

"I didn't do a thing," he replied, pressing a hand to her back. "Let's go upstairs."

They started in that direction, but Kate hung back. Eli turned and tried to read an unreadable expression. "You okay?"

She nodded slowly. "That was...intense."

"It was, but...he's going to be fine."

She gave a faint smile. "I saw you comfort your family. That matters."

She walked upstairs with Meredith, leaving Eli with the sense that she had so much more to say. He followed, glancing outside to see the clouds had deepened to an ominous gray.

After the conversation, he felt both the weight of peace...and the shadow of a storm.

THE SKY DID OPEN up that day, drenching Destin in a downpour that lasted for hours, but left the beach glistening and fresh. The weather and lack of a car forced Eli to concentrate on work, so he and Meredith battled the drawings, fixed the arch, and helped one of the other designers at Acacia Architecture put the finishing touches on a new business pitch.

By four o'clock, the world looked much more inviting than the computer screen and when Kate came up and announced that Atlas was well and truly napping, he didn't hesitate to ask her to take a walk.

"Yes, please, but—"

"I've got him," Meredith said, sliding her own laptop into a case. "And I'm not alone."

"You are not," Vivien said, swooping into the room from the deck where she'd been on a call. "I'm done for the day and would love some baby time."

"Then let's go." Eli draped his arm around Kate. "I've been cooped up all day."

A few minutes later, they hit the boardwalk in a familiar beat, heading off for their favorite activity. He and Kate had fallen for each other on beach walks back in the spring, and they hadn't taken enough since she'd been here this time.

When they walked in the dark, they usually wore sneakers, in deference to the possibility of stepping on a shell. But today, they both kicked off their shoes and let their feet sink into the cool sand.

The Gulf was restless, though. Not stormy, but churned up—like something beneath the surface had been stirred and couldn't quite settle. It matched Eli's gut, sensing this might be a difficult conversation. He'd felt it ever since Jonah left.

They headed down to the shoreline to walk in the

firm, wet sand, their bare feet leaving twin trails in the amber-lit beach. The waves reached for their ankles, retreated, tried again. The sun was still above the horizon but had lost most of its power.

"Good day of babysitting?" he asked, taking her hand.

"Exhausting," she admitted on a laugh. "For such a little guy, he keeps ya hoppin'. How did the architecture world treat you?"

"Good, good," he said. "Meredith is a little...odd."

"Really? I don't know her well enough to notice. She seems fine to me."

"She's fine, yes. But Mer doesn't really do 'fine.' She's more...fire."

She chuckled. "It's the beach, the old Destin magic. She's relaxed, I imagine, and taking a break from being a world-beater."

"You're probably right," he said. "I didn't know she *could* relax, but yeah."

They walked for a few steps, then he tightened his grip on her hand and eased her closer. "Thanks for your help this morning with Jonah."

"I didn't do anything but call in the big guns," she said. "You handled it."

"Well, I certainly had help." He looked toward the sky. "He never lets me down."

He felt, rather than heard, her sigh.

"You don't like that, do you?" he asked after a beat.

"What I like or don't like isn't important. We've discussed it before."

"In other words," he said slowly, "there's no need to rehash it."

She didn't answer right away, but slowed her step and looked out toward the turquoise water.

"Nothing you say is going to make me...believe." She stated that last word very softly, as if it terrified her. Well, it did terrify a lot of people.

When she didn't continue, he gave her hand another squeeze. "And?"

"And nothing. I just don't believe the same things you do, at least as far as religion and...God. I believe in the same family values and principles, though. I believe in showing up for the people you love, and you certainly did that for Jonah today—and in every moment you have with him. You love deeply—something I find infinitely attractive—and if that is a credit to your God, then good. I believe that's also a credit to...science."

He gave an easy laugh, choosing not to jump on the "*your* God" comment. He was everyone's God, but he knew better than to try and correct that. But science and love? That he had to question.

"How is love something you can credit to science?" he asked.

"Brain chemistry. Hormones, dopamine, synapses... science."

He had to bite his lip to keep from moaning in disappointment. "That's...clinical."

"It doesn't make love any less real," she replied quickly. "In fact, I would argue it makes those emotions more real. Instead of being some vague, kind of out-there feeling, love is based on physiological events in the body and brain. Very real."

He nodded, swallowing the ache rising in his throat. "Fair enough."

But inside, he felt a tiny tear in the fabric of his soul. He knew that his faith—the very foundation of his life— might be the thing that eventually broke them apart.

They walked a few more steps. A lone gull cried overhead, and the wind seemed to pick up.

"It's an issue, isn't it?" she finally asked, looking up at him.

"An...issue?"

She gave a light scoff. "I can read your every expression, you know. You're gloriously transparent, which is yet another thing about you I find infinitely attractive. But we—if I can be so bold as to call us a couple—have to face what is and what isn't an issue. I did with Jeffrey."

"And look how well that worked out," he said dryly, making her laugh.

"It was a very logical way to end a marriage. That's how I roll. Hey..." She elbowed him, lightening the mood. "You fell for a lab rat, so that's what you get. Logic. Science. Studies. Physical proof and unwavering facts."

He laughed again, wrapping an arm around her. "Okay, okay, doctor. How I feel about you is a fact."

"And so is how I feel about...faith," she added, easing the conversation back to the core point. "I get that your faith brings you comfort, Eli. And peace. I'm not knocking it. If it makes you feel good—helps you cope with everything you've been through—then I think that's a beautiful thing. It just can't and will never be *my* source of comfort."

Eli stopped walking and turned to her, needing to be very still to make his point.

"Kate," he said firmly. "I've heard that a hundred times. But that's not what faith is. Not real faith. It has nothing to do with being a 'source of comfort'—that's a side benefit. I don't lean on Jesus like a crutch. That's not what it is."

"Then what is it?" she pressed.

"It's...not about feeling good," he said after a breath. "It's not a fairy tale to help me sleep at night. And it sure isn't easy. In fact, having faith in this world, in this culture, is way harder than walking away from it. But I know He has a plan and a purpose for my life, and some of it is awesome and some of it actually sucks—like losing the wife I loved in a plane crash or Jonah's girlfriend getting hit by a truck. Faith is not a choice to me. It's part of my soul, which you probably don't believe we have because it can't be found on an X-ray."

She winced at that. "I get having a soul." But she didn't sound so certain, and turned to look out at the water. "But the Bible? Eli, you have to know how it looks to someone like me. A book written over centuries, passed through countless hands, languages, cultures...edited, changed, politicized. And you think it's the absolute truth? You don't find that a little... questionable?"

"There's historical backing, Kate. Plenty of it. Archaeology, written records, early manuscripts—"

"Written by people who believed the story," she countered. "That's not fact. That's confirmation bias. People recorded what they wanted to be true, and three hundred years after Jesus died, they decided which books made the cut and which ones didn't."

He crossed his arms. "And science doesn't have biases? You think researchers aren't influenced by funding, or ego, or politics?"

"Science changes with evidence. It grows. That's the point."

"So does faith," he said.

"No, Eli," she replied, gentle but insistent. "Faith resists change. It demands you hold the line even when logic says otherwise. Science is my religion. I trust what can be proven."

He looked at her, searching her face.

"But you *do* have a religion," he said. "You just said it. Everyone worships something. God puts a hole in our hearts and we choose how to fill it. I think the longing, the questions, the need to make sense of the world—that's not random. It's divine design. It's a pull toward Him."

Kate faced the water again, quiet for a long time. The breeze caught one more sad sigh as she finally turned back to him.

"I have to ask you something," she said in a low voice.

"Anything. I just hope I can answer."

"Could you..." She took a breath and looked hard at

him. "Could you really fall in love with someone who doesn't share your faith?"

"Well," he said with a smile. "I guess the answer is yes because...I already have."

She exhaled, a mix of relief and sorrow. "Eli..."

He stepped closer and took her hand. "Kate, I think about you when I wake up. When I fall asleep. When I see a beautiful sky, or hold that baby, or sit at my desk or take a bite of food. You're becoming as much a part of my fabric as...as God is."

She looked up at him, her eyes shining but unreadable. "I feel exactly the same way."

His smile wavered. "I sense a 'but' on the end of that declaration."

She tipped her head in concession. "But I'm not going to wake up one day and start believing just because it would make things easier between us."

"I know," he said.

"And I don't want to change you either. Your faith is...honestly, it's beautiful. But I can't fake something I don't feel."

"I don't want you to fake anything." He reached for her, pulled her close, and kissed her—long, deep, slow. When they pulled apart, her forehead rested lightly against his chin.

They stood there for a long time, waves brushing their ankles, the sun dipping close to the horizon. Then they walked back toward the Summer House, quiet but close, as Eli thought about the immutable fact he had to face.

He was falling in love with a woman whose heart didn't match his own—and no matter how much he wished faith alone could bridge the gap, some divides could be too big and too wide and too far to cross.

Was this one? He didn't know but, like always, he had to trust God.

Chapter Ten
Meredith

"Okay—backpack, water bottle, emotional baggage...you got it all?" Meredith eased the baby out of Jonah's arms with a sly sisterly smile as she helped him out the door the next morning for his second day of classes.

Jonah rolled his eyes as he gave Atlas to her. "You rehearse that one?"

"Nope," Meredith said, stroking the tiniest fuzz-covered head that ever existed. "Came to me in the moment. It's called talent."

He gave a snort and bent down to tie the laces on his battered sneakers, the kind he'd worn since high school. Meredith swayed Atlas a little, the move freakishly instinctive. The baby let out a delicate coo, then settled against her like he belonged there.

Jonah straightened up and looked over at them, the corners of his mouth twitching. "You look like Mom on the first day of school. Minus that blinding pink robe she wore."

"The breakfast robe," Meredith said on a laugh. "I can still see her standing in the driveway when we walked to the bus stop, waving like she was sending us to war."

"And packing us breakfast burritos that exploded in our backpacks because she couldn't figure out how to wrap them tight enough."

"She was better with the morning pep talks than the food prep." Meredith shifted Atlas and nearly melted at the way he shuddered when he sighed. "'Today is a fresh start,'" she mimicked their mother's chirpy tone. "'Go in there and show the world what Lawson kids are made of.'"

"We're made of burritos, Melissa Lawson." Jonah grabbed Meredith's keys and jangled them. "Thanks for the wheels, and the babysitting service."

"You're so welcome," she said, and meant it. "Everyone is off doing their own thing today, and Dad said I'm officially on a PTO day."

"Have you ever taken one of those in your life? Not that watching my kid while I'm in my first full day of kitchen lab is a vacation."

"It is for me," she said, stroking Atlas's head. "I get to be a world-class auntie, and don't tell me I can't do that mountain of laundry I saw in your room."

He paused in the act of sliding his backpack on, his gaze locked on her with love in his eyes. "You're so much like her, you know that?"

She knew exactly who he meant.

"She loved a good load of laundry," Meredith said on a laugh.

"She loved...being a mom."

The words made her heart feel like it was folding in half. "She was quite good at it, too."

They smiled at each other, and for a moment, the years fell away. Jonah didn't look like a single father starting his life from scratch. He looked like her big brother, gearing up for another day of school after pounding down three eggs and way too much toast while Meredith barely touched a yogurt.

"We had a good childhood," he said as if he could read her mind. "I mean, until we didn't."

She gave a sad smile. "Yeah."

"And you," he added, leaning in, "look pretty darn natural with that little beast." He gave her a look with enough weight to make it more than a casual compliment. "Honestly, Mer... when are you gonna find a good guy and be the world's most overachieving mother?"

She blinked. Her heart stuttered. She stared at him.

He didn't know. Of course he didn't. The words hadn't been said aloud yet. Not to anyone. And now, here he was, standing in front of her, innocently tossing a grenade into her morning.

"Uh...I'm so busy trying to be the world's most over-achieving architect."

Jonah chuckled. "You? Do both. But then, I suppose you need to find some idiot to fall in love with you."

She looked down at the baby, his eyes blinking up at her with sleepy trust. Her throat went tight. "Idiots I can find. It's the good ones that are few and far between."

"Hey." He touched her shoulder. "I was just kidding.

Any guy in the world would be lucky to have you, Miss Perfect."

She smiled and leaned over to kiss the top of Atlas's head. "Well, this is the only man I need for the time being."

Jonah gave her a hug and a kiss to his son. "Good luck. You're the best. I'll text if I get out early."

"Don't get out early!" she exclaimed. "Schmooze the professor. Get extra credit. Make your fellow students look lazy. Have I taught you *nothing* in life?"

He cracked up and jogged out the front door, keys jingling, bag swinging.

And then, for the first time in what felt like weeks, she was alone.

She turned slowly, the house unusually quiet. Atlas gave another tiny sigh, still nestled in her arms.

"Okay, little man," she whispered. "Let's own this domestic goddess morning."

She padded down the stairs to the lower level and set him gently into the cushioned bassinet next to Jonah's unmade bed. He didn't fuss, just gurgled sweetly and shifted his blue-eyed gaze to the window and the light.

Meredith crouched beside him. "You are dangerously precious, you know that? I'm aready in love with you. And I do have the power to give you a cousin, you know."

But would she?

Meredith had done an astounding job of compartmentalizing her pregnancy since she'd arrived, but could she do that forever? She was clearly staying here for a while...shouldn't she get a doctor? Tell someone? Do something?

It certainly wasn't like her to be paralyzed.

"Let's just start with making this room fit for two human males, shall we?"

She kissed his forehead and got up, grabbing the overflowing laundry basket near the door. It was loaded with bibs, onesies, burp cloths, and Jonah's many spit-up-covered T-shirts.

"Might as well do his sheets," she muttered, proceeding to strip the bed. And pick up clothes. And do a little cleaning in the bathroom.

Before long, she was up in the laundry room, with Atlas on the floor in the bouncy seat that Aunt Vivien had produced. It made him very portable.

"Do you think these baby socks multiply overnight?" she asked him. "Because I swear, I didn't even know socks this small existed."

She started the washer and moved into the kitchen, bringing the little guy along. There, she found sterile premade bottles in the fridge—it did help that the place was teeming with aunts who treated formula prep like an assembly line.

Atlas made a contented little chirp from the bouncy.

"Coming, sir," she said, swooping in to gather him again. "Let's change that diaper and then dine *al fresco*, shall we?"

A few minutes later, they were settled into the rocking chair, bathed in fresh salty air and shaded from the Destin late-morning sun.

She held him close, angling the bottle just right. His lips latched eagerly, his eyes never leaving hers. Something unspoken passed between them—a gentle tethering that was impossible to define.

As he suckled, Meredith gave in to a wave of peace. And not her usual peace—like the sight of an empty inbox or that last slash on a To Do list. This was a different kind of fulfillment. This was...deeper.

Could being a mother be the ultimate accomplishment?

She leaned her head back, rocking them both. Her palm drifted to her own abdomen, flat but no longer hers alone. There was a baby in there and she simply had to deal with that.

Carefully, without disturbing Atlas, she reached for her phone and opened her browser. With one hand, she searched for Destin OB/GYN offices and found a practice with good reviews.

Heart thumping, she called.

"Coastal Women's Health, how can I help you?"

"Hi," Meredith said, voice steady even as her throat tightened. "I...I'd like to make a new patient appointment. I'm pregnant."

Saying the words made it more real than the two pink lines ever had.

The receptionist was warm, professional. She answered the easy questions and, well, of course Meredith had her insurance information memorized. After reciting it, she mouthed to Atlas, "Have you met me?"

They settled on an appointment date a few weeks away, and Meredith hung up, staring at the baby in her arms.

Atlas blinked slowly, the corners of his mouth sticky and sweet, so she dabbed them with the cloth diaper that Grandma Maggie insisted all babies had to have in the house. It was a nicely functional little blast from the past.

"Well," she whispered, thinking about the phone call, "I guess it's official now, little man. You're going to have a cousin."

An unexpected tear burned her lid and slid out from under her lashes. Hormones, she told herself. And maybe hope. For a future she hadn't expected but might be what she wanted after all.

Holding Atlas certainly made her think so.

Rocking, she swiped the tears away, tugged the empty bottle free, and eased him onto her shoulder. He let out a soft burp—honestly, no one knew how to get him to do that like Aunt Meredith—then drifted to sleep.

She took him back downstairs, tucked him gently into the bassinet, adjusted the monitor beside it, and tiptoed upstairs to the kitchen, making sure the monitor receiver was on.

She was on her way to the laundry room when the office door opened and her father stepped out. "Oh, thank God you're here."

"I'm on baby duty," she said, holding up the monitor. "He just went down. What's going on?"

Dad ran his hand through his hair, looking a little frazzled. "There's a permit issue on the Hill View complex. They think I submitted the wrong elevation plans. I didn't."

"You sure?" she teased. "You've had the Kate distraction."

He didn't even smile. "They're threatening to shut down work until it's resolved. I need someone to go through the files with me. I know the originals are on the shared drive, but the update from the surveyor is missing."

"I know exactly where they are, and I have a good friend in the city manager's office. Also, that surveyor is always late, but I have his secret cell phone. Let me get my laptop and we'll fix this."

Relief poured over his face. "You're a lifesaver, Meredith. Seriously. I couldn't run this business without you."

But would she be a lifesaver when she had her own baby to care for? Probably. She was Miss Perfect, as Jonah constantly reminded her. *Perfect*. If that wasn't the height of irony, she didn't know what was.

Two hours later, the fire was out. The city had their corrected elevations, the right documents had been located, watermarked, and sent, and Dad had finally stopped pacing the length of the living room like an architect on the verge of spontaneous combustion.

Meredith shut her laptop and leaned back on the couch, balancing her notes on one knee. "Paper trail restored. Municipal gods appeased." At his look, she laughed. "And your God, too."

He winced as if the words hit him somewhere tender but before she could ask, he dropped into the armchair across from her, exhaling loudly.

"I swear to you, admin crap will be the end of me. I can sketch a cantilevered deck over a marsh in my sleep, but I will never understand the way permitting offices organize digital files."

"They don't," Meredith said. "That's the secret."

He pointed at her. "This is why you're taking over Acacia someday. Someday soon, I hope."

She laughed, a little too loudly, a little too forced. "Sure. Right after I solve world peace."

"I'm serious." Eli leaned forward, elbows on knees. "You've got the full package, Mer. The design instinct, the client polish, the project management skills... and, somehow, the patience to untangle the city's red tape like it's a word jumble."

Her stomach twisted.

He meant it as a compliment, as a proud father marveling at his daughter. And, honestly, she normally lived for his praise. But today, all she heard was a countdown clock ticking toward disappointment.

"Thanks, Dad," she said, softening her voice.

He smiled. "You make it easy. I honestly don't know how I got so lucky. Jonah, too, even if he's on a different timeline. Still, when I look at you, I just can't believe I had a hand in creating such a perfect creature. Oh, don't make that face. I'm not calling you 'Miss Perfect' like Jonah does."

"I'm not...perfect."

"Hah. Prove me wrong."

She glanced down, pretending to study her notes. It wouldn't be hard to make that point. Two words. Two harsh, impossible, really dumb words.

"I mean it, Mer. You're awesome."

Wasn't he going to stop? She was so not awesome.

"Thanks," she muttered.

He leaned in some more, still not done making her wallow in guilt. "You know, after your mom died, I wasn't sure either of you would come through it. Heck, I wasn't sure *I* would. But you...you just attached yourself to life. To the work. To me."

Because I didn't have anyone else. Because I couldn't let myself fall apart. Because I thought if I was perfect enough, you wouldn't leave me, too.

But she kept all that self-therapy to herself. Instead, she just swallowed the lump rising in her throat and lifted her chin. "Well. Somebody had to keep the firm from crumbling."

"You did more than that," he said. "You're one of the most grounded, moral, disciplined people I know. And that's rare, Mer. It really is."

She literally had to bite her tongue to keep from screaming, "*Stop!*"

How could she tell him? It would break his heart and his cracked-up impression that she was all that. She was none of that. She was the fool who made a series of decisions without thinking. The idiot who wanted pleasure and freedom from commitment.

She knew Trevor was temporary. She didn't know he was married, but she knew he was nothing more than a good time.

How could she ever tell the truth to this man sitting in front of her, singing her praises and calling her grounded and moral? This man who loved God and...her.

She couldn't. Not now, at least.

"You okay?" Eli asked.

She blinked. "Yeah. Just...tired." Did he notice how often she said that?

He leaned back in the chair, lacing his fingers behind his head. "This was supposed to be a vacation for you, Mer."

"It is," she assured him. "I'm loving the beach and Atlas. Even Jonah is...good." She almost laughed. After she broke the news, he would officially be "the good Lawson kid" again. Been a lot of years since he could claim that title.

She pressed a hand to her abdomen, unconsciously. She really should get this conversation and disappointment out of the way.

"Dad..." she started, voice low.

He studied her, his gaze expectant.

She opened her mouth, then closed it. She just couldn't break his heart. Not yet, anyway.

"Yeah?" he urged.

"Nothing, I just...I love you, that's all."

"I love you, too, Mer." Eli stood and walked over,

pressing a kiss to the top of her head. "You're everything I ever hoped you'd be."

"Thanks," she whispered, barely managing the word.

He left the room a moment later, whistling as he walked down the hallway.

She sat there and didn't move until she heard Atlas's tiny mew from the monitor, then headed off to answer his call.

She was a great architect. And a lousy daughter. But what kind of mother could she be? Right now, she wasn't sure and maybe the best thing to do was to hide away, give the baby up for adoption, and never face her father's disappointment.

July 29, 1992
Summer House – Living Room
Rainy and loud, like God is mad about something

It's official: the men have left the premises— estrogen is taking over.

Dad's in Atlanta for architecture business meetings (read: avoiding Florida in July), and Uncle Artie took Peter and Eli for a "men only" (puh-lease) fishing trip with his friend Seamus.

Which meant last night was just the girls. And what did the moms decide to do with this sacred, testosterone-free window of opportunity?

They threw a _Tri-Delt Melt, the_ official name of their sorority party night.

And, honestly, I might be ready to pledge. It was SO MUCH FUN.

So, it was me, Tessa, Kate, and Crista sitting on beach towels in the living room while Aunt Jo Ellen and Mom acted like they were college girls again. That was until Mom discovered her first gray hair! She freaked out and Aunt Jo Ellen plucked it right out of her head with her bare hands and announced "it shall be banned herewith!" and singed that sucker on the stove!

They broke into "Delta Tunes" which is apparently the destruction of songs from their era. My favorite was "These Boots are Made for

Rushing" because I've heard the real (ridiculous) song. I know new words now:

You keep sayin' you don't want to pledge now
But baby that's not how it's done
One of these days these Delts are gonna
rush all over you...

Something like that. Runner up: "(You Make Me Feel Like) A Tri-Delt Co-ed." Mom sang every note like a hyena.

Anyway, then we had pizza and Coke (pretty sure that's not what Mom and Aunt JE were drinking) and it was time for Tri-Delt Awards Night!

With great fanfare, Tessa was voted "Most Likely to Be a Pageant Queen" and Kate was "Most Likely to Stage a Coup." They named Crista "Most Likely to Win an Oscar" and I was —I love this—"Most Likely to Bring About World Peace"!

It went a little downhill then, with a Delta Dare Game, Secret Sister Nicknames (when we learned that Jo Ellen was "Boom Boom" for reasons NO ONE will tell us, and Mom was Macrame Mags because—get this—she ran a bootleg plant hanger business from her college dorm room). Who knew?

Anyway, we ended the night with Tessa's boombox out and somehow she found a song called "I'm a Believer" that brought the moms to their feet screaming about "Micky" and "Davy" and how Michael was the sleeper of this jungle of monkeys.

After that, they let us stay up late, play our own music (minus Jo Ellen's "no Nirvana after 9 p.m." rule), and turned the entire living room into spa night.

There was a lineup of Wet n Wild nail polish on the coffee table (the color names were borderline criminal so I went with Electric Grape #47), and we all did each other's nails.

Mom and Jo told us secrets about all their sorority sisters, including the fact that someone named Ruth Ann Bingham dropped out of school and ran off with a guy on a motorcycle but ended up married to a multi-millionaire who invented the snap-top ketchup lid!

I'll never look at a bottle of Heinz 57 the same!

Best part: when Mom laughs. The kind that starts in her stomach and tumbles out when she forgets to be "a proper Southern lady." She's usually so tightly wound that if you pulled her ponytail, she'd snap. But tonight, it was like she became someone else for a few hours—someone who remembered how to have fun and didn't care what anyone thought when she danced and sang.

And Jo Ellen? She's so much fun! She just

kind of brings out the best in Mom. She even let us paint her toenails Bubblegum Blitz and didn't flinch when Kate smeared some on the carpet. She said it gives the house character and without that, a house isn't a home! So cool but of course Mom went into full clean mode, whipping out the polish remover and scissors to snip out the pink threads. You can put Maggie in a party, but you can't stop her from cleaning.

By the end of the night, all four of us girls crashed in sleeping bags in the living room. The moms went out on the porch to "watch the rain," which is code for whispering secrets that can't be shared with teenagers.

I like this version of the moms. It makes me wish I'd known my mother when she was young and made macramé.

I wish I could bottle nights like this. I'd call that color Delta Love and add glitter because tonight, everyone sparkled.

~Viv (Secret Tri-Delt sister nickname is Snickerdoodle. Don't ask.)

Chapter Eleven
Maggie

Day Three of The Great Miami Caper unfolded with high hopes and good spirits. But not too much in the way of radio stations, since the fossil on four wheels only got a few. But Maggie really didn't mind and was, if truth be told, quite enjoying the sojourn so far.

They'd had a great night at a historic hotel in Apalachicola, which Maggie would forever call "Apa-coca-cola," and were still talking about the Key Lime pie they'd shared at an unforgettable little restaurant called Up The Creek.

Determined to make progress and get well and truly out of Florida's Panhandle and all the way to what Oscar labeled "a hidden gem of an island called Cedar Key," Maggie pushed the truck to its limit. Yes, it could theoretically go sixty-five, but she could sense that fifty-eight was about all the old clunker—and Maggie—had in her.

"I need music!" Jo Ellen said, finally giving up on the radio. "Wait. Wait. I'll ask my boyfriend." And out came the phone and Oscar.

Maggie peered at the long highway ahead, grateful

there was so little traffic on the slow but safe back highways.

"Oh, I did it! Get this, Mags," Jo said, waving her phone. "He just made me a playlist, and my grandson Matt taught me how to put that into Spotify—do you know what that is?"

"Is that like a Tide Stick?" Maggie asked, gripping the steering wheel.

"Oh, you're so funny. We'll have to listen through my phone, but that's okay. Yours has the GPS and we shouldn't run out of battery."

"Famous last words," Maggie muttered, keeping her eyes on the road as they went through a "town," though it truly was generous calling it that. Sopchoppy—really, what a ridiculous name—had one flashing light, a faded gas station with a hand-lettered "bait" sign, and at least one Dollar Store for every resident.

Leaving it in the rearview mirror, Maggie settled in and let Jo Ellen fire up some Motown and, God help them, sang along. The road had literally no cars, but an unending vista of flat scrubs, the occasional cow, a surprising number of churches, and bales of hay.

"This is perfect," Jo cooed, sipping on a can of Diet Coke. "I couldn't be happier. I knew everything would be perfect."

"Do you not understand the concept of a jinx?" Maggie fired back. "Plus, we're only..." She frowned when the truck made a weird thumpity-thump. "What was that?"

"I think you ran over a cow patty," Jo said with a snort.

"No, no. Listen. Do you hear that hum? Turn down the music." She tapped the brake and frowned, the noise getting louder. Then a low, whiny *wheeze*, followed by a series of clanks that sounded distinctly...bad. Really bad.

Jo Ellen leaned forward. "You're right. That's the sound of..."

"A jinx," Maggie shot back, underscoring it with a look.

"Oh, please, Mag— Oh!"

They both cried out when a puff of smoke curled up from under the hood. Was it a fire? An explosion?

"Pull over!" Jo yelled.

Slamming the brakes, Maggie yanked the wheel toward a patch of gravel. The truck gasped again, gave a last dramatic huff of steam, and rolled to a stop. The engine died and left them in silence but for a distant ticking.

"Is it going to blow?" Jo asked, scrambling for her seatbelt.

"I don't think it's going to do much of anything," Maggie muttered, already out of hers.

"Give it a minute," Jo said, "then start it up again. That always works with my TV or computer."

"Which were made in this century," she grumbled, pushing the door open. "Plus, cars don't work that way."

"How do they work?"

Maggie gingerly stepped onto pavement so hot she

could feel the burn through her sandals. "I don't know, Jo Ellen. And that is the problem."

"Well, I have Oscar."

"Yeah, he'll be a big help."

Shielding her face from the sun and smoke, Maggie walked to the front of the truck and stared at the hood.

"Do you at least know how to open it?" Jo Ellen asked as she joined her.

"Do you?" Maggie fired back.

"I'll ask Oscar."

Wiping her brow, Maggie bent down and tried to see if she could find a latch. Of course, she couldn't. She felt around, pressed everything she could stand to press—it was so hot—and swore mightily.

"Is this a Chevy?" Jo asked. "Or a Ford?"

"It's a pain in the— Oh!" She hit something and it unlatched, popping up and drowning them in a cloud of smoke and steam.

They stumbled backwards, automatically holding each other to keep from falling.

Maggie waved the smoke away, sputtering.

Jo Ellen, bless her sweet heart, put her hands on her hips. "Do you think it's the radiator?"

"Do you even know what a radiator looks like?"

"No, but that's what they say in the movies. It's always the radiator."

Irritation skittered up her sweat-soaked spine. "This is not the movies, Jo. Will you please use that phone for good and call Triple-A or something?"

"I would but I don't have a signal."

On a grunt, Maggie let her head drop back, but straightened at the faint hum of a motor. "Someone's coming."

"*Three* someones," Jo Ellen said, squinting down the shimmering road.

Maggie turned to follow her gaze, sucking in a breath at the sight of three menacing-looking motorcycles.

"Oh, dear," she muttered. "Now we might be in the movies. *Easy Rider.*"

Jo snorted. "They'll help us."

"Or kill us."

Undaunted, Jo stepped into the road and waved. "Hello? Help! Also, please don't be a gang!"

"We're on a back road in rural Florida," Maggie said. "It is absolutely a gang."

The bikes slowed as they approached, driven by three men in black leather vests with long gray beards.

"And ZZ Top is on tour again," Maggie said under breath.

Jo shot her a look. "We need help, Mags. Let's be nice, okay?"

Oh, sure. Let's be nice to the tattoo-covered Hells Angels in the middle of nowhere.

One of them parked, kicking his stand and whipping off his helmet. He was terrifying looking—with deep creases and that matted beard and skin that looked more like an alligator than a human.

"Ladies," he said, making a weirdly formal bow. "Looks like you might need some help."

"Just a..." Maggie swallowed and looked into his eyes.

"Phone that works." Oh, darn it! Did she just admit their phones didn't work?

Another man, tall and lanky and maybe a little younger, got off his bike. He wore a white T-shirt that had last been laundered when Reagan was in office, and his forearms were covered with words and eagles, and... was that a naked mermaid?

"My name's Brick," he said.

"Of course it is," Maggie whispered, getting a vile look from Jo and a soft snort from Brick. "This is Randy" —he indicated the first man—"and Angel."

"Angel?" Jo Ellen said on a laugh. "Well, we could use one of them."

"My real name's Gabriel," the third man explained as he, too, got off his bike, shaking back some silver locks of his own. "But what you could use is a mechanic, and my brother up in Crawfordville has a garage and a tow-truck."

Maggie breathed a little. "Well, that sounds... reasonable."

Jo Ellen stepped in, all honey and kindness. "We're so sorry to trouble you. Our truck seems to have...had an episode."

Randy crouched under the hood, and Angel joined him, while Brick smiled at Maggie.

"I take it you ladies aren't from around here?" he asked.

"Not far," Maggie said.

"We're on a road trip," Jo Ellen said at the exact same time, making Maggie fight the urge to glare at her.

"So are we," he said. "We take the same route every year in honor of our buddy Bear, who died right on this road."

Maggie nearly swayed. "I'm so sorry."

"Looks like your water pump blew," Angel said. "Maybe the thermostat, too."

"Translation?" Maggie asked.

Angel stepped away, wiping his hands on already filthy jeans. "Lemme call Mikey." He held up a flip phone. "I always got bars."

"And he's usually in one," Randy cracked.

He chuckled and made the call, and then informed them with his spare words that the tow-truck would be there in thirty.

"We'll wait with you," Brick said, looking at Maggie. "Not that I think anyone around here would harm you or you couldn't take them down with that sharp tongue of yours, but it'll be safer for you ladies."

"Oh, thank you," Jo Ellen cooed. "Let me get you some snacks and drinks."

While she went to the back of the truck, Brick smiled at Maggie, his leathery skin making her think he was every bit as old as she was—minus the nightly Retin-A and sunhat she wore while gardening.

"You think I'm going to kill you, don't you?" he asked with a sly smile.

She drew back. "I don't..."

He laughed and reached into his pocket and for a moment, she thought he was going to pull out a gun or a knife. But it was just an iPhone.

"Want to see my grandchildren? I got four, and they're darn near perfect."

"Oh." She couldn't help laughing at the unexpected statement. "I have four, too. And they're also perfect."

His brows shot up, impressed. "Well, lemme see 'em and we'll let Angel decide whose grandchildren are cuter. Don't put money on it, 'cause I'll win."

Jo Ellen set up a snack mix and some drinks like they were hosting a Bulldogs tailgate and they shared pictures and stories. The men were all Army veterans, retired, and, frankly, fascinating.

In addition to having four grandkids, Brick was a beekeeper. Randy taught line dancing at his community center. Angel volunteered as a tour guide at the Apalachicola National Forest.

And Maggie had to revise everything she thought she knew about bikers.

The tow-truck arrived—a rusted white beast driven by a man named Mikey who said nothing but spit sunflower seeds to the ground as he peered into the engine of Frank's truck.

"Water pump. Yep. Tomorrow."

"Oh, dear," Jo Ellen said. "I have to ask Oscar where we should stay."

"Is that your husband?" Randy asked.

"No," Jo Ellen said.

"Yes," Maggie replied right on top of her answer.

The men just laughed, but Mikey walked away to set up the tow, while Maggie and Jo Ellen looked at each other with a mix of confusion and worry.

"I guess we go with the truck..." Maggie said, glancing at the man as he spit again.

"You can't go in that tow-truck," Brick said. "Mikey doesn't have insurance for passengers." He thumbed to his bike. "But I do."

Maggie stared at him and then let out the most unladylike snort. "I don't think so. We'll walk."

Brick rolled his eyes. "It's seven miles up to Crawfordville," he said. "Be sure to get off 98 and turn on 319."

"Seven..." Maggie turned to Jo Ellen, who already had her phone out.

"My grandson put the Uber app on my phone, so..."

"There ain't no Uber out here," Randy said.

"We can get you there in ten minutes, ma'am," Angel added. "You can borrow our helmets."

He could *not* be serious.

"Gator Jack's can put you up," Randy added. At the women's matching dubious looks, he laughed. "No real gators. It's just a joint across the street from Mikey's shop that's got a couple rooms they rent to fishermen," Randy added. "Ain't the Ritz, but it's clean."

"Got a decent bar, too," Mikey chimed in as he dragged a chain—an actual chain—from his truck to theirs. "Passable burgers, cold beer, and a jukebox. And every night is Ladies' Night."

Jo Ellen turned to Maggie, who was starting to feel like she might sway in the sun.

"We'll change into sneakers and walk," Maggie insisted under her breath.

"You can," Jo Ellen said. "I'm taking the ride."

Maggie felt her jaw loosen. "Jo Ellen Wylie! Are you out of your mind?"

She leaned in. "A seven-mile walk in this heat would be the crazy thing. It'll kill us both. These men won't. Right?" She gave them a sweet smile. "You won't hurt a couple of grandmas in a bind."

Brick winked at Maggie. "Grandmas are our specialty."

Oof. Why did he make her laugh?

"Come on, Mags. You go with Brick."

He reached out a hand. "Yeah, *Mags.* Come with me. You'll have so much fun you'll let me buy you dinner."

She stood frozen in place as her entire life flashed before her—one that was always still and controlled and sharp-edged and fearful.

And then, shocking herself more than anyone, she nodded. "Okay. I guess I'm going to die on a motorcycle behind a man named Brick."

He let out a belly laugh. "Oh, no, honey. You're going to live a little."

Ten minutes later, Maggie was on the back of Brick's Harley, arms around a strange man while Florida pines blurred past them. The sun hit her face and for the first time in...too long, she laughed. Loud. Like she meant it.

Tomorrow, they'd deal with the truck.

Tonight? God help them—a *jukebox.*

~

Maggie climbed off the motorcycle with knees that had no interest in supporting her anymore. Brick caught her elbow before she could crumple to the gravel like a poorly pitched tent.

"You okay?" he asked.

She just gave him a warning look. "I left my dignity on the turn to 319," she said, brushing dust from her slacks. "Along with my equilibrium."

"Nothin' a cold brew won't fix." He pointed across the street to...a place. Yes, she could call that a place. A two-story *place* with a torn green and white striped awning and a faded sign that said *Gator Jack's* with an alligator as the apostrophe. "You two go in and square things with Mikey, then get set up in your room." His finger rose to the second-floor windows. Then back down again. "The boys and I will be waiting for dinner."

Her eyes widened. He was serious?

"I know it's four o'clock, but dinner's half price before five and we love us a good early bird special. Then, we'll dance."

They'd see about that.

She managed a tight smile and walked to Jo Ellen, who was positively as giddy as a girl getting off a roller coaster as she climbed off Randy's bike.

"Settle down, will you?" Maggie muttered.

"Don't make me quote your favorite character, Mags."

Maggie lifted a brow in question.

"'Fiddle dee dee!'" she exclaimed in a terrible

Southern Scarlett O'Hara accent. "I had fun and I'm not done yet."

Oh, heavens. There *would* be dancing.

They followed Brick's instructions—as he took their suitcases and they just *let* him. Then they found Mikey in the "shop" that smelled like old shrimp. Was bait standard in every gas station in this part of Florida?

Jo Ellen walked around in a daze, talking about how much Artie would have loved this place. After Maggie signed her life away and watched Mikey spit enough sunflower seed husks to sprout a garden, they made their way across the street to Gator Jack's.

Inside, it was all dark wood, neon signs, and the faint but permanent scent of stale beer and fried things. A scarred old jukebox stood proudly in the corner like it had survived three hurricanes and a few fights. A couple of locals sat at the bar, wearing ball caps and sunburned noses.

The bartender, a tall woman with bright pink hair and a T-shirt that said, "Bite Me, I'm Local," gave them a nod.

"Ladies? Brick got you settled. Room's upstairs. Here's the key and before you ask, it's got one bed, a queen. Sorry, it's the busy season." She lifted her brow as she held out a key. "Go through that hall past the bathroom, up to the second floor, first door."

Maggie opened her mouth.

"We're happy to share," Jo Ellen chirped, dragging her toward the hall.

"Is there a shower?" Maggie managed to ask as Jo pulled her away.

Pink Hair guffawed. "Of course! What kind of place do you think I run?"

Just then, Brick walked out of the men's room, shaking off his wet hands. "Hurry back, ladies. We'll order for you."

"Thank you!" Jo Ellen called, ignoring Maggie's glare.

"We are not—"

"Yes, we are," Jo said. "Let's comb our hair and freshen up. This is fun!"

There was no arguing with her, so Maggie went along with it, not willing to admit that a beer sounded really good. Had she had one in...ever? Not in years, but, hey, when in Crawfordville...

Two hours, one beer and *two and a half* shots of bourbon—she tried to sip but Brick wouldn't let her— later, Maggie gave up the battle.

She laughed at *everything* that blue-eyed, bearded redneck biker with rough hands and a sweet smile had to say. Brick Collins met her snark, sarcasm, and condescension with so much humor that she gave up the fight.

The Wild Turkey helped, too.

And then Jo Ellen came clip-clopping over in wedge heels—when did she put those on?—and said, "Randy showed me how to work the jukebox."

"That's good."

"It's great, because...listen."

After a beat, Maggie heard the iconic opening high-pitched organ notes that sent chills up her spine and whipped her back to the Tri-Delt House on the Georgia campus—which might have been the last time she had shots of bourbon...and this much fun.

"It's the Monkees!" Jo Ellen cried and started singing with Micky Dolenz. "'I thought love was only true in fairy tales!'"

"Stop," Maggie pleaded.

"When 'I'm a Believer' plays?" Jo Ellen scoffed, tugging Maggie from her chair. In her weakened one-beer-and-two-point-five-shots state, she let herself be pulled to a stand. "Come on, Mags! We always loved Micky the best!"

She snorted *again* and let Jo drag her toward the cleared space near the pool table, where two men were swaying off-beat with beers in hand.

Brick gave an appreciative whistle. Randy whooped and pointed at the jukebox like he'd just summoned the spirit of fun. Angel leaned against the bar and watched like he was their personal bodyguard.

Jo twirled and pointed at Maggie. "'Then I saw her face!'"

And, Lord help her, Maggie sang right back. "'Now I'm a believer!'"

They belted out every word that was burned into their memory and kept it going when "Build Me Up, Buttercup" echoed through the room. Then some Aretha, The Temptations, and the capper—The Archies singing "Sugar, Sugar."

Maggie utterly surrendered to the night, the memories, the laughter, and even Brick's arms when Percy Sledge belted out "When a Man Loves a Woman." She danced with him, giving in to the bliss of being held, swayed, and serenaded with lyrics that melted the coldest of icy hearts.

Even hers.

When things speeded up again, Jo Ellen did something between the swim and the mashed potato, and Maggie nearly lost it laughing.

The bar, now full, clapped along. Someone—maybe the pink-haired bartender—shouted, "Go, Grandma!"

The whole time Maggie felt young, free, and ridiculously alive.

They didn't make last call—not for lack of trying. By the time they headed upstairs, Maggie had a stitch in her side from laughing. The tiny room was cozy, clean, and cooled by a noisy fan that didn't even bother her.

The sheets were crisp, their PJs comfy after showers, and Jo Ellen and Maggie shared a queen bed as they had for two solid years at the Tri-Delt House.

As they finally settled in, Jo sighed and proclaimed it, "The best night ever."

Maggie closed her eyes and snuggled under the blankets, thinking about Brick's funny lines and how good it was to...not care. Tomorrow, she would care again. She had to.

As Scarlett would say, tomorrow was another day. But this day? One of the most exhilarating experiences she'd had in seventy-eight years.

Chapter Twelve
Tessa

Tessa stepped into Dusty's home with a whole different mindset than when she'd been here for the open house. For one thing, she wasn't late this afternoon, and she really would meet with the selling agent. For another, after the Realtor gave her an official tour, she had plans for a dinner date with the man who owned the house. A date that Tessa was looking forward to even more than the showing.

She tapped on the front door and it instantly opened, revealing a woman around Tessa's age with thick brown hair and a sparkle in her espresso eyes.

"Tessa Wylie?" She extended her hand as she opened the door wider. "I'm Lorna Gonzalez, the listing agent. It's lovely to meet you."

"Hello, Lorna." Tessa shook her hand and stepped into the cool house, which felt spotless and staged, and every bit as appealing as the last time—minus the equally appealing owner. "Thank you for the showing, since I missed the open house you held."

"Oh, it's my pleasure." She gestured her into the house and tugged at the lapels of a crisp navy jacket. "I turned the A/C down to 'please don't let me ruin another linen blouse with a hot flash' level," she joked. Then she gestured to Tessa's arms, bare in a sleeveless dress that she'd picked more for the date than the showing. "But if it's too cold..."

"I'm fine," Tessa assured the other woman, glancing around. "Anxious to finally see the place. I don't need my own agent, do I? Because I'm just starting the process, and I haven't found one—"

"Absolutely not," Lorna assured her. "Let's take a peek around, and if it isn't quite what you're looking for, let me know what is, and I bet I can find it. I know Destin and the whole surrounding area like my own name. I was born and raised here."

"Really? I spent summers here as a teenager," Tessa told her. "From Ithaca, New York."

"Oh, speaking of cold."

"It is, but our summers in Destin were special. In fact, that's how I met Dusty—well, he was Dustin then."

Lorna smiled. "I knew him as Dustin, too, but Kelly pinned the nickname on him and it stuck. She said she refused to be married to Dustin from Destin."

Kelly...his late wife, Tessa recalled. "So you knew her as well?"

She nodded. "We were friends since childhood," she said. "Losing her was...hard."

"I'm so sorry," Tessa said, reaching out to her. "Dusty hasn't talked a lot about her, but it's clear they had a happy marriage."

"Very much so," Lorna said. "But years of it were spent with him taking care of her. And I can't blame him for wanting to leave this house, but I tell you, now? You cannot recognize it as the ranch they bought shortly after they got married. Total gut and reno. Come on, let's take a tour."

Tessa appreciated the easy transition back to business, as she followed Lorna into the kitchen. The agent carried a tablet open to the listing but didn't need it for reference, moving through the house as if she knew every inch of it as well as her own.

Efficient and not at all pushy, Lorna pointed out every feature and all the upgrades to the remodeled kitchen and family room, which was lined with sliding doors that overlooked a deck and a spacious backyard.

A *dry* spacious backyard.

"Don't tell me, you were hoping for a pool," Lorna said, obviously adept at reading a buyer's expression. "You could easily put one in. There's plenty of space. Come look."

Outside was beautiful and lush with palms and foliage, but all Tessa could see was what it *wasn't*—the Gulf with sunsets and white sand and an endless horizon.

"You don't look thrilled," Lorna said, eyeing her.

"I'm living in a lovely place on Gulf Shore Drive."

"*Ooh*. Wear your money." Then her eyes widened with a soft intake of breath. "And you're selling?"

"It's not mine," she admitted. "I'm staying with friends—actually, the family we vacationed with when I was a kid. They owned the house and did a massive rebuild."

"On Gulf Shore?" She narrowed her eyes, thinking.

"The three-level showstopper with turquoise shutters? Not far from the marina?"

"That would be the one."

"Oh. How could you leave?" She pressed her hand to her chest, reflecting Tessa's precise sentiments.

"Because it's not my home," she replied, realizing yet again how much that bothered her and how ready she finally was to put down roots. "I want to buy but, yes, I'm spoiled by the view and location. I'd give my right arm to be able to see even a sliver of the Gulf."

"You and everyone else who comes to Destin, or anywhere up and down 30A," she said, referring to the beach highway that had become synonymous with this part of the Panhandle.

"Can I have a water view, if not water*front*?" Tessa asked, already knowing the answer.

"Not for under seven figures and, even then, it'll likely be a fixer." Lorna added an apologetic look. "Now, if you're handy like Dusty…"

"Not in the least." She glanced back into the house, accepting reality. "So, if I give up water, then I want something new or recently remodeled, close to my friends, and big enough for at least one office to run my business."

"This house is all of that and more," Lorna assured her. "Come on, let's see the rest."

They continued through the rooms and while Tessa liked it and could even see herself living and working here, it was just a little too…landlocked. And despite an excellent renovation, she knew a man had lived here with his sick and dying wife.

The house simply wasn't for her.

"Not quite what you want?" Lorna guessed when they worked their way back to the kitchen.

"I'm just starting to see what's out there, and I'm afraid I'm looking for a unicorn."

"Not if I'm your agent," she quipped, gesturing toward the table. "If you don't want this house, why don't we get specific about what you do want, and I'll find it for you?"

Tessa took a seat and let out a sigh. "Okay, but be prepared for a few things. One, I don't know what I want until I see it."

"Totally normal."

Tessa shrugged because maybe it was. "And two, I've never owned a home before."

That made Lorna look up, surprised. "Well, what a wonderful new adventure for you," she said with the practiced ease of someone who sold for a living. "Let's make that happen, shall we? I'll start with a peek at MLS right now. About two thousand square feet and in this price range?"

"Yep." Tessa leaned back while Lorna tapped the tablet, looking around and thinking more about the man who'd lived here than the square footage.

"I have to admit," she said, "the last person I would imagine as a caretaker *or* house remodeler was wild and rowdy Dustin Mathers."

Lorna smiled and her fingers slowed, following

Tessa's gaze and train of thought. "It was Kelly," she said. "That woman was like the balm on Dusty's broken life."

Tessa frowned, angling her head. "Broken?" she asked. "I just thought he was...immature and maybe a little reckless. I guess I didn't think it was worse than that."

"So much more." Lorna set the tablet down. "I hope I'm not talking out of school, but since you knew him, it's only fair you see the side he kept covered. His father was an alcoholic. A mean one, too. And his mother? She wasn't around much. I heard she'd come back now and again, then disappear. I have no idea why, but I doubt it was good. Did you ever meet his older brother, Brendan?"

She knew none of this. Were these people the ghosts mentioned in Vivien's diary?

Tessa shook her head, her heart already aching for the man she had a date with—something she suspected Lorna didn't know or she wouldn't be spilling this much tea.

"Well, you won't ever meet Brendan because he spent years in prison and came out...rough. Their dad died pretty young, and I honestly thought Dusty was headed in the same direction as his brother but, then, *wham*. He and Kelly got together and a year later? He was a changed man."

"Really?" Tessa tried to imagine a woman having that kind of power and patience. "She must have been... something."

"She was awesome," Lorna gushed. "Helped him get into school and get a degree, then an advanced degree that led to a very successful therapy practice. He's volunteered for years at AA, helping people going through what his father did. Then Kelly got diagnosed with a rare blood disorder, spent her life in and out of the hospital, and he was...everything to her."

Tessa blinked, her heart cracking with a million different emotions. Pity, admiration, and a new respect for a boy she'd always thought was just young and dumb.

And, if she was being honest, she also felt a twinge of envy, which was shameful, since Kelly was gone and Tessa was sitting here considering buying her house.

Still, she was human and couldn't help wondering... what would it be like to be loved that way? Well, she knew. Her father had loved her mother that way. But Tessa had never had a relationship like that in her whole life.

So maybe it wasn't envy, exactly, but a deep and powerful longing. Oh, men had pursued her—always. But no one ever wanted to *sacrifice* for her. It hurt to think about.

"It all went on for a long time, too, Tessa," Lorna continued, oblivious to the effect her story was having. "Through all the years, Dusty never wavered. Not once. My husband and I watched him carry her through that. And then Kelly's father died, and her mother came to live here, and that woman was no picnic. She also got very sick, and he took care of *both* of them. Gave his mother-in-law his office as her bedroom until the day she died, and ran his counseling practice from the garage back then. Didn't sleep much, but he still showed up for everybody."

Tessa could feel the prickle at the back of her eyes. She pressed a knuckle gently to one of them. Dusty was changed all right, by life and duty and a history she'd known nothing about.

"That sounds like a lot for one person," she said.

"It was. And, yes, he had support from friends and his clients. Just recently, after he hunkered down and spent two years renovating his house like his very life depended on it, he told me he wasn't sure who he was anymore."

Tessa listened, rapt.

"He said he'd been so busy keeping people alive—and counseling his patients—he didn't know how to live just for him." Lorna gave a tight smile. "I think he's finally out of the fog, and ready to start a new life. I really admire him for that."

"There's obviously a lot to admire," Tessa said, mulling over all this new information.

Then Lorna gave a dry laugh. "Oh, but you're not here for all that, are you? You're not buying Dusty, you're buying a place to live and"—she tapped the screen with a long nail—"I have a townhouse right here that does have a hint of a water view from the rooftop." She made a face. "Would something like that work for you?"

She stared at Lorna, still thinking about the beach bad boy turned into a halo-wearing angel of mercy when the door from the garage opened behind them, and they both turned.

Dusty stood there in khakis and a short-sleeved

button-up, holding a bouquet of flowers from the market. "Hello, ladies."

Lorna smiled and gestured to the flowers. "Oh, for me?"

"Only if she made an offer," he joked, coming all the way in. "Actually, they are for my dinner date." He handed the flowers to Tessa. "Trying to make up for the many sins of my past."

She wasn't sure how to react, other than to accept them with thanks, but Lorna's brows shot up.

"Dinner date, huh?" She gave Tessa a sly look. "And here I am talking on and on."

About Dusty, Tessa knew she meant. "No, you're finding me my dream house."

"This isn't it?" Dusty asked.

Tessa gave him a warm smile. "Very close," she said. "But I've decided to keep looking for my unicorn."

"Welcome to the club," he teased.

"And you both have me to find *two* unicorns," Lorna said, flipping the cover of her tablet to close it. "I shall make it my goal."

"No rush here," Dusty said, walking out of the kitchen. "I have a few things to take care of while you finish up."

He disappeared into the living area and down the hall, leaving Lorna and Tessa in an awkward beat of silence.

"I should have mentioned..." Tessa said softly.

"No, no. You don't...no." She regarded Tessa with a

long, warm look. "Anyway, now you know you couldn't do much better than Dusty Mathers."

"We're just old friends, honestly."

Lorna shrugged, obviously doubting that. "It's been two years and he's not a man who should be alone. He needs someone lively and beautiful. And..." She leaned in and lowered her voice, "he's looking for waterfront, too. Imagine what you could do together."

Tessa just laughed at the implication while Lorna stood and slung her bag over her shoulder.

"Have fun tonight," she added. "That is what he needs more than anything. In the meantime, I'll keep looking, Tessa, and we'll be in touch."

With a wave, she let herself out while Tessa sat stunned and holding sunflowers and...maybe some stupidly high hopes. For a house and a man like Dusty Mathers.

Dusty drove them to a precious Italian restaurant near the harbor, tucked under an awning of bougainvillea. The drive didn't take long, and the conversation was easy —about their mutual house hunt and how much they wanted to be able to see the Gulf, hopeless as that seemed. They chatted about the weather, the changes in Destin, the latest on Jonah's travails since the barbeque.

Tessa let all that she'd just learned about the man next to her settle on her heart. Everything she thought she knew about Dusty Mathers had turned upside down in the last hour.

She tried to set it aside as they were seated at an outside table, and he surprised her by suggesting they have wine. Did Lorna say he didn't drink? Or just that his father had?

It was a stark reminder that she shouldn't take everything the hard-selling real estate agent just shared as gospel truth.

So she also ordered a crisp Pinot Grigio and decided the job of revealing his personal history was Dusty's, not Lorna's. She'd let the evening unfold as if she hadn't just been given a glimpse into his life.

After a moment alone, he leaned in, putting both elbows on the table, giving her a chance to really drink him in.

She liked a man with a beard, and his was clean-cut and the perfect amount of silver and black. He wore dark-rimmed glasses, but they didn't hide the glint in his deep brown eyes. His shoulders had the breadth of a man who was no stranger to the gym—or, maybe in his case, building materials.

She even noticed clean, blunt-cut nails and the fact that sometime in the past two years, he must have stopped wearing a wedding ring—there wasn't even a tan line.

"God, you're gorgeous," he whispered, his gaze as intense as hers must have been.

"Oh." She had not been expecting the heartfelt

compliment. "Flowers *and* flattery. You must really want me to buy your house."

He chuckled. "No, I think we'd be having a different conversation if you were gung-ho to buy. And the statement stands, Tessa. You're the same jaw-dropper today that you were in that white bikini that was made simply to torture helpless boys with raging hormones."

She leaned back, her jaw loose. "I can honestly say I never thought you noticed."

He snorted. "No one didn't—and probably still doesn't—*not* notice Tessa Wylie." He made a face. "A couple too many negatives in that sentence, but you get my drift."

"Thank you, Dusty. Honestly, I never got that vibe from you."

"Did that bother you?" he asked with a tease in his voice.

She inched closer. "Maybe. Did you pretend not to notice me just to get under my skin?"

"I wish I were that clever," he admitted on a laugh. "Truth?"

"Only the truth."

He took a minute to think and during that time, the waiter brought their wine and Dusty asked if she wanted to split fried calamari to start. After they ordered dinner, toasted, and sipped, he put his drink down and looked at her.

"Blame Eli," he finally said.

"Ah, yes. He had 'dibs,' as you mentioned." She rolled her eyes at the memory of young Eli's sweet crush on her.

"I honestly thought the sun rose and set on that guy," he told her. "I mean, he was a bit of a dork, but in a way that I longed to be. He had his act together at eighteen, and after spending some time with him last weekend, he *still* has it together. And he's grieved, so I'm all the more impressed by him."

She studied him, letting the cold wine play over her tongue. "It was nice of you to back off even if it did shake my confidence."

He hooted softly. "Nothing should shake your confidence. Anyway, we were friends. I was such a mess, you and I could just have fun. And we did." A slow smile pulled. "Do you remember the bonfire when we had to call the fire department?"

"Kate just reminded me of it the other day—not that I forgot." She took a sip, letting her mind slip back in time. "But do you remember the time we climbed the fence into the Coastal Community pool at four in the morning?"

He threw his head back with a hearty laugh. "Hey, you dared me during truth or dare. What else could I do?"

"You could have told the truth."

"No, I couldn't. The question was what one girl had I never kissed that I most wanted to." He pointed at her. "You asked it, by the way, and Eli was right there ready to kill anyone who said your name."

She shook her head, laughing. "I have no recollection of that, but I do remember a bunch of us walking down Gulf Shore Drive, singing something by The Cars—"

"'Just What I Needed'," he said, and at her questioning look, he explained, "That was the song by The Cars. Don't make me sing it."

"Yes!" She gave a clap at the memory. "And you had the words all wrong. You kept saying, 'I guess you're just what I needed, I needed someone to read!'"

"And you kept getting in my face saying, 'It's feed and bleed, you idiot.'"

"Oh. I'm sorry I called you an idiot," she said, reaching over the table. "That was rude."

"Also true. I kinda liked it, anyway." He turned his hand and captured her fingers. "It was like your special name for me. You didn't call anyone else an idiot."

"Oh, Dusty." She bit her lip, unable to ignore what she now knew about the childhood that kid had. "I'm still sorry I said that. But I have zero regrets about breaking into the community pool."

"Until we heard sirens," he reminded her.

"We made it out unscathed," she said, laughing again. "And we're no worse for the wear."

The memories continued as they shared the appetizer and ordered blackened fish for dinner, which was almost as good as the conversation. It flowed with no pauses except for belly laughs.

He was skilled at asking questions—she assumed from years as a therapist—and over a shared tiramisu for dessert, he let her go on and on about her event planning business, even filling him in on her years with Ritz-Carlton.

"I lived in Ritz hotel suites for so long, I never paid a

dime in rent or mortgage," she explained. "And that brings me back to house-hunting. I believe it's time to settle down."

"I'm so glad," he said, putting down his fork. "Otherwise, I doubt I would have run into you. I don't go hang out at the beach anymore, and you certainly don't need a therapist."

She cocked her head. "I could have used one after my father passed and maybe when my new friend and only employee went behind my back and found the son I'd given up for adoption."

She'd told him the entire story about Roman during the first course, and he hadn't seemed at all surprised. But then, in his job, he'd surely heard it all.

"But I'm glad this house-hunting secret of mine reunited us." She took one final bite, and narrowed her eyes. "You've come a long way since those days, Dusty. You're nothing like I remember."

"Thank God," he said. "I didn't have the best upbringing," he confessed, and she waited for him to elaborate. He just lifted a shoulder. "And I loved my wife, but taking care of her took a toll on me."

"I bet it did," she said, thinking again of all Lorna had shared. "There's a special place for you in heaven."

"And I hope I don't get there for a long time," he said. "I'm fifty-two and...ready to have a different life."

She smiled at the confession, leaning in. "Tell me about it."

He met her gaze, and there was a flicker of something real that Tessa felt right down to her toes. Then he picked up the check and tossed a credit card in the folder. "Let's walk around the harbor and I'll share everything."

"I'd love that, and thank you for dinner."

A few minutes later, they strolled the boardwalk, which had plenty of tourist traffic on a warm June night. The breeze carried a briny scent and felt absolutely delightful on her bare shoulders.

But not nearly as delightful as the charming and attractive man at Tessa's side. She was pleased that instead of mulling over his past, she'd let the meal, the conversation, and the lovely glass of wine cast a glow over an evening she definitely did not want to end.

"So," he said, taking her hand in a move that felt natural. "About my new life."

She looked up at him, vaguely aware that she was holding her breath for what he would say. He certainly wasn't leaving Destin, was he? With a thriving practice here?

With a start, she realized she didn't want to hear that or anything, frankly, about this new life that would mean she couldn't have any place in it. The thought made her breath catch as she slowed her step.

She *really* liked him.

"As you know, I'm a therapist, and we make the worst patients," he continued with a laugh. "But I am self-aware enough to know what I need in my life."

"Tell me," she said softly, clasping his hand tighter. "I really want to know."

He walked them to the railing over the water, leaning against it, looking down at her with something she couldn't quite define in his eyes. Hope? A promise? A secret? Something that made her heart beat faster.

"I spent two years renovating that house," he started. "And it was quite cathartic. With every room I finished, I felt like a piece of my soul was...better. Cleaner, brighter, newer, less..." He closed his eyes. "Exhausted and sad."

She let out a groan. "I can't imagine how difficult it must have been to take care of the woman you loved and ultimately lose her."

"No, you probably can't, but that's okay. I don't really want to talk about it, or any dark parts of my life. I renovated myself, too."

She felt a smile pull. "How does that work, exactly?"

"I'm changing where I live—if I can sell my house and find something perfect—and how I live. I'm dedicating myself to pleasure, fun, laughter, and life."

"Those are...good pursuits," she replied. "It kind of sounds like old Dustin from the beach."

"Not *that* much pleasure," he joked. "But I won't do serious again. I won't do a lifelong obligation or spend any time with people who drain me—other than my patients, of course. My personal life..." He lifted his brow. "Light, easy, fun, and filled with"—he inched closer—"someone like you."

She stared at him, her smile wavering as she tried to understand what he was saying.

"Me?"

"Still the most fun woman I've ever met," he replied.

That's what she was...fun. For some reason, her heart

dropped to the wooden dock below her feet and left a hole of emptiness behind.

"Tessa, I'd love to keep seeing you," he said. "I like laughing and not being...solemn. I want a friend—maybe more—but I don't want..."

"A commitment," she whispered the word, sorry it slipped out, but it did.

He gave a light laugh. "For lack of a better term, yeah. I want to put myself first for a change and spend time with someone like you—easy, breezy Tessa Wylie."

And she nearly swayed on her wedge-heeled sandals.

What was he saying? That she was a good time girl—the very name of her boat—so he could have all fun and no future?

Well, yeah. That was precisely what he was saying. And up until this point in her life, that's what she had been.

Searching her face, he brushed some hair away and let his knuckles graze her cheek as he got closer, clearly about to close the space that separated them.

"You would be the first woman I've kissed in two years," he admitted gruffly. "That is, if you let me."

She sighed. "Let's wait on that," she said. "Because the truth is..." She took a deep breath and made a quick decision. She wasn't going to lie or play along. Not this time.

"The truth is..." he urged.

"Dusty, I've spent my life being the girl people fall for when they want to be entertained and amused. Not the woman they want forever."

Dusty exhaled. Long and slow. "And you want... forever." It was a statement, not a question.

"That's as optimistic as a house with a water view," she said, trying to make the confession lighter. "Let's just say you're not the only one looking for a change." She swallowed and waited a beat before adding, "It just might be that we've changed in different ways."

He looked deep into her eyes, quiet for a minute or so.

"Okay," he finally said. "But you're not scaring me off."

"I'm not trying to. I just want you to know that I'm... serious."

"Why don't we just keep it open to see what happens?" he suggested. "I like you, Tessa. One more date or two? Maybe three?"

She smiled, touched by his persistence and candor, but strong in her position. "Well, it seems we're looking for the same thing in real estate. Maybe we can do some house-hunting together."

"We'll start there and see where it goes."

They took a few steps to walk together, neither one of them able to let go of their clasped hands.

Maybe she hadn't found forever yet.

But at least she was done pretending she didn't want it.

August 4, 1992

Let the record show: I survived three hours of heatstroke, foot blisters, and sunburned sarcasm in the name of civic responsibility. All thanks to Seamus Donahue, who, in addition to being Uncle Artie's fishing pal is also a Do Gooder, as my father calls them.

And Seamus apparently believes four Wylie-Lawson teenagers are the answer to an environmental crisis.

Technically, this was a beach clean-up event hosted by Seamus's church or something, and they do it after some huge annual party in Miramar Beach that leaves the place covered in trash. Seamus wanted "positive role models" for the kids he brought from Destin and Fort Walton. So naturally, he called Artie and asked for the Wylie-Lawson Dream Team.

Plot twist...it was not a dream. It was a sweaty, chaotic circus, and only one of us showed up prepared to lead it. Three guesses and the first two don't count...

Kate Wylie, no surprise to anyone, came armed with sea turtle migration charts, two mesh trash bags, and enough facts to host her own PBS special. She all but made flashcards for the younger kids.

And she was good, too. She got this whole

group of fourth grade boys to stop whining about the heat by convincing them they were on an undercover mission to save a baby sea turtle named Radar. They _loved_ her.

But you know who didn't love her—or at least appreciate her?

Eli the Moron who practically tripped himself following Tessa to help her so she didn't have to break a sweat.

Of course she wore cutoffs the size of a Band-Aid and a tank top that said SUN'S OUT, FUN'S OUT. Instead of helping Kate explain the difference between recyclable and non-recyclable trash, she taught three middle schoolers how to do the Running Man in the sand while holding orange Gatorades.

She did not bring gloves, but she did bring cherry lip gloss and glitter sunscreen.

Eli, in his infinite wisdom, decided his job was to keep Tessa "hydrated" and laugh at every dumb thing she said.

Tessa: "Do cigarette butts even count as trash? They're like, so small."

Eli: guffawing like she was Jerry Seinfeld.

Kate's response? "They're toxic to sea life and take ten years to decompose."

Sometimes I love that girl...which makes me wonder how DUMB is Eli that he doesn't see Kate's pure quality?

Peter spent most of his time helping a little boy with a stutter. He walked beside him, picking up bottle caps and gum wrappers without a word. I don't even think Peter knows how kind he is.

It was pushing noon when Seamus called everyone to the picnic tables under a pavilion. He wanted to thank the volunteers and asked if one of the teens wanted to say a few words. Most wanted to get to the waves.

But not our Lady Katie.

She gave this perfect speech about how important it is to take care of beaches and our environment and something about eco-systems and turtles.

Eli clapped politely.

But when Tessa tripped on a cooler, caught herself from face-planting, and bowed like she meant to do it?

He practically gave her a standing ovation.

What is <u>wrong</u> with him?

I shouldn't care. He's my dumb brother and I'm just glad I don't act like that around Peter. (Or that Peter doesn't act like that around Tessa!!) 'Cause, trust me, I could. Meanwhile, Eli acts like Tessa invented sunshine.

I think he's got it backward. And it bugs me more than it should.

Especially because Kate noticed. She

watched him watch Tessa. I saw it—just the tiniest flicker in her eyes. I'm the only person on Earth who knows she likes him, so I'll never tell.

Anyway, he's too busy handing Tessa his water bottle like she just won Olympic gold in trash collection.

Boys are hopeless.

Love,

Viv

Chapter Thirteen

Eli

The sea air clung to Kate and Eli as they got back to the Summer House with sandy toes and light hearts. They lingered in the sunlight on the boardwalk, still laughing about the fact that Kate had once again lost her glasses in the sand. And, once again, Eli found them.

Eli gave her a warm smile, affection washing over him. "Now that was medicine," he said.

"Hours of it," she agreed, brushing sand off her bare legs.

They'd taken a long walk with towels, water, and an umbrella, getting complete privacy and some alone time on the beach. After an hour on the sand and a swim in the Gulf, they finally made their way home, hot and tired and as close as they'd ever been.

"I warned you we'd lose track of time," Eli said, wrapping his arm around her waist. "Not that I'm complaining, although I am ravenous."

"Same." She tipped her head up and kissed him, quick but sure. Then she drew back and gestured toward the house. "Back to reality?"

"Diapers and client calls and a six-bedroom house

that suddenly feels too small?" He sighed. "It's what we got."

"It's not too small," she assured him, digging out the wayward specs and sliding them on. "It's just not what you expected this summer."

"I'm fine if you are willing to run away and have secret beach time with me." He kissed her this time, much longer than hers. "Because that is the summer I expected."

Kate brushed her fingers down his chest, and for a moment he caught a glimpse of something in her eyes that made his heart ache. She seemed unguarded, like she was starting to believe in them as a couple.

"I had no expectations," she said softly. "So I can't possibly be disappointed. Unless there's no leftovers from the pasta dinner Jonah made last night. Then I'll be bereft and hungry."

"Let's go find out," he said, leaning in for one more kiss. "And if everyone is off doing their own thing, we can eat on the deck just the two of us."

"Mmm. I like the way you think, Mr. Lawson."

They made their way to the pool level, which was empty, rinsed off their feet in a small shower Eli had installed, and headed inside the hushed downstairs living area. Jonah's door was closed, and no sound came from his room.

"Jonah's studying," Kate whispered.

"Words I haven't heard very often in my life."

She smiled. "He only had a lab this morning and said he was going to hit the books all afternoon."

"Or maybe he's..." Eli hesitated when he heard a voice behind the closed door, low, in a quiet conversation. "On the phone."

They'd made it to the bottom of the stairs when Jonah's door opened.

"Hey," he said gruffly.

They both turned and Jonah walked closer, unhappiness visible all over his face.

"Either you are studying too hard or something's wrong," Eli said, frowning at his son.

"The latter." He huffed out a breath. "Can you two talk for a minute?"

So much for continuing their impromptu date upstairs. But Eli didn't hesitate, stepping right back down and, bless her, Kate did, too.

"Of course," they said in unison.

"What's going on?" Eli asked as the three of them went into the living area.

While Kate and Eli sat on the sofa, Jonah dropped onto an overstuffed chair with a deep sigh, running his hands through already tousled hair.

"Is Atlas okay?" Kate asked, leaning forward in concern.

"Meredith took him when he woke up," he said. "She said she'd feed him because I was on the phone." He swallowed visibly. "With Carly's parents."

Eli grunted softly. "What did they say?" he asked.

Jonah barked a joyless laugh. "Nothing terribly nice."

"But what were the specifics?" Eli pressed.

"Like, they wanted to know where Atlas is, who's

taking care of him, when I'm bringing him back, why I haven't contacted them. That stuff."

"You haven't contacted them?" Eli asked, his voice rising in disbelief.

"I sent Carly's sister a text and they know I'm here with family. They know he's fine."

"That's all?" Eli drew back and glanced at Kate. Her arms were crossed, her expression unreadable.

"It's been a couple of weeks, Jonah," Eli said. "You owe them updates. You should be sending them pictures, reassuring them Atlas is in good hands. You shouldn't ignore them, son."

"I'm not," he shot back. "I don't know what to say. I mean, their daughter died. Is it right to send pictures and say, 'Look how cute your grandson is?' That doesn't feel right, either. I just don't know what's the right thing to do."

"The right thing to do is not cut them off or antagonize or worry them. They have enough on their hearts right now." Once again, Eli looked at Kate, expecting her to back him up.

But she remained silent, clearly deep in thought, wearing her most analytical expression.

Finally, she leaned forward. "How did they contact you?"

"They called."

"So they've had your number," she said, glancing at Eli. "If they were worried or antagonized, they would have called sooner. My guess is they're using this time to get their legal ducks in a row."

"Legal ducks?" Eli scoffed. "Their daughter was tragically killed. I'd be surprised if they made it out of bed or brushed their teeth every day."

"Exactly," Jonah said. "And I didn't want to make it worse by sending pictures of Atlas."

"It might make things better," Eli said. "How did you leave it?"

"They want to see the baby."

"All right," he said, calm and deliberate. "Then we invite them, and we host them for as long as they like."

Jonah blinked. "What?"

"They're grieving," Eli continued, feeling certain about this approach. They would offer hospitality, love, kindness, and peace. That was truly the faithful way to handle the situation, and God would bless them. "They just lost their daughter. And now they're trying to understand where their grandson fits into their lives. We open the door. We show them love. That's what Carly would've wanted."

"They didn't sound very... loving," Jonah muttered.

"They don't have to sound that way," Eli said. "They're scared. Angry. Hurting beyond description. Of course they have to come and stay here. Let them see Atlas is safe and loved and healthy. Do you want me to—"

"They might try to take him," Kate said flatly.

Eli turned toward her, blinking at the statement. "We don't know that."

"We don't know that they won't," she replied. "You can't just open this house to complete strangers."

"They're Atlas's grandparents! They have as much right to love him as I do."

"They want to take him from Jonah," she countered. "They've said they would. What if they kidnap him in the middle of the night?"

Jonah sucked in a breath and Eli whipped around to look at him.

"Do you think they might?" he asked.

"I honestly don't know them that well," Jonah said. "I mean, I don't think so but, you know, in their minds, I kidnapped Atlas."

"You brought your motherless newborn to the safety of his extended family," Eli replied firmly. "You hardly kidnapped him. There are no police at the door."

Jonah blew a breath, looking from one to the other, scared and confused.

But Eli wasn't confused. He knew exactly what to do. "We will give them the benefit of the doubt and treat the Danes family like our own." He dropped his elbows on his knees and locked his gaze on Jonah to underscore his point. "Because they *are* family, and they deserve respect and kindness."

"Eli." Kate took a breath, her tone cool as she put a hand on his arm. "I appreciate your good heart, but we have to be cautious and logical."

"There's nothing illogical about this family losing their daughter and wanting to see their grandson," Eli said, feeling very much on the side of the other family in this. "It's emotional and gut-wrenching."

"It is," she agreed, "but we also have to be smart." She

shifted her attention to Jonah. "First things first. Out of the gate, you need to contact a local lab and arrange to do a paternity test to put any question about that to bed."

Jonah let out a quiet sound—almost a whimper—and dropped back in his chair. "There's no question."

"Then you'll easily prove that," she continued. "Then, we hire a family attorney to draw up whatever paperwork we need to name Jonah as Atlas's sole legal guardian. Didn't you say your name is on his birth certificate? Perfect. We'll get custody contracts, power of attorney, emergency filings—whatever it takes. We need to be in front of a judge before they are."

Eli felt his chest tighten. "Before we even *meet* them?"

"Absolutely," she said. "Before we let them in the house, before we set a place at the table, or let them hold that baby. Hospitality can come later. Right now, Jonah needs to dot every I, cross every T, and be prepared for a fight. That should be our strategy."

Eli managed a breath, the pronouncements leaving him reeling, stirring his gut. "I don't like that *strategy*." He hit the word hard. "It feels cold and untrusting, and it's not how you treat family."

She rolled her eyes. "Tell that to the person whose child has been kidnapped by an ex-spouse who wants custody and can't get it. We have to get the law on our side."

He understood what she was saying, but it didn't feel right. "I don't like doing all that before they've forced us into it," he said. "It's not..." He wanted to say *biblical*, but he knew Kate wouldn't understand that. And maybe she was correct about lawyers and tests, but that didn't feel right, either.

"What do *you* want to do, Jonah?" he asked, knowing the final decision belonged to his son.

"Part of me totally agrees with Kate, but I also think they just want to see him and maybe the best thing to do is have a relationship with them without, you know, lawyers and contracts."

"And the test?" Kate asked.

"Yeah, I can do that for sure. I do think that makes sense, but..." He groaned. "I don't want to get in some kind of legal battle."

"You might already be in one," she said. "So you'd best be prepared."

"Or maybe you can avoid one," Eli countered. "With kindness, love, and the creation of family ties."

Kate sighed. "I'm just saying...be smart."

Eli swallowed hard. "And I'm saying...be wise. Honestly, there is a difference between the two."

Poor Jonah looked visibly rattled.

"I need some air." He pushed up and walked to the sliders they'd just come in, yanking them open and leaving with another noisy exhale.

The silence he left behind was heavy, and the tension thick.

Eli turned to Kate. "You think I'm naive."

"I think you're a good, kind man," she said. "And since I was raised by one of those, I have a lot of respect and understanding. But good doesn't stop bad things from happening."

"Well, Kate, that's where faith comes in," he said. "My gut says we're causing trouble where we don't need to if we go on the offensive. Let's treat them like family. That's the right thing to do."

No surprise, she looked away, jaw tightening. "Faith didn't stop Carly from dying."

"No," he agreed. "But as I've told Jonah, a bad thing doesn't mean we have to respond badly. I believe that opening our home to their family and building a relationship with these people who are Atlas's maternal grandparents is the right thing to do."

She didn't roll her eyes again, but a single exhale was enough for him to know what she thought.

"You don't think he should take a paternity test, Eli?"

"I never said that," he replied. "And I'm not opposed to contacting an attorney. But the first thing we must do is invite them to be our guests. Frankly, I can't believe it hasn't happened yet."

"Because Jonah *ran away* from them," she reminded him. "He already showed us that he doesn't trust them."

"He panicked two days after he was dealt a crushing blow in life—a kid who's already lost his mother to a tragic accident. Things are better now. You have to have faith."

She snorted. "No, Eli, I don't. You have to have realism. And legal backing."

They stared at each other. The only sound Eli could hear was his pulse hammering in his head.

The moment stretched, balancing like a coin on its edge. It could fall at any minute, heads or tails. Who was going to win? And what was at stake?

Everything.

Eli broke the silence. "This is it, you know."

"This is...what?"

"The thing that could break us. Our biggest obstacle. Our most foundational difference." He couldn't hold back the words, knowing they had to be spoken. "We could survive a family feud or the possibility that your father put mine in jail. We could overcome a thousand-mile distance and completely different lives. But this? This is the real test of what we have and if it could last."

Kate nodded slowly. "I know."

Again, they looked at each other, silent. Eli would never give up his faith, and Kate may never understand it. If that were true, they were doomed.

"Can we just deal with Jonah and Atlas's grandparents first?" she asked gently. "I'm not ready to fight you on...God." She wrinkled her nose. "He might win."

Eli smiled and leaned into her. "Yes, let's deal with Jonah. But I stand my ground—I want to believe that opening the door to grieving parents can be an act of peace."

"And I want to believe that protecting Jonah and Atlas isn't an act of war."

Eli put his arm around her, holding her as they watched Jonah come back to the slider and step inside, his shoulders squared. Happy to show solidarity, they both stood together and faced him.

"Decision?" Eli asked.

"I'm going to do both," he said. "I'll do the paternity test. I'll get a lawyer. But I invited them all to come and visit us. I told them they were more than welcome to stay here, get to know Atlas, and we can all talk about how they can be part of his life."

Relief and gratitude washed over Eli. "Good call, son."

Kate's brows lifted, her mouth opening—then closing. Whatever she wanted to say, she'd chosen not to.

"I hope so. I'm going to break the news to Atlas," Jonah joked, then pointed upstairs. "And then I'll call a local lab and find out how one goes about proving paternity."

Eli nodded and put a hand on his shoulder. "I'm proud of you, son," he whispered, and never meant it more.

When he left, Kate turned to lean into Eli, letting her head drop on his shoulder but not meeting his gaze.

"We're different," she said softly.

"We are," he agreed. "It would be boring if we were the same."

"It would be easier and make more sense." She looked up at him, a world of emotion in her mahogany eyes. "I need things to make sense, Eli. It's important for me. I must have logic and proof and evidence and tangible... everything. That's how I'm wired."

He didn't know where to begin to answer that. How to tell her that he did have tangible proof of God—every time he looked in the sky or picked up Atlas or listened to

Meredith laugh. She already probably thought he was a weakling for wanting to win a custody battle with hospitality and not contracts.

He'd also fight in prayer, but she wouldn't understand that, either.

"Let me show you," he said on a whisper, not really sure where the words or the sentiment was coming from.

She lifted her brows in question. "Show me what?"

"The power of something you can't see or feel or touch."

She looked dubious. "How?"

He had no idea, but he was trusting God. "You'll see. You'll know it when it happens."

She gave a sad smile, half pity, half amusement. But he didn't care—the answer to this dilemma was in bigger hands than his.

Upstairs, they heard some chatter, a surprised laugh, and the baby crying.

"I'm going to see if there's any chance that a mere strand of pasta is left over," she said, inching away.

He just nodded and let her go. Alone, Eli stood in the quiet room, listening to the echo of her retreating steps. Something inside him—a sliver of certainty, or maybe fear—settled deeper.

She didn't believe. And no matter how much he loved her, he knew faith wasn't something he could compromise.

And now...he wasn't sure she'd even meet him halfway.

Chapter Fourteen
Meredith

"They're coming? Here?" Meredith froze mid-shake, the baby bottle still in her hand. She stared at Jonah, who leaned against the kitchen counter like he'd been tossed there by a rogue wave, his expression unreadable.

He nodded, scrubbing a hand through his already-mussed hair. "That's what I said. Carly's parents want to see their grandson."

"Here?" she repeated. "As in this house?"

He lifted a brow. "Do you see any other houses around here full of Wylies and Lawsons and drama and sand in the sofa cushions?"

She blinked, a long To Do list suddenly forming in her head. "How much time do we have? What room will they stay in? Is her sister coming, too? We'll need space. There's a twin bed in the nursery, which won't work. I'll move out of the upstairs guest room and crash down there. Or do you think we should put a queen bed in there—oh, does the sofa pull out? They may want to be with him. I can help clean. It should all be clean and tidy and—"

"Perfect?" Jonah deadpanned, staring at her with a hint of amusement in his exhausted gaze.

"Well, why not?" she fired back. "You want to impress them, right? To know Atlas is in a clean and comfortable environment?"

He gave a low grunt and headed to the fridge, opening it and staring at the contents like it was the horizon, calling him to escape.

"And now," he muttered, "we have yet another opinion on how to handle this."

She frowned. "What do you mean?"

He grabbed a yogurt and peeled off the foil top. "Let's just say Dad and Kate weren't exactly on the same page."

Meredith arched a brow as she placed the bottle under hot water, still not happy that the contents weren't yet precisely 98.6, the gold standard of formula warmth. "What does that mean? Like, disagreeing on what to serve them? Or how long they should stay?"

Jonah found a spoon and dug in. "Try good cop-bad cop. Christian and atheist. Grace and science. Black and white."

Her eyes widened. "Wait. What?"

He shrugged. "Don't worry. I handled it."

"You *handled it*?" She laughed a little, disbelieving. "You're a sleep-deprived single dad who still uses his sweatshirt as a napkin. What does 'handling it' even look like?"

Jonah leaned against the counter, then pointed at her with a spoon dangerously close to dripping peach Yoplait on the floor. "Like letting both of them talk at me for twenty minutes, then agreeing with two differing opinions. I handled it," he repeated, "so they can be equally annoyed and call it compromise."

Atlas, seated in the bouncer on the kitchen island, chose that moment to let out a high-pitched coo and thump both his feet against the padded edge like he had something to say about it, too.

Meredith sighed and snapped the bottle cap to test the temperature. "I didn't realize Kate and Dad were that...different."

Jonah scooped the last bit of yogurt and tossed his spoon into the sink. "Yeah. They are. Which is kind of the point. But also, kind of the problem."

Meredith paused, satisfied with the temperature, but not her brother's vague response.

He'd been around here longer—he knew them better. Would he tell her if there were any red flags? Would he even notice if Dad was flying headlong into a relationship that would break his heart?

"Do you think she's not right for him?" she asked.

"I told you, I think Kate is pretty amazing. She's helped me so much."

"I know she wrote a letter of recommendation for your culinary program, but..."

"But nothing." He stepped closer to Atlas and leaned over, tapping his nose with a smile. "She's been..." He blew out a breath and his shoulders dropped like a weight had been removed. "Don't balk at this, but in some ways, she's been like a mother to me."

She shouldered Jonah away from the baby to lift his little body. "What does that mean?" she asked him.

"I'll feed him," Jonah said, reaching in to lift the baby up. "It means she's been steady and supportive. We cooked together a lot when I came here back in the spring. It was Kate who made me believe I had real talent in the kitchen. I never expected that. No one's ever done that for me lately."

Meredith nodded, the comments tweaking at her. "Well, with all due respect and not wanting to start an argument, Jonah, you were the one who took off and drove a van up and down California, keeping Dad and me at arm's length for years."

He shrugged, but didn't disagree.

"And if Carly hadn't kicked you out and demanded you get your life together, would you have ever come back to us?"

"What does that have to do with Kate?" He pried the bottle free from her hands while Atlas smacked his lips together.

"I mean, *we* could have supported you and spotted your talent," Meredith said. "You never gave us a chance."

"This isn't about you, Mer. You asked about Kate, and I answered."

"I asked if she was right for Dad, not you," Meredith countered.

Jonah's lips twitched. "I wondered when the interrogation was coming."

"I've been busy," she muttered, looking away for something to clean. "With...stuff."

"Stuff." He slipped the bottle between Atlas's lips. "Let me guess. You've scoped out every preschool within a hundred-mile radius, alphabetized the pantry, and reorganized all the linen closets by function."

"And color," she quipped. "I'll get started on the preschools tomorrow."

He gave in to a smile, never able to resist her comebacks.

"Look, Jonah." She cocked her head, not interested in a fight. Not now. "I just want Dad to be happy. He deserves someone who really gets him."

Jonah's gaze relaxed just a touch. "Then maybe, *Miss Butt-In*, you should try actually getting to know Kate before you decide whether she's worthy of him."

Meredith nodded, since he was right. "I haven't had the chance," she said softly.

"Then make it." He stroked Atlas's cheek with tenderness she honestly hadn't known her brother had in him. "I get the protectiveness, Mer. He's our dad. But you don't have to protect him from love. Or conflict. He's stronger than that."

She watched Jonah adjust the baby expertly, his large hand cupping the soft curve of Atlas's head as he greedily took the bottle. It made something in her chest ache. He looked like a dad. Natural and loving.

Could she be that kind of mother?

Jonah kissed Atlas's temple then turned. "I'm gonna

take this guy outside. He needs some fresh air. And so do I."

He stepped onto the deck, leaving the door open—they never closed it in this house—as she heard footsteps and a woman clearing her throat.

Kate. Oh, goodness. How much of that had she heard?

"Hey," Kate greeted as she came into the kitchen.

"Hi, there," Meredith replied. "Jonah's out on the deck with Atlas if you're looking for him."

"Actually, I was looking for you."

She swallowed. Had she eavesdropped?

"Well, here I am. What do you need?"

"Time," she said simply. "And despite the fact that Eli and I just walked for way too long, I'd love to hit that sand again, maybe with someone not as fast. Take a stroll on the beach with me?"

Yep, she'd heard every word.

"I'd love to," Meredith said, mustering her best casual tone.

Kate glanced toward the deck again, then back to Meredith. They held each other's gaze for a minute, a challenge and a question in the air.

A question that Meredith was ready to ask, but she wasn't sure she was going to like the answer.

The sun cast a shimmer that made the Gulf look like a brushed sheet of light. The tide was low, leaving a wide stretch of white sand between the boardwalk and the surf.

They left their shoes near the house and strolled barefoot to the waterline. The conversation—if she could give the small talk they exchanged so weighty a name—floated between Meredith and Kate, light and inconsequential. Surely they were both waiting for the perfect moment to get into something more serious.

"This sand is ridiculous," Meredith murmured as her toes curled and disappeared with each step. "The color of powdered sugar."

Kate chuckled. "I once broke your father's heart by explaining the color is the result of finely eroded quartz from the Appalachian Mountains." She gave an apologetic smile. "Blinding him with science."

"You people ruin everything," Meredith teased, jabbing her gently with an elbow. "Don't ever try to explain how rainbows work, or I'll cry."

Kate grinned, her hair tousled by the wind as they reached the calm surf and stood for a moment, letting it froth around their ankles. "Deal. I'll leave the famous Destin magic intact."

The laughter faded, and Meredith felt the real reason for this stroll settle on her shoulders as they started to walk. She inhaled slowly, tasting salt and tension on the breeze. The silence stretched just long enough to feel awkward, and finally, she just...went for it.

"So," she said, eyes fixed on the horizon. "You and my dad. Is it serious?"

Kate didn't miss a beat. "Don't start picking out what

color you want to wear to the wedding quite yet, Meredith."

The joke landed wrong—Meredith's smile twitched, then faltered. Even the *mention* of a wedding made something inside her tighten.

She cleared her throat. "Have you two talked about that kind of thing? Marriage? The distance? I mean, your job at Cornell is...pretty solid. Impressive, actually. Are you expecting him to move there?"

Kate turned to look at her, one brow arched. "Wow. You don't play, as your brother likes to say."

Meredith shrugged, not about to apologize for directness. "Sorry. I care about him. A lot. And I know he's my dad and I'm his daughter, but we've got a special bond forged by a shared love of architecture."

"And grief," Kate added. "He's your only parent and he's a magnificent one. I understand, respect, and absolutely love your closeness. When he talks about you, well..." Kate laughed. "I was pretty sure you hung the moon even before I met you."

The compliment warmed, and relaxed, her. And reminded her just how far the mighty were about to fall.

"Trust me, I didn't hang anything. But I guess you understand that I want to be certain you're both, you know, on the same page. With...life."

"Life?" Kate glanced out at the water. "We haven't talked about long-term logistics. No one's booking U-Hauls or applying for out-of-state driver's licenses. We're just taking the summer to see if this is real. If what we've felt from the minute I walked up to this house is, well, more than just my childhood crush."

"On him?" she asked, surprised.

"I kept it on the DL," Kate joked. "I threatened your Aunt Vivien with her very life if she told anyone or even mentioned it in her infamous diaries. And he had Tessa fever, so it was a moot point. But this time, thirty years later...well, it's good. It's special. And we both want to know if the long-distance thing we've kept alive for a few months actually holds up in the bright light of daily life. That's all."

"Is it holding up?"

"We're discovering things," Kate said with hesitation. "About each other, and ourselves."

"That's nice and vague."

Kate let out a short breath of laughter. "It's also true."

Meredith slowed her step. "Like what are you discovering, exactly?"

Kate paused, too, then tilted her head. "He's kind. Grounded. And deeply generous in ways that sneak up on you. Obviously, handsome and delightful and good-hearted."

"Check, check, and triple check," Meredith replied. "I hear a 'but' on the end of that list of attributes."

Kate nodded. "But he's also..." She seemed to search for the word. "Committed. In every sense of the word."

"You mean his faith," Meredith guessed.

"His religion is part of it, yes."

Meredith folded her arms, brushing back a strand of

hair blown over her eyes. "I'm sure this is not news to you, but my father isn't just *religious*."

"I know, he hates that word," Kate agreed.

"He hates it because his belief system is *foundational*, not a list of...of...rules. It's how he makes every decision—big or small. Personal, professional, emotional. It's not a decorative accessory. His love of God *is* who he is, and it dictates his actions and decisions. I know he doesn't evangelize about it—that's not his style. But once you really know him, it's clear."

Kate was quiet for a few footsteps, then she asked, "He wasn't always like that, though. Right?"

Was there something *hopeful* in that tone?

"Why?" Meredith asked. "Do you want him to go back?"

Kate pushed her glasses onto her head and looked hard at Meredith. "No. I don't *expect* him to stop believing because I don't, if that's what you're implying. I'm merely curious where it came from, when it started. His siblings aren't relig— believers. And Maggie isn't exactly Mother Teresa."

Meredith snorted at that.

"Was it your mother's death?" she asked. "I'm just wondering where these beliefs came from."

"He would say it came from God," Meredith said evenly.

Kate sighed. "That does seem like the kind of answer Eli would give."

"It started before my mom died," Meredith added, staring down at the shell her toes had uncovered. "People always think his belief came from grief, but it didn't. It deepened, sure. But he was already on that path. So was she—you know she'd already cracked a Bible before she died. They were both what is called 'Christian curious' nowadays. Then she passed away and he turned to God." She slid a look at Kate, a frown forming. "He hasn't told you all this?"

She shrugged. "Bits and pieces. I think he doesn't want to scare me away and he sort of dances around the topic of his faith."

Meredith turned to her fully, hands tucked into the pockets of her cutoffs. "Well, it's an awfully big thing to dance around."

Kate looked down at the water, silent for a long time. "You're protective of him, Meredith. I understand. But he's a grown man and knows what's what."

"He does, but sometimes he's too good, too trusting, and too...faithful. If God tells him you're the one, he'll go all in." Meredith studied her for a moment. "You haven't said where you stand on the issue of faith. Atheist? Agnostic? Reformed Catholic or...what?"

"I did say," she replied. "I'm a scientist."

"That's not a religious system or belief."

"My world is built around observable data, verifiable results, controlled environments. Capacitors, not catechisms. Energy storage, not spiritual epiphanies. I don't believe in anything I can't test, touch, measure, or reproduce. It's not about being cold or cynical. It's about being...precise and *real*."

Well, faith was real to Eli Lawson, Meredith thought.

"So you think his beliefs are...woo-woo? For the desperate and heartbroken?"

"You're putting words in my mouth," Kate replied. "I never belittle what he believes, but I'll be perfectly honest, it's very difficult for me to grasp. Supernatural? A supreme being in the sky? Miracles and answered prayers and...a book written by...who knows?"

"Eli knows," Meredith said quietly. "He'll tell you exactly who wrote it."

Kate's shoulders slumped slightly. "I know. I know. It's just hard for me. Hard to believe in something I can't understand or prove."

"Then watch him," Meredith said, gentler now.

"What do you mean?" Kate asked, sounding genuinely curious.

"Like I said, my dad's not an evangelizer. He doesn't quote scripture or pray in public or leave Bible verses in people's mailboxes. He thinks that's a shortcoming, but I think he doesn't see that he *lives* his faith in a million different ways. In his strength and clarity and kindness and inner peace. That all comes from his unwavering trust in God, who he sees, hears, measures, and tests every single day."

Kate was silent, then sighed. "We're talking about how I feel about God, but the real question is how I feel about Eli."

"And?"

"I love him," she said simply. "I really do."

Meredith's throat tightened.

"But this?" Kate went on, waving a hand toward the

sky, the sea, the invisible chasm between them. "It's a big thing. A deep divide. I keep asking myself—if I can't believe in what he believes, will he still believe in *me*?"

Meredith studied her, the woman who made her dad light up when she walked into a room, who had been kind to Jonah, who had written him glowing letters and shared meals and laundry and lullabies. She wasn't evil. She wasn't selfish. She wasn't even trying to change him.

"You said you only believe in what you can test," Meredith said. "What you can measure. Touch. Prove."

Kate nodded.

"Does that mean you don't believe in love?"

She didn't answer, and the expression that crossed her face—pain, uncertainty, something raw—was gone almost as quickly as it came, but clearly, the question had hit the mark.

"I'll need some time to think about that," she whispered.

"Come on," Meredith said when they reached the boardwalk where they'd started. "Jonah might be father of the year, but he can't burp that baby for love or money."

They smiled at each other and as they picked up their shoes and headed into the Summer House, Meredith put a light hand on Kate's shoulder.

She certainly didn't want any animosity with the woman her dad loved, just a genuine connection. Kate met the gesture with a warm look, both of them silently agreeing to table all the unanswered questions. For now, anyway.

Chapter Fifteen
Maggie

The palm trees were lit from below like runway models, casting long, glamorous shadows across Ocean Drive as Maggie rolled down the truck window and let the humid, sea-soaked air warm her face.

They hadn't planned to arrive in Miami Beach at this time, but stopping in the little hotel in Fort Lauderdale like their itinerary said seemed like a waste. Maggie had stuck to her decision not to tell anyone in Destin where they were or what they were doing. No one had asked too many questions in her brief texts and one call, but she sensed that couldn't last too much longer.

She hoped they could get to Miami Beach, pick up the car early, then zip back to Fort Lauderdale by seven or so.

Whoa, had she calculated that wrong. Who knew so many cars could be on the roads, jamming South Florida like it was Mardi Gras in New Orleans? The traffic had been ghastly, giving Maggie a headache and a handache from a constant death grip on the wheel.

They'd stayed on the beach road to avoid I-95, of course—some fears couldn't be conquered—and that was an absolute nightmare where clearly everyone made up their own driving rules and speed limits were casual suggestions.

Now it was too late to turn back, and way too late to get the car they'd come to pick up.

Jo Ellen had used the Great and Powerful Oscar to get a hotel recommendation in Miami Beach, and made a reservation for that night.

If they got there in one piece. That was looking like a longshot as they crawled along Ocean Drive, which was more of a street party than a road.

"Oh, my word," Maggie muttered, watching a shirtless man on rollerblades weave between slow-moving convertibles while holding a neon cocktail in each hand. "We've landed in a spring break documentary."

Jo Ellen leaned forward in the passenger seat of Frank's beater truck, clutching the itinerary printed in a font so large, Maggie could read it from the driver's seat.

"This is exactly what I thought Miami Beach would be like," Jo cooed. "I half expect to see Don Johnson in a white suit with his gun drawn any minute!"

A man walked by wearing nothing but a bathing suit that made him look like a professional grape smuggler.

"Careful, Jo. Having your 'gun drawn' might mean something completely different down here."

Jo Ellen snorted. "Look around, Maggie. It's so alive!"

"Oh, it's alive. It's practically vibrating with..." She searched for the right description, seeing nothing but lithe bodies, long hair, and tiny threads pretending to be clothing. "Youth," she finished on a sigh.

"Well, then we'll stand out like that man's bright pink drinks," Jo said. "By the way, is everything made of blindingly colored lights down here?"

She wasn't wrong—the neon was relentless. Pink and turquoise signs blinked like they were in competition. Music thumped from somewhere, and every building looked like the set of a movie made in the 1920s.

The sidewalks teemed with the beautiful people, from scantily clad girls to a statuesque woman walking a poodle in a rhinestone vest.

"That dog's better dressed than me."

"You did buy a leopard caftan in Winter Park," Jo Ellen reminded her.

"A moment of absolute madness." Maggie clucked. "Why did you let me shop after day drinking?"

"Because we accidentally got on the highway that afternoon and you'd earned an espresso martini."

"Which was *nothing* like coffee," Maggie tsked. "That waitress lied to us."

"Turn here—this is our hotel."

"Oh, good heavens." Maggie eased the truck under the overhang of The Selina South Beach, which looked like *Travel + Leisure* magazine had collided with a rock concert and taken a detour in the Caribbean.

The valet entrance pulsed with pink light and a sunburst chandelier. A man in linen pants and no shirt danced next to a pile of suitcases.

Maggie pulled up to the curb and turned off the engine but didn't move. "Why do I feel like they're not expecting two widows in sensible sandals with a travel cooler full of pimento cheese?"

Jo Ellen patted her hand. "We're women of the world."

"We're women of a *different* world."

Two valets immediately opened their doors and greeted them, promising to watch the truck while they checked in.

Stepping onto the asphalt, Maggie was immediately hit by a wall of humid air and cloying perfume. She tugged down the hem of her shirt and squared her shoulders, heading inside like she was bracing for battle.

The lobby was all white couches, tropical plants, and glowing artwork. A wall mural read *SUMMER NEVER ENDS* in swirly letters above a pair of lime green angel wings. In front of it, two young women posed for pictures, wearing matching dresses that seemed to be missing waists, backs, and half of their skirts.

Maggie wrinkled her nose. "I feel like Miss Pittypat when Scarlett scandalized Atlanta at the Confederacy fundraiser." She pretended to fan herself, making Jo Ellen laugh.

"We're not in Atlanta anymore?" Jo Ellen joked.

Maggie shot her a look. "You mean Kansas, and that's *Wizard of Oz*, which, coincidentally, was made the same year, 1939."

"And looking around?" Jo Ellen elbowed her as they approached the front desk, manned by a...person. "This place makes me feel like *I* was made that year, too."

"You practically were," Maggie sniffed. "Let me handle

the young'uns." She strode up to the desk and stared at a... well, she just wasn't sure. The receptionist wore bright green eyeshadow, had yellow hair about a centimeter long, and each earlobe featured a hole large enough to drive through.

"Welcome to The Selina!" A deep voice, so she was going with 'he' and hoped that didn't get her kicked out. "Are we checking in, ladies?"

"Yes," Maggie said. "Magnolia Lawson and Jo Ellen Wylie. One room, two queens, ocean view, one night." One long, miserable, noisy night.

"You got it, my two queens." Grinning, he tapped the keyboard, a frown formed, and then grew deeper. "Can you spell those names?"

She did, shifting from one foot to the other.

"I am sorry. I'm just not seeing a reservation for tonight. Do you have a confirmation number?"

"I'm sure we do." She turned to Jo Ellen, who had walked across the lobby and was gawking at the place like a true tourist. "Jo! I need you!" She frantically waved her over then turned back to the desk. "It was booked directly through your website. Pre-paid in full." She fished into her bag. "Do you want the credit card we used?"

He shook his head, then tapped more keys. "Huh. Looks like the reservation was made but never confirmed on the system. Unfortunately, we are fully committed tonight."

Maggie blinked. "Committed?"

Jo Ellen stepped up beside her. "That's hotel-speak for full."

"I *know* what it means," Maggie snapped. "I was just giving him a chance to rephrase before I set this entire lobby on fire."

Ear Holes smiled nervously. "We'd be happy to arrange for you to stay at our sister property about ten minutes west, Selina Marsh Landing. It's not on the beach but—"

"It sounds like the Everglades." Maggie narrowed her eyes. "We wanted oceanfront."

"I'm sure it's a lovely hotel," Jo Ellen said sweetly. "But we chose this one very specifically because we're celebrating a milestone."

"We are?" Maggie asked under her breath.

Jo Ellen leaned in and stage-whispered, "It's our sixtieth anniversary of...being together."

Maggie blinked at her, startled.

"No!" Ear Holes gasped. "You two?"

"It's true," Jo Ellen said brightly. "We met in college, and it was love at first sight. We've laughed, cried, survived heartbreak and hot flashes together. Side by side, till death do us part." She wrapped an arm around Maggie and pointed to her. "And when this beautiful woman doesn't get what she wants, death can't be far away. For you. Don't make my darling Maggie upset on this trip."

He just stared from one to the other, jaw loose.

"This is the anniversary trip we've planned our whole lives," Jo Ellen said.

"Wow. That's...incredible. Congrats, ladies. You

don't see that much with women your age—not that you look old. You're gorgeous! Good for you!"

"Oh, it's been a celebration!" Jo was clearly high on her own fiction. "We were just in Vero Beach and had the best sea bass of our lives. And before that? Watched a real rocket launch in Titusville. Have you ever seen one of those?"

Ear Holes shook his head so hard the wide-open windows of his lobes actually quivered.

"And before *that*," Jo Ellen said, her voice growing excited, "we went shopping in Winter Park and, oh, we met a biker named Brick who took quite a shine to my Maggie."

Maggie coughed into her hand to keep from laughing.

Jo Ellen beamed. "So, you see, this hotel is the final cherry on top. And we'd hate to end such a beautiful trip in a parking-lot motel across the causeway."

There was a pause.

Then—miraculously—Ear Holes tapped his keyboard again. "Let me...see something. We may have had a cancellation this afternoon."

Jo Ellen squeezed Maggie's hand under the counter. Maggie just turned her head so he didn't see how badly she was trying not to laugh.

She stared at the words "Summer Never Ends" with only one thought: she *couldn't* love Jo Ellen more.

Two minutes later, they had keycards in hand and matching lavender welcome drinks with dried orchids on top.

As they walked away, Ear Holes congratulated them

again and Maggie punctuated the whole thing by draping an arm around Jo Ellen.

"Too much?" Jo murmured. "I know you hate it when I make up things to get what we want."

"Are you kidding?" Maggie squeezed her. "Don't make me kiss you on the lips...sweetheart."

They giggled their way to a room that was a fever dream of Miami Beach chic with whitewashed walls, terrazzo floors, sleek wood paneling, and an enormous window with a balcony. There was a record player on the dresser and a minibar that was calling Maggie's name.

Jo Ellen dropped her purse and flopped on the bed. "We did it, Mags. We road-tripped to Miami Beach, didn't die, and scored a room without using any weapons. Well, one of my stories, which could be considered a weapon. Think I should write a book?"

Maggie walked to the window, pushed open the slider, and looked out at the pink-lit skyline before turning back to her friend. "You know what I think?"

Jo Ellen lifted a brow.

"I think we are still young."

Jo Ellen grinned. "That's because of sixty years with me, darling!"

"It really is." Maggie went straight to the minibar. "I'm ready for room service, but first, let's pregame."

"Let's *what?*"

"It's what the kids call it," Maggie said, yanking open the fridge door. "You drink before you go out, or, in our case, stay in. Either way, it's fun."

Maggie pulled out two tiny cans of something called

White Claw and handed one to Jo Ellen. "Cheers to the man with holes in his ears."

"He thought we were a cute couple."

Maggie lifted her can and popped the top. "Well, we are!"

THE CAR GLEAMED like a cherry on top of the sundae of life.

Parked under a striped awning at Suncoast Classic Motors, the candy-apple red '57 Thunderbird shimmered in the morning light, top down, white leather interior glowing like a fresh manicure. Even the whitewall tires looked buffed to a mirror finish.

"Oh, my word," Maggie breathed, stopping dead at the sight. "That car is...sexy."

Jo Ellen let out a low whistle. "I feel like we should be wearing scarves and red lipstick. We really *are* Thelma and Louise. They were in a Thunderbird! Oh, no, Maggie—it's bad luck."

"Hush, and don't make me sorry I let you watch that."

Maggie walked a slow circle around the car, her fingers twitching with the urge to touch. She didn't know what she expected after all that fuss Frank Cavallari made about this being Betty's antique dream car, but this was no rusted relic. This was a statement.

"This is so Betty," Jo Ellen said, following Maggie's train of thought.

"Like that ridiculous fur coat," Maggie muttered. "Gorgeous and useless."

"Maggie." Jo elbowed her. "The woman is dying. If she wants this car, she should get it."

"We're here, aren't we?"

"Ladies?" A dark-haired middle-aged man dressed in a suit came out the door. "Can I help make your dreams come true?"

Maggie looked him up and down, but Jo Ellen stepped forward, no doubt to stave off sarcasm that wasn't going to make this go any easier.

"This is our car." She pointed at it.

"Sorry, but she's spoken for," he said. "I have another—"

"It's spoken for us," Maggie interjected. "We're here on behalf of Frank Cavallari. That's his lovely truck for the trade-in and we have a cashier's check for the rest, the paperwork, the phone number, everything you need."

"Oh, you're Maggie and Jo Ellen. He told me to expect you." He reached out a hand to shake hers. "I'm Rodrigo and I will get everything set up inside. Why don't you sit in the car and get comfortable with her? I'll come and get you momentarily."

When he left, Maggie and Jo Ellen climbed in with the necessary amount of reverence.

Inside, the Thunderbird had a bright white dashboard lined with chrome, a big circular speedometer, and a bench seat that seemed tailor-made for teenage makeout sessions. The steering wheel was the size of a pizza pan, and the whole thing smelled faintly like leather and wax, all warmed by the Florida sunshine.

Jo Ellen was nearly vibrating. "Maggie, this is what joy looks like. Candy-coated and completely impractical."

"I'm not usually a car person," Maggie said.

"You don't say."

She gave a dry laugh. "But this is—"

"A stick shift," Jo Ellen interjected, putting her hand on a shiny ball that stuck up on the end of a wand between them.

"Isn't that just the thing you use to put it in Park and Reverse?"

Jo Ellen made a face. "Pretty sure this H-shaped diagram with the numbers one, two, and three is for shifting. And that pedal?" She pointed to the floor. "Is what my husband used to call a clutch."

"A...*clutch?*" Maggie choked the words. "I have no idea how to drive a clutch."

"Don't tell Rodrigo or he won't let us have it," Jo Ellen said, jutting her head toward the door when the man came out. "And I'll ask Oscar for some tips."

But somehow Maggie didn't think even that robot could help her now.

Inside the much cooler showroom, they followed the slick-looking salesman to a glass-enclosed office to sign their lives away. Rodrigo seemed a little surprised that they were driving all the way back to the Panhandle, but Maggie decided to let Jo Ellen do the talking.

Sometimes, that really was better. Especially when all Maggie could think about was...a *clutch*. And it wasn't her favorite beaded handbag.

They gave away Frank's keys for the truck, signed a mountain of documents, and drank some bitter and tasteless coffee.

"Well, we're committed now," Maggie murmured to Jo Ellen, who was madly tapping her phone, no doubt begging Oscar for a driving lesson.

Two men in white shirts came in, looking crisp and efficient. "We transferred all your belongings from the truck to the T-bird," one said.

"We reset the top, too," the other informed them. "And we fit all your stuff inside. Cooler, bags, and the... bike helmet."

Maggie and Jo Ellen shared a surprised look.

"I bet Brick slipped that in there so you didn't forget him," Jo Ellen teased. "Probably wrote his number inside."

Maggie rolled her eyes and signed the last page of a contract, the one that probably included fine print that legally acknowledged she could drive a stick shift.

After she put down the pen, Rodrigo dropped the keys ceremoniously into her hand and gave Jo Ellen a packet of papers the size of the Yellow Pages, prattling on about temporary tags and a bill of sale for registration. But all Maggie could do was stare at the keys and think about...the clutch.

"She's all yours," he said. "Happy trails, ladies."

"Oh, I'm sure they'll be...interesting," Maggie muttered, her hands already sweating as she imagined gripping that gearshift like she was in a racecar at Indy.

Jo Ellen grinned. "Oh, this is going to be so much fun."

Outside, with Rodrigo looking on like a proud papa, Maggie opened the driver's side door, slid into the low-slung seat, and looked down at the clutch. She breathed the words that would define the next thirty minutes of her life...

"Oh, *hell*."

Jo Ellen, already shoving the papers in the glovebox, glanced over. "Come on, Mags. How hard can it be?"

Very.

The first attempt launched them half a foot forward before the engine stalled with a cough.

The second attempt got them rolling five feet before a grinding sound made Jo Ellen scream and seize the door handle like it was a lifeline.

By the third attempt, Maggie was sweating through her cotton top and swearing like a sailor as she caught a glimpse of the shock and horror on Rodrigo's face in the rearview mirror.

"Give it gas! More gas!" Jo Ellen yelped. "And put your foot on the pedal at the exact second you move that stick. Oscar says it's like choreography."

"Oscar can bite me!"

The Thunderbird jerked forward like a toddler learning to walk and sputtered into the street with a horn blast from behind. Somehow, Maggie managed to jam it into second gear without turning the transmission into shrapnel.

"We're in traffic!" Jo Ellen, queen of the obvious, shouted over the noisy motor.

"I *know!*"

A sleek white BMW honked as it swerved past them, and Maggie gave the driver a prim, queenly wave. "Sorry, darling, we're learning."

Jo Ellen leaned closer, clutching her phone. "Oscar suggests we...pray."

"Finally, something smart from that dimwit."

They somehow navigated through the South Beach traffic without getting arrested or rear-ended, though there were several close calls, one heated middle finger, and a woman on a scooter who shouted, "Learn to drive, ya old bag!"

"God bless you, too!" Maggie yelled back.

By the time they hit a red light on Collins Avenue, Maggie had found something resembling a rhythm. Her left leg ached from the stupid little pedal, her jaw was tight from the tension, and her soul had left her body no less than five times.

"You know what?" she said, flexing her fingers on the wheel. "I feel like Scarlett after Rhett left her stranded with a sick horse, a half-dead woman, and a newborn."

Jo Ellen peeked through her fingers. "Traumatized?"

"Determined to get home." Maggie threw the car from Neutral into first gear with increasing confidence.

Small screech of the clutch, but it caught. "As God is my witness, I will never avoid a highway again."

"You're not going on the *highway,* are you?"

"I might. We can make it to Orlando today. Honestly, Jo, this thing drives like it was dipped in caffeine."

Jo Ellen moaned. "Well, bad news, honey. If you want to get to the interstate, you have to turn left here. But forget an arrow—there's not even light. And lots of oncoming traffic."

"Oh, boy." She pulled into the left lane, said the prayer Oscar recommended, and stepped on the gas like it was a palmetto bug on her patio.

Before long, Miami was finally in the rearview mirror and Maggie was zipping up I-95 like a pro.

"You know what?" she said to Jo Ellen. "Roger would be so proud of me."

"I'm proud of you," Jo said, putting a hand on her arm. "You are my idol, Maggie Lawson. I never met a woman like you, and I never will again."

Maggie laughed. A deep, from-the-gut laugh that wiped out decades of fear.

"Thank you for pushing me. I feel like I could take on anything. Drive Route 66. Race a dune buggy. Parallel park on Peachtree Street."

"You're drunk on power."

Maggie turned the wheel with one hand and passed a truck that was just going too slow. "I'm drunk on freedom. Being afraid is the same as being in prison. We're out, sister."

Jo Ellen hooted. "We should get a car like this!"

"Don't tempt me."

They sped north, the T-Bird humming along, and Maggie let herself feel it—that buzz of youth, that hum of strength, that knowledge that she could do something scary and still keep going.

Chapter Sixteen
Tessa

"Well, that was...educational," Tessa said, tugging the passenger seatbelt across her body after climbing into Dusty's surprisingly luxurious truck. The silver Ford they'd taken on their day of house-hunting was solid but high-end, the kind of vehicle that said, "I've done well but I also like to haul stuff."

Like everything about Dusty Mathers, it appealed to Tessa. The truck, the man, the banter, the insight, the honesty, the humor, and the effortless exchange of conversation and information—it *all* appealed to her.

"I didn't know they still made linoleum that color," Dusty cracked as he touched the ignition button. "Would you call that rancid mustard? Or baby-food peas?"

"It was Sherwin-Williams Light Trauma," she quipped. "And that kitchen? I've seen bigger galleys on fishing boats."

Dusty shifted into Reverse and backed out over the cracked concrete driveway. "How about the office? A generous term for a closet, don't you think? Not only would I not have a couch for my patients, I'd barely have room for a desk."

As he drove off, the house faded from view. "Goodbye, beige ranch with mismatched window shutters circa '77," she said wistfully.

"With a bathtub if you want a water view," he added, cracking her up.

"Lorna is texting us the address for the next house," Tessa said, taking out her phone to read the message. "Can you bear another? She has high hopes for this one."

She'd also said she wanted to "kill two birds" by taking them together to listings, since they were essentially looking for the same thing in their next home. But Tessa had the feeling Lorna wanted to *mate* birds, not kill them.

The woman hadn't bothered to correct the listing agent at the first house when he'd assumed Tessa and Dustin were a married couple.

She whispered that "it was just easier" than trying to explain the truth, which didn't seem *that* complicated to Tessa. What she wanted, Tessa suspected, was for her friend Dusty to get a new romance in his life.

Did Lorna know what Dusty really wanted?

"You've heard of the first pancake theory, right?" Dusty said, pulling her from her thoughts.

"Must have chocolate chips and blueberries?"

He laughed. "You gotta burn the first one."

"That's the waffle theory, and yeah, I guess. But now we've burned three. That's officially a failed breakfast."

He threw her a look. "I didn't take you for a pessimist, Tess."

She sighed. "I hate compromising, and I have a

feeling I'm about to. Anyway, here's the address." She read the numbers and glanced at the listing. "Oh, wait. This one actually says 'water view.' Fingers crossed."

"Don't cross—hold." He reached out his hand for hers. "Maybe my bar is really low, but...don't you think this is fun?"

She slid her hand into his, aware of a rough palm and strong fingers and a good, solid feel. "And fun is what you wanted," she reminded him.

He chuckled. "You didn't answer my question—do you think this is fun?"

"I guess it depends on how you define fun," she said on a laugh, because it was easy to play along.

Did "fun" mean good times and lots of drinks and easy, meaningless conversation? Or did fun mean inside jokes and quick looks that communicated plenty— because even after only seeing three houses together, they had quite a few of those, too.

"And she *still* doesn't answer."

She laughed. "You're such a therapist. You think everyone has to answer every question and reveal their inner workings."

"Don't you want to?"

She considered the question and all the ways to respond. Of course she wanted to share her innermost thoughts and learn his, but that would just lead her deeper into feelings and she was already drowning in them.

"I've never been to therapy," she admitted.

His brows flicked in surprise. "You're absolutely next level at avoiding a question, you know that?"

She laughed and shrugged. "I'll answer when I'm good and ready."

"When will that be?"

"Umm, when one of us finds a house we think is perfect?"

"So, never," he said with a side-eye. "I don't want to wait that long. Let's do a free therapy session tonight."

"Is that what the kids are calling it now?"

He laughed. "Come on. One more date. We'll make it special. What would you like to do?"

"I'm supposed to go to the marina and check on my boat. It had some service done on the engine and I need to run it."

He took his eyes from the road to turn his whole head and give her a surprised look. "You have a *boat*?"

"I do. And you'll love the name—*Good Time Girl*. I got it as payment for an event I handled for a rich guy renting down the street."

His brows flicked, impressed. "Can I come with you tonight to check the engine? I know, a bold and presumptuous question, but it's one you have to answer. Yes or no?"

She just looked at him, holding in the real answer, which wasn't yes or no. It was, "I don't know because I like you so much it's starting to hurt, and you don't want what I want."

"Only if there's no therapy," she finally said.

"Oh, you can't stop me," he teased. "Every conversation I have is therapy."

"That's terrifying," she muttered, looking back at the phone. "This house does look nice. Super updated, three beds, two baths, and a pool that's situated 'on the water,' whatever that means."

"If there's a sliver of blue beyond that backyard fence, I will throw down an offer before you can spell your last name."

"Just know I will fight you," she countered. "Bare-knuckle. Realtor gets to pick the winner."

"The Realtor," he said, "is counting on it. You know that's why she's doing this, don't you?"

"Yes, I do. Full disclosure, she prattled on about you before you showed up the other evening."

"Oh, no." He pretended to touch something over his head. "Is my halo on straight?"

She laughed. "It's glowing."

He grinned and glanced sideways at her, a longer look than was strictly safe while navigating the turn. "You're good at this, you know. The banter. The vibe."

"Well, I *have* been dating since Blockbuster still charged late fees. Got a little practice."

He laughed again, but it faded into something quieter. "I know you said you never married, but you never said why."

"*And* the therapy starts."

"Tessa." He gave her hand a squeeze. "I want to know you."

Her heart shifted. Didn't he see where that would lead? Maybe that didn't scare him, but it freaked her out. She'd just like him *more*.

"I don't let men...into my heart," she said, surprising herself at the candor.

"Why not?"

"Hey, you're the therapist. You tell me."

He smiled and turned, following the GPS on his dashboard. "That's not actually how therapy works. I guide you to figure it out yourself."

"I thought you had the answers."

He shook his head. "No, you have the answers. I just help you find them. Let me ask it this way—when someone asks you why you never married, what do you tell them?"

She exhaled and looked out the window, even though she knew the answer.

"Please don't evade, answer with a question, or otherwise sidestep."

She smiled at that. "I tell them that my dad was picture-perfect—the greatest guy I ever knew and truly my hero, role model, and favorite person. No man has ever measured up."

He thought about that for a moment, quiet, like he was filing it away. "Is that true?" he finally asked.

She searched her heart for the absolute truth, but his GPS chimed in first.

"Your destination is on the right," the mechanical voice chirped.

"Saved by the robot," she joked.

He just gave her a sly look. "We'll pick this back up on the boat tonight." Then he jutted his chin toward the house. "I do believe there is a classic Florida retention pond in the backyard. Does that count as a water view?"

"For the alligator that lives there," she said, pointing at the ominous sign that was visible from the street.

They toured the house, but her heart wasn't in it. The kitchen was beautiful. The pool sparkled. The third bedroom would be perfect as an office. But the pond was brown and brackish and filled her with dread.

As they stepped back onto the front porch, Dusty looked at her. "Not it?"

"No," she said quietly. "It's not. You?"

"Most certainly not." He nodded slowly. "You okay?"

She just smiled at him. "I guess."

He put a casual arm around her and walked to the truck. "Nothing a sunset cruise and a little free therapy won't cure. You still up for it?"

She looked up and into his dark eyes, wishing she didn't like him so darn much. But she did.

"Yes." She added a smile. "How's that for a straight answer?"

"In my business, we call that progress," he said on a laugh.

"How DID I not know this was what you meant by 'boat ride'?" he asked. "I thought you had a little flats boat or something. You negotiated for *this* as payment from a client?"

She gave a saucy smile. "I saved his butt and he owed me. She's sweet, huh?"

He lifted his bottle in a toast. "As is her owner."

"Thank you." She adjusted the wheel as they rounded a sandbar, taking in the dramatic vista.

The sky looked like a watercolor painting—pink bleeding into peach, melting into soft gold. The harbor was so calm it barely lapped the hull, and the motor purred beneath them like a satisfied cat.

Tessa had slipped *Good Time Girl* out to the bay with Dusty sitting beside her at the helm, nursing a bottle of Heineken and looking impossibly at ease.

"I told you," she said, nodding at the horizon where Destin shimmered like a mirage. "I know all the secret sunset spots."

"You weren't lying," he murmured, eyes on two seagulls swooping overhead. "This is...whoa, I don't even have the right words."

"You're a therapist. Don't you have *all* the words?"

"I leave the pretty ones to people like you."

"Is that a compliment or a classic Tessa Wylie-style deflection?"

"Yes. You ready for a drink now that you've navigated us away from land, Captain?"

"Yes, please. Same as you."

He reached into the cooler wedged beside the seat and grabbed her a beer, opening it, then handing it to her.

She tapped her green bottle to his. "To free therapy."

"Oh, you want some now?" he asked before taking a sip.

"Not me, my favorite idiot. *You.* You are going to unpeel your onion, and I'll be the therapist. Come on, let's drop the anchor and get comfy."

A few minutes later, the Sea Ray was bobbing in the water, and they were stretched out on their backs, side by side on the bow.

He propped his arms behind his head, regarding her from under his lashes, which were easy to see since he'd left his glasses on the console.

"So where do you want to start?"

"Your emotional damage from..." She bit her lip. "That linoleum today. Don't you need closure?"

Chuckling, he looked at the sky. "Tip number one: never go for closure. You want to open all the dark, soft, wounded areas."

"God, your job sounds like fun. And I thought stringing vineyard lights for atmosphere was challenging."

"It can be fun," he said. "Sometimes in those wounds, you mine gold."

She regarded him through narrowed eyes, wondering where his gold was and how she could get it. "Then tell me why, Dusty Mathers, you were such a bad, bad boy and now you are a good, good man."

"I think that's a country song."

"Now *that* was a Tessa Wylie deflect," she volleyed

back. "Answer or I'll make you swim laps around the boat."

He laughed, but the smile disappeared after a moment. He turned a little, facing her, letting his fingertips graze her shoulder.

"Two words," he said gruffly. "Dumpster fire. That's the only way to describe my childhood."

"I heard a rumor," she said softly. "Dad drank and your mother..."

"What mother?" he scoffed. "My dad was a nasty SOB who once made my brother shovel dog poop with a soup spoon. In July."

"Wow."

"Yeah. And my mom? Wasn't even a ghost. Ghosts show up sometimes. She didn't."

Ghosts. She remembered the diary entry again. "It explains a lot of your behavior, Dusty."

"Not all of it," he said. "Crappy childhood is a good excuse, but as you love to point out, I *am* an idiot."

"Far from it."

"I did one good thing in my life," he said.

"Kelly?" she guessed.

His whole expression changed. "Yeah. She was the first, last, and only perfect thing that ever happened to me and I still can't figure out how or why."

Tessa turned toward him, the only sound the slosh of waves against the hull. "Tell me about her."

He thought for a long moment. "I just did—she was perfect. Grounded. Brilliant. Warm. When she found out she couldn't have kids, she just accepted it. When she found out she was going to die, she was more worried about everyone else than herself. She trusted God, her family, and, for some reason, me."

"How did you meet?"

"We met when I was…well, let's say I wasn't the guy you see now. I was twenty-three, angry, hungover most mornings, but I'd gotten a job volunteering at a group therapy place for court-mandated teenagers."

"Which are…"

"Kids who get told by a judge to get help for drugs, underage drinking, shoplifting, gangs. I'd been in a time or two in high school and got to be friends with the people that ran the clinic. I was trying to clean up my act, so they helped by giving me a job…ish." He sighed deeply, lost in his memories. "Kelly was in her first year working for a mental health non-profit and she came in to do an audit. We spent five minutes together and I knew then and there I couldn't live without her."

Everything in Tessa just melted. "Oh. That's… romantic."

"Or I was being an idiot again," he joked. "That woman taught me everything from how to fold fitted sheets, to paying taxes and making meals that weren't frozen. She was the first grown-up I ever met who wanted to keep me and, honestly, she helped me become a real… man." His voice cracked on that word.

Tessa's throat tightened. What would it be like to not think anyone wanted you? That was an emotion Tessa never had, and for that, she was grateful.

"But she got sick," he continued. "It was slow and ugly, an insidious blood disease that sounds like a toy but sure isn't."

"What was it?" she asked.

"It's called aplastic anemia, which is a rare condition where the blood marrow stops producing new cells. Hers was chronic, started kind of quietly with fatigue and bruising and infections. One day, it all blew up into a semi-permanent residence at the ICU with lots of trans-fusions and, ultimately, internal bleeding that couldn't be stopped."

"Oh." Her whole body ached just thinking about it, and she put a comforting hand on his arm. "God bless you for going through that."

"The last three years were sheer hell. I took care of her full-time." He swallowed. "But she died at home, which was nice, in the bed we used to share. I was holding her hand."

She closed her eyes, empathetic pain punching her.

"And now?" he added, his voice reed-thin. "Now I want easy. I want fun. I want to sleep in the middle of the bed and not wake up to check if the person next to me is breathing."

Tessa didn't respond right away. She watched the sun wink over the horizon, slow and golden and impossibly still. She let her mind replay every word he'd just said, imagined him feeding, loving, bathing, and hand-holding his sick wife.

She couldn't help realizing all that told her about this man.

"At the risk of not getting paid for my therapy services," she finally said, forcing herself to keep her voice light. "Can I ask you a question you might not like?"

"They're the best kind."

She sat up a little. "Why are you lying to yourself about what you want from a woman?"

He just looked at her, silent.

"I mean, you say you want fun and frivolous, and no commitment or caretaking, just a great time with someone who may or may not stick around, you don't really care."

He flinched. "I don't know if that's exactly what I said."

"It's exactly what I heard."

"Fair enough," he conceded. "And you don't think that's true?"

"Not one syllable."

He blinked. "What?"

She was being honest now, and couldn't stop. "I don't think you want just fun and easy. No one who's had a love like you've had wants to face the possibility of never having it again. No one who has loved with that much ferocity can exist without something like it in their life."

He stared at her, silent.

"I get that you don't think you will want it again. I get that you want to figure out how—or if—you can be alone without losing yourself. You want to believe you can survive without it. I get that."

He took a shaky breath. "And?"

"And you *are* surviving," she added. "But you're lonely as hell."

"Wow." He exhaled. "Hey, if the event planning thing doesn't work out for you, you might have a future as a therapist."

"I just like you, Dusty," she whispered, the truth bombs obviously still detonating. "And I can see through you and into you. Also, if you think any of that made me like you less? You'd be dead wrong. It was like a love potion and I'm...feeling drunk. And, apparently, quite honest."

For a long moment, he just looked at her, the storm of emotions in his eyes subsiding, leaving a hint of a smile.

"So, you like me, huh?" He inched closer, his smile widening.

She put a hand on his chest, holding him back with a sure touch, not quite ready to give up the fight to the inevitable kiss.

"Why do you say you want a good-time girl, Dusty? Why not go find another real thing? Something that lasts?"

His mouth twisted into something sad and raw as he moved away and let his head drop back. "Now we're getting to the wound."

"Open it," she urged.

He closed his eyes. "Because I don't deserve that *twice*. I barely deserved it the first time. Kelly was the kind of woman you only get once in a lifetime."

"That's not true."

"You don't know that," he shot back.

"I know *you*." Her voice cracked a little, but she didn't care. This was serious and important and needed to be said. "You're kind and funny and—God help me—*brilliant* at figuring people out. You don't have to earn love by being perfect, Dusty. You just have to let someone in. I know because I never have."

"Would you?" he asked. "I mean...if the right guy happened to be on the bow with you in the sunset?"

Tessa froze, heart hammering. "I don't know," she whispered. "I don't think I've ever offered that to anyone before."

He reached for her hand and eased her closer, his fingers warm, his grip gentle. Neither of them moved for a long time.

Then, slowly, like gravity was pulling them together, he leaned forward and kissed her.

It wasn't wild. It wasn't rushed. It was careful and warm and deep, like they both knew this was a line they couldn't uncross.

And when he finally pulled away, she sat back hard against the bow bed, breath gone, heart racing.

"Wow," she murmured.

He didn't answer. But he looked at her like he was afraid to say anything that might break the spell.

She wanted to say something. Wanted to ask him to try, to risk, to want more.

But she didn't. She could only be so honest, so she drifted back into character with an easy laugh and a wink. "I think I like therapy."

He grinned and they just rested there without saying

a word until the sun had disappeared over the horizon. Eventually, they pulled up the anchor and rode back to the marina. The whole time, her heart felt like a tangle of nerves and hope.

Because she didn't want to be his *no-strings girl*.

And she wasn't sure he'd ever let anyone have his heart again.

Chapter Seventeen
Jonah

Sweat. Water. Panic.

Jonah thrashed left to right, covered in perspiration—or was it seawater?—knowing one thing. Only one thing. The baby was...*gone*. He was gone! Where did he go?

One moment, Jonah was walking along the beach with Atlas—just like they had that morning, those tiny toes squirming against his chest, sun on his shoulders. Then the sky had gone black. The waves rose like giant fists, swallowing the shore, pummeling them to the sand.

He lost the baby in the surf. But someone kept calling him.

"Jonah! Jonah!"

Who was that? Wait. He knew that voice. He loved that voice. It was his mother, screaming his name as he jerked from side to side, searching and *searching*, but all he could hear was his mother calling.

Her voice from the sidelines of a football game. Her voice from the front door when he was on his bike. Her voice from...heaven.

She was calling him from a place where he'd never been and would never go.

"Jonah!"

Where was she? And where was the baby? He tried to shout, but every time he opened his mouth, nothing would come out, and saltwater slipped between his lips.

Finally, he saw a woman in the surf. But that wasn't Melissa Lawson. That woman had curly blond hair tumbling over her shoulders. She wore a Baby Bjorn around her neck. It was empty.

"Where is Atlas?" she screamed.

Carly.

"You lost him, too?" Her voice roared like the waves. "You lose everybody, Jonah! You are cursed!"

Her face turned dark, covered in blood and tears and—

He shot up from sweat-soaked sheets with a soft cry. He was trembling, a black, hot pit of fire in his stomach, tears pouring down his cheeks and into his open mouth.

He gasped for air, the sheets tangled around his legs and his skin clammy with sweat. The monitor light glowed, green and silent.

Blinking into the near darkness, he peered at the bassinet where his baby son slept peaceful and safe, his little chest rising and falling with life. No waves, no voices, just...baby's breath.

Letting out a groan of raw relief, Jonah flung the covers off and swung his feet to the floor. It was second nature now, this middle-of-the-night check-in. But tonight, it wasn't just duty. It was panic.

He stood on shaky legs, trying to wipe away the terror

that had gripped him. The words that Carly had shouted at him.

You lose everybody, Jonah! You're cursed!

Of course he was. He was living under a dark shadow of disaster and so was anyone who had the misfortune of loving him. Mom. Carly. Who was next?

Now adjusted to the darkness, he gazed at Atlas, his heart breaking. Exhaling shakily, he reached down, gently brushing the baby's round, fuzzy head. Not him. Please, God, not him.

"Sorry, bud," he whispered. "Just a bad dream."

And of course he was having nightmares, now that he knew Sally and Gary Danes would be knocking at the door in exactly two days, threatening to take his child away. They'd called earlier that evening and said they'd be here on Saturday morning, the day after tomorrow.

Except tomorrow was already today.

So, no, the dream wasn't random. It was a stark reminder of...everything.

Was poor Atlas doomed at birth? Did this curse cross generations? That thought seemed awfully...*biblical.*

The word landed in his head as if it were an actual direction. Like a GPS voice saying, "Turn here. Go there."

To...the Bible?

He switched on the light next to his bed, the one Aunt Vivien said was specially designed not to wake a baby.

His heart thumped like a warning bell in his chest, the words echoing. *You lose everybody! You're cursed!*

His gaze drifted toward the dresser, to the Bible his dad had left for him right after he'd arrived with Atlas. It was untouched, still at the same random angle in the same spot Dad put it. Jonah hadn't so much as cracked it. But it was there, full of...Mom.

Could he find that passage again? The one Dad read that had Mom's handwriting? "Taste and see," it said. With his initials.

Had she written anything else that could help him?

He pushed up and grabbed the book, opening the cover, which announced that this was A Journal Bible. Underneath that, someone had written a short note.

For my friend, Melissa Lawson—may you find Him on every page.

With Christ's Unending Love,

Deborah Sutherland.

It was dated...four months before the day she died.

He vaguely recalled a producer at her TV station named Deborah who'd spoken at his mother's funeral, but he didn't remember a word she'd said. She must have been important to give Mom her first and only Bible.

He flipped the parchment-thin pages, opening to the one marked with a long blue ribbon, hoping it was the passage Dad had read.

But it was just a bunch of gibberish evidently written by someone named Isaiah. The only ink on the page was the word "Jesus" with a question mark, but that was definitely his mother's feminine, tidy handwriting.

He stared at how she'd written the word "Jesus" as though she'd taken her time with each letter. He recognized her distinctive J with a curve at the top, a long-buried memory punching into his consciousness.

He could hear her voice...feel the touch of her hand over his.

"Just imagine an umbrella, Jonah. See? That's your J. The first letter of your name. J is for Jonah."

A tear fell and landed on the page. The ache for her rose up and strangled him, as it still did from time to time, even fifteen years after losing her.

He turned a few pages, feeling a different pang. Suddenly consumed with the need to find more of her writing and a message that had to be for him, he started flipping madly through the pages.

He found something titled "The Book of Jonah" that gave him hope, but it was just that old Bible story about some dude swallowed by a whale.

She hadn't even written a word in that book, which he thought was weird. Where did she write?

The paper made a rustling sigh as he turned, finding his way to a fog of words titled "Ezekiel." Wrath. Wheels. Warnings. Something about dry bones. Wait a second. Is *that* where Mario Kart got the character name?

Toward the last third of the whole book, there was much more of his mother's writing in the books that even a heathen like Jonah recognized as the gospels.

John had held Mom's attention, with scribbling up and down both sides of almost every page. Words under-lined like *grace* and *love* and *abide in Him* with three exclamation points. Full paragraphs highlighted in yellow, pink, and green. Notes and questions on both sides, filling in the lines he imagined made this a "jour-nal" Bible.

But no message to poor, cursed Jonah.

"Come on," he muttered as he flipped from section to section. "There has to be something in here for me."

He turned back to Psalms, which looked promising—lots of cries for help and ill will on enemies. Plenty of underlined verses, not many notes.

Then he landed in Proverbs and noticed the frequent mention of the word "son"—and nearly every time, she'd circled it and written his initials again. *JFL.*

With a kick of hope, he flicked through the pages, and stopped at one that was covered in her writing. Proverbs 17 was starred, underlined and highlighted.

He skimmed the words about strife, prudent servants, and deceitful lips.

Why did she—

And then he saw it. Highlighted in neon green with the word GRANDCHILDREN written in capital letters. He squinted at the scripture, reading out loud.

"'Children's children are a crown to the aged, and parents are the pride of their children.'"

His throat tightened as he lifted the book to read the tiny script she'd written.

"Children's children are my grands!!" She'd actually drawn a little crown, which was so Mom, it almost hurt.

His gaze dropped to the note beneath it, again reading the words out loud.

"'Dear Lord, let me be a grandmother someday. Let me hold Jonah's baby and hear that child's voice. Let me kiss Meredith's little girl (has to be!) and rock her to sleep. Let my children know they are not the end of a broken line, but the part of one that is highly favored. Bless these babies that aren't yet conceived, knit them with love, and help them know You above all. That is this Someday Grandma's prayer.'"

He couldn't breathe.

Her words hit with the weight of a thousand tears and fifteen years of grief.

Bending over the book, he gave in to a full-body sob and let the tears pour over his face and onto the page. His shoulders heaved, his chest let out a groan, yet all he could feel was...peace.

Absolute, indescribable peace.

He didn't look up until Atlas kicked his little night sac, and let out a weak pre-cry, the one that sounded like a mouse squeak.

Jonah was next to him in an instant, lifting his tiny body to hold him against his chest.

"Atlas," he whispered. "Your grandma prayed for you before you were born. Well over a decade before. Did you know that?"

He whimpered, eyes glued shut.

"Well, it's true," he said, the tears flowing. "She blessed you before she knew your name. Before Carly, before anything, before she died. She blessed you and me and the whole next generation."

He stroked the warm, bald head and kissed him again.

"She knew," he said. "She knew I could be a father.

And that my child and your child and all the little Lawsons that will come in the future would be a blessing. Not a curse! No word of a curse!"

Atlas made that "eh eh eh" sound that was a sure sign he was waking.

"Good. I want you to wake up," Jonah said. "I want to tell you all about your most amazing Grandma Melissa. She was beautiful. Funny, smart. Never dropped the ball in life, you know? And still she found time to pray for you and me."

Tears fell again, and Jonah wiped his face with the back of his hand, rocking the probably very confused and hungry baby. His baby. Her grandchild.

"A blessing," he said, suddenly understanding the meaning of the word in a way he never had. "That's what you are, Atlas Lawson. I thought I was broken, you know? But I'm not and you're not. We're part of a family that is absolutely amazing and blessed."

"You certainly are."

Jonah jerked his head up to see his father standing in the doorway, his face streaked with tears. He wore nothing but sleep pants, holding the small monitor receiver over his bare chest. He raised the device and gave a sleepy smile.

"It was my night to be backup, remember?" he said in a thick voice. "So...I had the monitor."

"And heard everything."

Eli stepped into the room and reached out both arms, enveloping Jonah and Atlas in a hug.

"Everything," he confirmed. "And, no surprise, she

said it better than I ever could. The woman had a way with words, didn't she?"

Jonah managed a soft laugh. "She sure gave me the right ones tonight."

Eli patted his shoulder and inched back to look Jonah in the eye. "She's right, you know. We—you and Atlas and all of us—are blessed. I'm not afraid of Carly's parents or imagined curses or whatever the future holds. I'm completely confident we're on the right side of this story and it's going to be a good one."

Jonah let out a sound that was half sigh, half moan, with no desire to argue. In his arms, Atlas nestled closer and opened his mouth.

"He agrees," Jonah said. "And he's about to make sure everyone knows."

Eli chuckled. "Let's go get him his three o'clock bottle."

"You take him up," Jonah said, handing the baby over. "I just need a minute."

"You got it." Dad took Atlas, cooing soft words to him as they walked out and up the stairs.

Jonah took a few seconds to gather himself, trying to fully understand what just happened. Something, every-thing, had changed. The world shifted. His heart felt... different. Renewed and reborn and different.

With an exhale, he scooped up the Bible, not really sure why. Maybe because he wanted to read Mom's prayer again, this time with Dad. Maybe he just wanted to talk about this book that obviously meant so much to both his parents.

Holding it against his chest, he took the steps two at a time, reaching the main floor just as a shadow moved on the stairs.

"Jonah?"

He turned at his sister's voice, seeing her padding down barefoot. "Everything okay?"

"It's so okay, I don't even know what to say." As she reached the bottom step, he held out both arms, the Bible in one hand. "C'mere, Mer Bear."

"Seriously?" She gave a sleepy laugh at the nickname he was sure he hadn't used since before their mother died. "What's going on?" she asked groggily. "Where's the baby? Is that a Bible? Are you crying?"

"Too many questions. Come on. Dad's in the kitchen with Atlas. Let's have a family hang."

She gave him a face like he'd lost his mind—and he kind of had, in a good way.

"Dad?" she whispered as they joined their father, who held Atlas in one arm and warmed a bottle with the other.

"Meredith? Why are you up?"

"I understand there's a family *hang*." She threw a look at one man, then the other, her expression darkening. "Why are you two crying?"

Dad didn't say anything as he tested the temperature, giving Jonah a look that said the moment was his to share or not.

"Look at this, Meredith," Jonah said, flipping open the Bible. "Just read this."

She scowled. "I can't see a thing."

"I installed undercounter lighting just for moments like this," Dad said, tapping a switch and giving the room a golden glow. "Well, maybe not this," he added, whispering to the baby in his arms. "But life does have a way of surprising you, doesn't it, young Atlas?"

Meredith and Jonah shared a look and a smile, then he went back to the Bible, flipping madly. "Let me see... Joshua, Kings, Job—where do I go, Dad?"

"Two more books. Psalms, then Proverbs. It was Number 17. The one about grandchildren."

"Grand... What is going on?" Meredith asked, her voice sounding a little tense.

"Just look." Jonah frantically searched, then found the beautiful writing next to a few words he'd never, ever forget.

Children's children are a crown to the aged, and parents are the pride of their children.

He was a parent now!

"Look what Mom wrote." He turned the book and nudged her closer. "And, Mer, you better have a girl."

"What?" Her head shot up with a gasp and even in the dim glow, he could see her face go pale.

"Just read Mom's prayer," he said. "Read it and weep," he added. "I sure as heck did."

Silent, she leaned over and squinted at the words he was already thinking about having made into a work of art. Could he find someone to do calligraphy of her prayer and hang it in—

"Oh." Meredith straightened and put her hand on her chest.

"I know, right?" Jonah asked on a laugh. "Blessing."

"Are you all right, honey?" Dad came around the island, the bottle already nestled into Atlas's tiny mouth, held in place by his father's capable hand.

"Yes, I'm..."

"Overwhelmed," Jonah supplied. "I was, too. But her words, her prayer, it changed everything for me. And she wants you to have a girl." He snorted a laugh. "You better get out of the office and on the dating apps or something, 'cause—"

She silenced him with a raised hand, her face as white as the quartz countertop she gripped as though she needed stability.

"Mer?"

"Honey?" Dad inched closer. "What's wrong?"

She swallowed visibly and took a step back, her lower lip quivering like it did when she was a little girl and about to give in to a rare bout of crying. Very rare— Meredith was made of tough stuff.

But right now, she looked like she was a house of cards, about to collapse.

She took a slow, deep breath and pressed both hands on her chest. "I'm..." She wet her lips and looked like she might sway.

Instinctively, Jonah reached for her arm. "What's going on with you?"

She sighed and closed her eyes. "I have to tell you... something."

Chapter Eighteen
Meredith

This middle of the night rendezvous probably wasn't the ideal moment to break her news—and Dad's heart. But Meredith had no choice.

She finally had her father and brother as a captive and private audience. Moreover, their mood was clearly softened by the whisper they believed they heard from Mom.

And maybe her mother had reached down from heaven and guided Jonah to that scripture because the words encouraged Meredith in a way she'd never expected. If Mom, then a newbie Christian who hadn't even gone public with her faith, prayed for the seedling that Meredith carried in her belly, then it all felt...right.

She hoped.

It wasn't going to feel right to Dad, not when he found out how this baby had happened.

"What is it, honey?" her father asked tenderly, adding that look of kindness that was so authentic, it often twisted Meredith's heart. No one was as good as this man. And what Meredith had done—even without knowing Trevor's situation—was so *not* good.

He'd take it personally, of course. He'd think he'd

failed as a father, when she was the one who'd failed as a daughter.

Time ticked and the clock over the stove flipped to 4:00 A.M., and she knew she had to speak. She slid onto a barstool, vaguely aware that she laid her hand on the open Bible as if it might support her.

"You're shaking," Jonah said, his gaze following the gesture. He put his hand over hers and searched her face. "Meredith. What's wrong?"

Across from them on the other side of the island, Eli rocked side to side with Atlas tucked into one arm, a bottle in the other.

"Nothing," she lied, then gave a soft laugh. "Or everything. Depends on your perspective."

Still regarding her closely, Dad's finger absently stroked Atlas's cheek, moving in a rhythm that matched the way the baby suckled. For a moment, she was mesmerized, staring at the simple gesture, feeling her heart ripped into a million pieces.

She watched his finger, the tiny movement demonstrating so much love, it squeezed the breath out of her lungs.

"You're scaring me," Dad said softly, the words pulling her gaze from his finger to his face. "Whatever it is, you can tell us."

"Seriously," Jonah added, looking hard at her, his own expression strangely at peace for the first time since she'd arrived. Maybe since Mom died. Goodness, what had just happened to him?

She looked from one to the other. Her father. Her

brother. The two men who knew her best. Who loved her best.

And she hated what she was about to do to their image of her.

"I met someone." Her voice cracked. "A guy."

Jonah's brows lifted. "That's what this is about? A dude?"

Eli gave a soft, relieved laugh. "It was bound to happen, although I can't imagine you left the office long enough to go on a date. Who is he?" He smiled, his sky-blue eyes glinting with hope she was about to destroy.

"Yeah, well, who he is isn't important or the point of the story."

Her words held enough weight and warning that Dad's smile immediately disappeared.

"What is the point of the story?" he asked, the first tension evident in his voice.

Oh, no. This was going to hurt...everyone.

"The point of the story is..." She dropped her gaze to the Bible, staring at her mother's writing, though it was too small and far away to read. "Grandchildren."

No one spoke. In fact, no one breathed. The only sound was tiny Atlas smacking his lips around a baby bottle.

She finally looked up and right into her father's already hurt eyes. "It appears there's going to be another one."

She heard Jonah whisper, "What?" but didn't look away from Dad.

His face flashed a thousand different emotions in a

nanosecond, but mostly shock. And disbelief. And, oh, yeah. Disappointment.

Then it was gone and he just stared, his jaw loose, his brows drawn in confusion.

"I'm pregnant," she said softly. "And I'm very much alone in the situation."

"What?" Jonah repeated his question, louder this time. "Who's the father? Where is he? How can you be alone?"

She swallowed, waiting for Dad to say something, but he seemed frozen. His mouth almost moved, but nothing came out. Maybe he was praying. Maybe he was trying not to scream and wake the whole house. Maybe he was putting together the words to disown her.

"Meredith." It was all he could manage, the color draining from his face as he processed this news.

She sighed. "The father's name is Trevor Whitlock, and I think I mentioned him to you before you came down here with Aunt Vivien in March. But it's over. I'm alone now."

Her father took a deep breath, then lifted Atlas an inch higher. "Jonah, can you take him, please?"

"Of course." He shot around the island to ease the baby out of Dad's hands without waking him. Seconds ticked by even though they did the hand-off in record time. And with each passing heartbeat, Meredith watched her father's face and tried to brace for the reaction.

His chest heaved with a battle for air. His eyes narrowed. His jaw locked.

Here it comes. The great big, "How could you?" or, "What were you thinking?" or, "You've ruined your life!"

But he didn't do any of that.

Instead, he turned away, lifting his arms slightly, palms up, eyes closed. "Thank you, Lord, for this incredible gift." He mouthed the words, but she heard them. "Please help us as a family. Please give me your words. We need you."

Wait. *What?* What did he—did he just *pray?*

Then he opened his eyes and looked right at Meredith, his arms still out as he rounded the island.

"One thing you are not, Meredith Lawson, is alone."

She hesitated. "You aren't mad?"

"Next-level furious," he said gruffly. "Could definitely murder someone. But not you. You're my daughter. Come here."

She practically fell into his arms, but the hug felt... undeserved. She inched back, knowing there was even more bad news.

"Dad, it's worse than you think. It was a brief and meaningless liaison." She flinched as she said the word.

"I'm getting that impression," he said, stroking her hair and bringing her back to hug. "And I'm trying to tell you that I'm not upset. Well, I am, but I'm also processing the fact that you're having a baby. A baby!"

Not upset? He would be.

She swallowed and pushed back. "There's more. I didn't know this. He didn't tell me, but he's married, Dad."

He winced and let out a grunt and a moan like the words punched him in the throat.

"I swear I didn't know. I would never have—"

Pain contorted his features as he grimaced and took the blow. "What a horrible man," he murmured, barely audible over Jonah's grumbling and name-calling.

"He doesn't want anything to do with the baby," she said.

"Of course not," Jonah snapped. "Because he's sub-human."

"Jonah." Dad held up a hand, quieting him and getting control. "Are you sure about all of this?"

He sounded like he wanted it to be a bad dream that he'd wake from. And, oh, how she longed for it to be just that.

"I'm positive," she said. "I talked to him, and he freaked. That's when he told me he was married, which I swear he never, ever mentioned or implied."

Jonah swore under his breath again, holding Atlas tightly. He looked like he might really want to punch a wall.

"And he's probably already gone from Atlanta, on to his next Beans & Buns franchise," Meredith said.

Dad made a face. "The coffee guy from downstairs?"

She nodded. "I mean, I could find him if I wanted to, but to be honest? I don't ever want to see him again. If I..." She took a shuddering breath. "I'm going to do this alone."

"Meredith." Dad breathed her name, the three syllables laden with pity and fury and love.

It was the love that nearly broke her. "Dad, I'm sorry. It was a huge mistake. I don't know what I was doing. I just...I didn't care because I was lonely and dumb and wrapped up in work and I know that's not an excuse, but I—"

He put his hand on her lips, quieting her verbal spew, then drying her tears with the same fingers that just stroked baby Atlas. Only now they were trembling. The rest of him, however, was solid as a rock.

"It's okay," he said in that tender, deep voice. "It's fine. You made a bad decision and—"

"I ruined my life! It was so, so stupid! I don't know how I got pregnant—"

"Oh, I do," Jonah chimed in, smirking.

"I'm sure you're thrilled," she shot back.

"Not to be the family screwup for a change?" His brows rose. "I don't hate it, but I also don't hate *you*, little sister. I'm here for you. Whatever you need." He leaned in, confidently holding his baby. "I mean that, Meredith. I will do everything from teach you how to change diapers to get the guy *unalived*, as they say—"

"Stop." Dad held up a hand. "I mean it. Stop saying things like that. Of course you'll support her. We all will. Meredith, I am here for you. We all are. You do whatever you need to do, just give me a healthy grandchild." He glanced toward the Bible. "I believe your mother is insisting on a girl."

"Oh, Dad." She nearly buckled. "I know you're disappointed. I know you are."

He looked like he wanted to disagree, but Eli Lawson

didn't lie. He was disappointed, but love always won with him. He merely nodded, then shook his head, then hugged her again.

"I'm just...blown away."

"I know and I'm sorry."

He gathered himself again and narrowed his eyes. "Are you one hundred percent certain this man—this Trevor—doesn't want anything to do with the baby? That he couldn't show up and try to take it?"

"Geez, it's a veritable epidemic around here," Jonah muttered.

"He couldn't have been clearer. The, uh, relationship ended after a few dates. I didn't..." She shook her head. "Anyway, when I told him, he basically said, 'Go away, it's not my problem.' I don't want money, Dad. Or anything. I can do this myself."

"You can with family," her father said. "And in this case, I don't think it would be a bad idea to get something in writing so he can't come back to haunt you."

"Yeah, we're not hosting the scumbag for a family weekend," Jonah said.

"How far along are you?" Dad asked, searching her face as if he hadn't really looked at her closely enough.

"I think I'm technically seven weeks, and no, I haven't done anything but frantically take four, okay, five tests and make a doctor's appointment. I came here because I didn't know what else to do. I wanted to tell you in person, and I wasn't sure if I should keep the baby—"

"What?" For the first time, her father looked truly stricken.

"Adoption," she said quickly. "I know I have choices and, you know, Lacey told me how great Roman's life has been, so I—"

"You can do whatever you want," Dad said. "But I, for one, would love another baby in this family."

"Mom, too." Jonah tapped the Bible. "I mean, she all but flew in here on a cloud to help you out tonight."

Meredith gave a mirthless laugh, her shoulders dropping as weight fell off them. "I know, right? Score one for Melissa Lawson."

"Score *two* for Melissa Lawson," Dad said, looking from one to the other. "The two greatest kids a man could have."

"Oh." Meredith bit her lip and looked at Jonah, whose eyes glistened with tears.

"I wouldn't go that far, old man," Jonah said on a tight laugh. "But if we're decent, don't give away all the credit. I know a little bit about being a father now, and, whoa. You've done a good job in the face of tough circumstances."

Meredith let out a breath she might have been holding for this whole conversation, leaning into her father, knowing every word Jonah said was true.

"Dad. I'm so sorry," she moaned out the apology. "I am ashamed and angry at myself and so broken to think I've disappointed you. I love you so much and I respect you and I know you have such strong faith—in me and in God. I've let you down."

He cupped his hands on her cheeks, looking into her eyes. "You, my dear daughter, are forgiven. All we have to do now is be a family. A growing one."

Tears burned again as her knees nearly buckled from the love she absolutely did not deserve, but he gave so freely.

"I love you, Meredith," he said, his voice breaking. "Nothing—*nothing*—you could do would change that."

"I don't think I'm ready to be forgiven," she said gruffly.

"You already are," he said. "That's how grace works. You don't have to earn it. You just have to receive it."

She let out a whimper. "I hope I can be half the parent you are, Dad."

"Same," Jonah chimed in.

Her father smiled and leaned back, waving Jonah and the sleeping baby closer. "Come here, everybody. Come to me."

As Jonah came around the island, Meredith pointed at the baby. "Did you properly burp him?" she asked.

"Maybe not as *properly* as you would," he joked. "But does he look gassy? Kid's in dreamland." Holding Atlas confidently with one arm, he put the other around Meredith. Dad wrapped both of them in a hug, forming a circle.

A beautiful, forgiving, loving Lawson circle.

They stood that way for a long, quiet moment, the room soundless until Dad let out a sigh and Meredith knew exactly what was coming next. And she never needed it more.

"Heavenly Father," he whispered. "We are humbled by your blessings. We thank you for this family, and for the love we have. We thank you for Melissa, and we know she's with you this very moment, basking in your glory. Tell her she showed up tonight and helped make us whole again. We remember her, every day, as a beautiful mother who raised exceptional children, and still has her hand on us, even though she isn't here."

Jonah sniffed and Meredith felt a tear meander down her cheek.

"Father," he continued. "Please bless baby Atlas and the precious new life you have just planted in Meredith's womb. Grow them into healthy, strong, kind, and loving children who honor you with their lives. Protect Meredith as she starts this journey into motherhood and help us all as we embrace this new life and change. We love you, Father, and ask all of this in the name of your son, Jesus."

For a moment, no one spoke, but they stood in perfect silence, holding the beauty of Dad's prayer in their hearts.

Then Atlas belched like a truck driver and all they could do was laugh.

"I told you to burp him properly!" Meredith said, poking Jonah's arm.

"I don't think it gets any more proper than that," Jonah said on a laugh, shifting the baby in his arms. "Also, that's usually a precursor to a loaded diaper, so I'm going to take him downstairs, change him, and my prayer?

When he cries in three hours, send in the cavalry to help me."

"Done and done." Meredith gave him another hug and kissed Atlas's head, sighing as they disappeared down the stairs, Jonah singing a mangled version of *You Are My Sunshine.*

Turning to Dad, she reached out her hand. "I don't know what to say. You're amazing."

He just smiled. "Don't beat yourself up, honey. You're not the first smart person to make a dumb mistake. When's that doctor's appointment?"

"It's two weeks from now, here in Destin." She lifted her brows. "Would you come with me?"

"I'd love to go with you," he said.

"Oh, Dad." She threw her arms around him, still not able to comprehend that all her stress was for nothing with him. "Can I ask one more favor?"

"Anything," he said with a confidence that only he possessed.

"Can we keep this a secret between us for now? I don't want Aunt Vivien or Grandma Maggie to know yet."

"They won't judge you, Meredith."

She gave him a "get real" look and he laughed.

"Okay, my mother will judge. But she'll get over it. Everyone will be excited."

She nodded. "But please, at least let me get a due date and closer to the three-month point. Don't tell Kate," she added, knowing she had to be specific. "Please?"

Eli hesitated, then nodded. "Okay."

They both stood in the stillness for a few seconds, then her father turned off the lights. They walked upstairs together, and Meredith stood in the hallway outside her room, hand on the door.

"Goodnight, Dad," she said, her voice quiet but full. "I love you."

"I love you, too, Mer. Sleep well."

"I will...now. Thank you." She stepped into her room, pulled the covers back, and slid into bed. And for the first time in weeks, she didn't feel alone.

And since her own mother had prayed for this baby, Meredith had a pretty good feeling she'd be having a girl. Maybe she'd name her Melissa. And they'd call her Missy. Mom always said she loved that nickname.

"Oh, Mommy. Mommy, Mommy, *Mommy*," she whispered, fresh tears forming as she smashed her face into the pillow. "I miss you so much."

Even though it hurt, she went to sleep with hope in her heart.

August 22, 1992

I just turned off my flashlight because it's almost one in the morning and Mom would have a fit if she caught me up this late, but I had to get this down while it's still fresh. Tessa just came in, barefoot and sand-dusted, and nearly stepped on Crista, who is asleep in her classic starfish formation between our beds.

I was waiting up—not intentionally, but sort of listening for the back door to creak.

Tessa didn't notice I was awake until I whispered, "What happened?"

She didn't even pretend not to know what I meant. Just sat down on the edge of her bed like all the air had gone out of her. Her hair smelled like bonfire and ocean. Her lip gloss was gone.

Tonight we all went down for a last-of-summer beach bonfire. Kate made s'mores like she was being graded on them. Peter played guitar badly (but at least not the Eagles this time), and I spent most of the night trying to keep the wind from blowing marshmallow ash into my eye. Around 9:30, three guys showed up — brothers in a family staying at the Seabreeze condos for the week.

One of them—a 16-year-old with sun-bleached hair and eyelashes that should be illegal—immediately locked onto Tessa.

His name was Kyle. Of course it was.

But we renamed him "Luke" (as in Perry, as in 90210, as in CUTE with a capital Q, as in exactly what Tessa said).

Kate rolled her eyes so hard at that I thought she might pull a muscle. I don't blame her. Luke/Kyle <u>was</u> cute.

Naturally, he zeroed in on Tessa. Well, she had broken out a Billabong crop top like she was a surfer queen and wore that little gold anklet which is like catnip to boys. She laughed at his dumb jokes (which were beyond dumb—what Kate calls DD's—double digit IQ).

He kept leaning closer like Tessa was some exotic foreign creature he was desperate to impress. He asked all about Ithaca like he was seriously considering transferring high schools just for the chance to bump into her at a Wegmans.

Eventually, the two of them wandered down toward the water —not out of sight or anything, just sitting on the damp sand with their knees up and their heads tipped back like they were watching stars or planning a wedding. The rest of us started packing up around 10:30. Kate said she wasn't going to wait around to see if Luke Perry had a curfew. It must have been midnight, 'cause Tessa came in a few minutes later.

She tried to be quiet, even though I expected

her to sigh and swoon and do that thing where she reenacts every moment like she's starring in a movie.

She didn't.

She sat down and told me—so quietly I almost missed it—that she kissed him.

Not her first kiss. (Which, okay, <u>shocking</u>, but also not shocking.) But then she said...he wanted more.

I didn't ask what "more" meant. I'm fifteen. I know what it means.

She shook her head and told me she said no and stopped kissing him.

She said he was cool about it — joked that he'd come warm her up when he visited Ithaca, which made both of us say "eww" at the same time.

But then she just looked so sad and said, "Is that all boys will ever want?"

How would I know? The only boy who ever sort of flirted with me did it by launching a grape into my soda.

Then she said something I'll never forget: "I want someone to actually like me. Like, for real."

And that's when I realized Tessa—who is sparkly and makes the world spin faster—might be lonelier than any of us. She's the girl everyone looks at, but maybe no one really sees.

She laid down a minute ago. Turned toward

the wall. I heard her sniff—just once—like she was trying to bury it in the pillow. I pretended to be asleep. But I felt something weird happen in my chest.

Because I always thought girls like Tessa didn't cry. Guess they do.

Love,

Viv

Chapter Nineteen
Tessa

The house was too quiet when Tessa padded barefoot into the kitchen late Friday morning, hair still damp from her shower after a long run on the beach.

Where was everyone? Tessa reached for a banana, then put it back. She wasn't hungry. She was restless. And ready to go.

She glanced at the time. Just past noon. Lorna had texted a message that morning that she had a very promising house to show her after lunch.

Just *her*. No word about Dusty. She hadn't heard from him since a late-night call a few nights ago, when he'd said something vague about having "a lot on his plate."

With a grunt, Tessa faced the fact that she didn't want to go alone. House-hunting was a two-opinion job.

Grabbing her phone, she texted Kate. No doubt her sister was somewhere with Eli. But she'd try to lure her anyway.

Tessa: *Got time for a secret errand? Meet me in the driveway in ten.*

A minute later, her phone chirped.

Kate: *I'm downstairs putting Atlas to sleep. Be up in five. Do I need bail money or just good shoes?*

Tessa smiled, happy for the company, even if it meant coming clean with the secret she'd kept for several weeks.

True to her word, Kate came up and, in a few minutes, the two of them were climbing into Tessa's sedan with plenty of time to make the house appointment. Next to her, Kate fished out her prescription sunglasses.

"I love that you don't even ask where we're going," Tessa joked as she hit the ignition.

"Please. I wanted the distraction. I was feeling sorry for myself."

"Why? Where's Eli?" Tessa asked.

Kate buckled her seatbelt. "He stuck in the office with Meredith. Said something about how busy they are. He was terribly vague and had already bugged me once this morning."

"He bugged you? Eli?" Tessa frowned. "I didn't know he was capable of bugging anyone but Vivien when we were thirteen years old."

"Oh, you know. He got...Bible-y."

"Bible-y?" Tessa laughed. "What does that mean? He parted the Red Sea? A live re-enactment of the Prodigal Son?"

She sighed, clearly not appreciating Tessa's humor. "He just was distracted. When I came into the kitchen this morning, his Bible—or his late wife's, I think—was open on the counter. He must have been reading it in the middle of the night."

"Maybe while he fed Atlas," Tessa suggested. "Wasn't he on monitor backup last night?"

"I guess. I don't know." Kate shifted in her seat and looked out the window, quiet for a beat.

"What's wrong?" Tessa pressed. "You still haven't asked me where we're going."

"Okay. Where are we going?"

"Tell me what's wrong first."

Kate sighed. "I just...I don't know. I mean, I know I came down here this summer to see where things were—or could go—with Eli and I'm having so much fun with him. I love the guy, not even going to lie."

"And..."

"And I can't compete with God."

"Is he asking you to?"

Kate didn't answer, but she sighed for the tenth time in as many minutes. "It's a gulf between us," she finally said. "Sometimes I feel like it's created such a distance. Like, I wasn't invited into that part of his life."

"I'm sure he'd love to invite you into that part of his life," Tessa replied. "In fact, I know he would."

"Maybe, but I don't...want to."

"Ah," Tessa said, imagining she sounded like therapist Dusty as she navigated traffic. "Now we're getting somewhere."

"Where?"

"To church?" Tessa teased.

But Kate didn't laugh. "It's so important to him. It's not just a personality trait. It's not just, oh, Eli is into God and prays for everything. No, it's like *who he is.* I can't be part of that. I don't want to, honestly."

Tessa let that settle, and couldn't help but ask what seemed to her to be the obvious—and dumb—question. "Would you really give up a man because he's...too good?"

Kate smiled. "Tess, I don't believe in things I can't see. Except..." She let out a little moan. "I suppose there are things that can't be seen, and we do 'believe' in them."

"Like love?" Tessa suggested.

"That's exactly what Meredith said." Kate groaned and dropped her head back, clearly in anguish over this. "Please tell me where we're going and don't make me talk about this anymore."

Tessa threw her a look, and decided she looked miserable and should have her request honored. Kate hated talking about feelings—it just wasn't logical enough for her scientist sister.

"We're going to see a house," she said.

Kate blinked. "A house? For...?"

"Me."

Kate's eyebrows rose. "Wait. You're house-hunting?"

Tessa gave a sheepish grin. "Yep."

"I didn't know you were even thinking of moving out."

"I didn't think I'd still be here three months after being discovered squatting in the back bedroom."

Kate winced. "I hate that you did that."

"Well, it's over and forgotten—except by me. I'm ready to not be The Thing That Wouldn't Leave."

"What does that make me?" Kate asked.

"The Guest That Eli Invited," Tessa shot back. "You're practically family except for, you know, the religion thing."

Kate rolled her eyes. "You *are* family. You and Lacey are joined at the hip and running a business."

"She's on her Jacksonville jaunt with her new man, and we can work remotely, or she can come to my house, where I'll set up an office," Tessa said. "I don't have to live at the Summer House to work with Lacey. It's not my house. It's theirs. And it gets crowded. I heard that Crista might be coming down in July—the place is jammed regardless of the oodles of bedrooms."

"Huh. So, this is a surprise," Kate said slowly as she processed the news. "How long have you been looking?"

As she drove into a sweet residential area, Tessa told her the whole story, starting with Dusty's house being the first. She explained that they were both essentially on the hunt for the same house in the same price range, so Lorna always brought them on showings together with hopes that one of them would like the property.

"You have been seeing him a lot," Kate said. "I didn't know it was just house-hunting."

"It's not. I mean, I...don't want it to be." She glanced at her sister, ready to open up. "I really like him, Kate. First man in a long, long time I'd like to seriously think about settling down with."

Kate's jaw dropped. "Tessa, that's wonderful."

"Not really. We actually have our own philosophical impasse. He's widowed two years, and after all that caretaking? He just wants 'fun' and, usually, that's where I come in. But this time, I want more."

"And you should have more," she said. Of course Kate, her counterpart since conception, immediately got all that and needed no detailed explanation.

"I hope he's here today," Tessa said as she turned onto the street. "I actually miss him and haven't seen him for a few days."

She drove down a shaded street lined with low-slung ranch houses, their yards peppered with oaks and scrub palms. And, sadly, no sign of that upscale truck she liked so much.

"I still can't believe you're buying a house," Kate said. "It's such a commitment."

"Right?" Tessa scoffed. "I know it's a big move for me. But I'm ready. I'm ready for a lot of things, actually, but..." She glanced around. "I don't see one of them here."

Surprised at how deep her disappointment was, Tessa parked in front of a brick ranch with a weathered front porch and three mismatched lawn chairs.

"I already don't like it," she admitted.

"Then why look?" Kate asked.

"I don't know. Truth is, I haven't liked most of the houses we've looked at. Dusty is more forgiving, and handy, so fixers have an appeal. I want something bright and beautiful with no need for a new floor or bathroom counter...and a view of the water." She snorted. "That's my impossible dream, but I simply do not have a million-plus at my fingertips."

"Have you found anything close?" Kate asked.

"A few, but nothing I'd commit to. I have found Dusty..." She gave a sad smile. "And apparently I don't have whatever that would cost, either."

"Don't sell yourself short, Tess. It's early and he's probably falling just as hard for you. If he has eyes and a brain, he is."

"I really hope so," Tessa confessed. "Because I really like this guy."

Kate looked past her, over her shoulder. "Lorna?" she guessed.

Tessa turned to see the Realtor striding to the car, dressed in flowy linen pants and a loose floral top, smiling like she had the keys to heaven.

"Ready to see it?" she asked as Tessa opened her door.

"Always. Let me introduce you to my sister, Kate."

They all greeted each other, then Lorna led the way with chatter about good bones and functional layout and "so much potential." Tessa managed not to ask about Dusty, hoping that maybe he'd driven with Lorna and was inside.

No such luck. Even worse, the place was cute, but dark and dated.

After they'd done a quick tour, Tessa stood in the doorway of the kitchen, eyeing the '80s-style walnut cabinets and imagining what could be done to them—but not by her.

"This is Dusty's dream house, not mine. Has he seen

it?" She hoped she didn't sound like a desperate teenager trying to finagle a date with her favorite boy.

Lorna shook her head. "No, he's, uh, backing off the search for a while."

Tessa's heart squeezed, more at the tone than the words—and the fact that he hadn't told her. "He's decided to keep his house?"

"Actually, I think I have an offer on it. And Dusty? He's spreading his wings. He's asked me to find a Realtor in Vermont, which is random and shocking."

Tessa tried not to react. "He mentioned a cousin in Vermont and the possibility of going there," she said.

But that was a long time and lot of feelings ago. She'd completely forgotten that, especially since he never talked about it during any date or boat ride or long walk or romantic dinner.

But...*Vermont.*

"I guess that kind of changes everything," Tessa added under her breath, but Lorna heard, and winced.

"Tessa, I have to be honest. I thought you two had a real shot," she said quietly, her words echoing Tessa's deepest feelings. "But he's...scared."

"Oh, please." Tessa gave her hand a flippant wave as if this news didn't affect her a bit. "He's had his soulmate, Lorna, and no one gets two."

Lorna made a face. "I promised Kelly I'd help him," she said softly. "She wanted him to find love, but he's not ready."

"I know," Tessa said. "And I'm not ready for a kitchen

that needs this much work, so this is a miss for me. But thanks so much, Lorna. We'll keep looking."

For a house...and a forever man.

They said a warm goodbye and then she and Kate headed out, not speaking until they were back in the car. Tessa slid into the driver's seat, hands gripping the wheel, but didn't start the engine.

"Guess that's that," she said. "Another one bites the dust and all."

Kate reached across the console and took her hand.

"I'm so damn tired of doing life alone," Tessa admitted, tears threatening to wreck her mascara. "For once, I wanted something more. I thought he might be it."

Kate leaned over and wrapped her arms around her. Tessa let herself fall into the hug, pressing her face against Kate's shoulder like she had when they were little girls and the world felt scary.

"I'm going to end it tonight," she whispered. "I deserve better than being somebody's 'good time.' And he should have told me he was looking in Vermont."

"Yes, he should have." Kate kissed her temple. "And, yes, Tessa Wylie, you deserve everything and more."

They sat in silence for a while before Tessa turned to her. "Can I give you some advice, Kate? Not that I'm a relationship expert, but I love you and I know you and I've watched you with Eli."

Kate grimaced. "You're going to tell me to work it out."

"Yes," Tessa said. "Don't let him go because he has

some beliefs that don't align with yours. You two have something real. Don't let fear ruin it."

Kate closed her eyes.

"I mean it," Tessa said, driving home her point. "His faith and your lack of it is not an insurmountable problem. He's not running away, he's not afraid of the future, and he's not saying one thing and…moving to Vermont. He's a good, good man who we've known our entire lives. Please give him a chance. You deserve everything, too. And I think Eli Lawson is ready to offer it."

Kate just looked at her, then nodded. "That's good advice, Tess. Thank you."

But would she take it? Tessa didn't know, but she hoped so.

THE SUN WAS JUST DIPPING behind the tree line when Tessa pulled into Dusty's driveway late that afternoon. She sat in her car, hands still on the wheel, taking in the comfort and arches off the porch he'd rebuilt himself, phrases from Vivien's old diary entry she'd read last night floating through her head.

She's the girl everyone looks at, but maybe no one really sees.

Maybe she had been that girl for fifty years, but that could change. Now. Tonight.

She climbed out slowly, the pavers warm through thin sandals, and walked toward the house with the weight of everything she hadn't said yet pressing on her chest. From an open window, she heard the faint strains of something old and acoustic that made her heart ache.

He opened the door a second after she knocked.

"Tessa," he said, surprised, stepping back. "Hey."

He looked like he'd showered after a long day—hair damp, a clean T-shirt clinging to his chest.

"Can I come in?" she asked. "You're not in the middle of a session?"

"No, I'm free. Come in." He stepped back to let her in, quiet as she entered the house. She'd been here several times, and it was starting to feel somewhat familiar and comfortable.

But his expression was anything but comfortable. He watched her warily, quietly, then gestured toward the kitchen.

"Too late for coffee, too early for wine. What can I get you?"

"Nothing," she said. "I need to talk to you."

"Oh." He exhaled softly. "The dreaded words."

She smiled but didn't elaborate, walking to the counter to take the same stool at the island where they'd had their first conversation.

"I saw Lorna today," she said as he sat next to her. "She showed me a house."

Dusty nodded slowly. "Yeah. She told me you were going."

"She said you have an offer. And that you're going to Vermont."

"Thinking about it and..." He winced. "I should have told you that myself."

"You think?"

He looked away, quiet and clearly embarrassed.

"When were you going to tell me?"

Stabbing his fingers into his silver-streaked hair, he pulled it back with a huff. "It's not quite that...black and white."

She waited for him to elaborate.

"I'm not sure I'm going, but"—he looked up at her—"you scare me, you know that?"

Drawing back, she let out a soft laugh. "I wasn't expecting that."

"I wasn't expecting *you*," he retorted. "What I planned was a nice, quiet life of being a widower and therapist. I was going to live in dreamy isolation with no one ever caring where I was or wasn't. Absolute monk-like solitude that would allow all the pain of the past to finally go away."

She had no idea how to respond to that.

"And along comes Tessa Wylie," he continued with a wry smile. "And she's just as bright and beautiful and wild and wonderful as she was thirty years ago. Only now she's lived and she's smart and she's got a good heart and she drives a boat and makes me laugh and has interesting opinions. She makes me...*feel things* I never wanted to feel again."

"Oh." The single syllable slipped out.

"So I'm running," he finished.

"Why?"

Dusty exhaled, shaking his head. "Because I never, ever, *ever* want to love and lose again. I never want to know that pain—hell, I'm still feeling it. I never want to go unprotected into life and have my heart and soul crushed and chewed up and spit out."

She stared at him, a thousand responses vying for their shot.

I would never do that! It is better to have loved and lost. Please give us a chance. All we have to fear is fear itself.

All of them, every single cliché, sounded utterly hollow in her head.

So she just spoke the truth.

"Well, I do," she said softly. "I want to feel the kind of love that turns your world upside down and brings tears to your eyes just thinking about it. I want my one and only, Dusty. And, you know what? I would take one *day* of that kind of love because I've never felt it."

He seemed to inch back at the power of her words, staring at her in stunned silence.

"So, I'm here to say goodbye," she finished.

"Really?"

"Well, what else would we say when you take off for Vermont? And, don't worry, you're not responsible for me. You never led me on or made promises you didn't keep. We're good."

"Oh, Tessa." He dropped his head with a grunt. "I'm just not ready for what you want yet."

She lifted a shoulder, undaunted, because *she* was ready. "But why run away to Vermont?"

"Because it's far from you."

She flinched. "Ouch."

"I meant that as a compliment."

"I've heard better," she cracked.

"Listen, Tess. This scares me. You scare me. Love scares me. And the kind I see with you..." He shook his head. "No, sorry. I can't take that chance again."

The words twisted her chest. She wasn't worth a risk, even the risk of real love.

"I should go," she said quietly.

He moved then, stepping forward. "Tessa—wait." He reached for her and drew her closer, touching her cheek with the gentlest brush of his fingers. "I thought you were just fun and then I found out you were...so much more."

The words were barely out before he leaned in and kissed her—slow, full of regret, and everything he couldn't say. She kissed him back, because it might be the last time, and she wanted to remember exactly how a kiss like this felt.

When they parted, she stepped back, taking an unsteady breath. "Bye."

"Bye, Tess."

She turned and walked out the door, waiting until she was halfway out of his neighborhood before the first sob escaped.

And once it did, there was no stopping it. She cried like she hadn't in years. For what was, what could've been, and what Dusty wasn't brave enough to try.

Guess what, Vivien? Girls like Tessa *do* cry. A lot.

Chapter Twenty
Maggie

"I know you want to get back, Mags, but we're coming up on ten hours in the car." Jo Ellen re-situated herself in the low-slung seat next to Maggie, wrapped in a cardigan she'd "borrowed" days ago and apparently was never giving up.

"I can read the clock, Jo. You know I have to be there when Atlas's grandparents arrive tomorrow morning. I need to stake my claim and make those people tremble in fear of me."

Ever since Eli had texted earlier today to suggest Maggie cut her visit short since those Danes people were coming to Destin, Maggie couldn't settle down.

Jo Ellen, bless her heart, had agreed that they should abandon West Palm Beach, where they'd been lollygagging like the rich and famous, and drive straight through to Destin to make it home by nightfall.

But they hadn't counted on an accident that practically shut down the turnpike and had them sitting in a line of traffic ten miles long for more than two hours. That turned an already grueling eight-hour drive into...a nightmare.

Now it was ten o'clock on Friday night and she was

not in her jammies sipping Sleepytime tea and judging other people's bad decisions on *House Hunters*. Instead, she was pedal-to-the-metal in the dark on Interstate 10, driving a manual transmission sports car that obeyed her every command.

For the most part, the experience had been heady. But there were some moments that had been...hairy. Like that truck she nearly went *under* instead of *around*. Still, all in all, the scaredy-cat driver had become a road warrior, high on her own success.

"We can still stop and sleep somewhere and get up early to make it to Destin before they arrive," Jo Ellen said, her voice taut with the same exhaustion that pressed on Maggie.

"We're not giving up now! We're half an hour from 331, the exit to Santa Rosa Beach."

"We're going to pull into Frank and Betty's after eleven," Jo Ellen reminded her. "Do you know any eighty-year-old awake at midnight?"

"Frank said it was fine, he'd distract Betty, and we could just leave the car parked in the driveway and he'd surprise her tomorrow morning."

"And you think we can get an Uber in Santa Rosa Beach at that hour?"

"I think we can do anything," Maggie shot back. "And that includes sneaking into our apartment like a couple of wayward teenagers. And I will show up bright and early on Saturday, ready to make sure those people know who's the boss of this family."

Jo Ellen yawned, thankfully too tired to argue.

"Can you even see where you're going?" she asked after five minutes of blessed silence.

"I can see," Maggie lied, blinking eyelids that felt like sandpaper.

In truth, the darkness smudged the edges of the world and made everything blurrier than it should be. The overhead lights were few and far between, saved for exits. The rest of this absolute wasteland of highway was pitch black.

Taillights bled red, when there were any at all for her to follow. And the headlights barreling from the opposite side of I-10 were small suns, searing into Maggie's retinas. But she didn't flinch. She didn't squint. She didn't slow down, even when that speedometer neared her age.

She gritted her teeth and kept driving.

A few minutes later, Jo Ellen groaned. "Oh, Maggie, I hate to say this, but I have to go to the bathroom."

"Hold it."

"Look, I'm sorry for being human," Jo Ellen muttered. "But there's an exit sign and a gas station."

Maggie curled her lip. "Another lovely restroom in a BP? Ah, nothing like using a key hanging off a two-by-four to open a world of rust-stained sinks and seat-free toilets. No, thanks."

"But you know my bladder. I believe you called it the size of a cashew."

"A half-cashew," Maggie corrected, then sighed. "Okay. We'll stop."

"It's this exit, Mags."

"Right here? This exit? Whoa..." She swerved into

the right lane—no, she didn't look, *sorry*—and blew down the ramp a little fast.

"Maggie!"

She slammed on the brakes and they screeched, which made her foot slip off the brake pedal and onto the gas, launching them forward.

"Oh, dear. Sorry!" She had a panic moment, veered into the other lane, and then straightened, finally stopping at the bottom of the exit ramp. "Whoops."

"Well, now I don't need to use the bathroom," Jo Ellen said without missing a beat. "Just get me a new Depends."

Maggie snorted and mumbled another apology as she gingerly picked up speed and turned right, but the words got trapped in her mouth when she spotted a flash of red and blue in the rearview mirror.

"Wait. What?" She hit the brakes so hard, they bucked, and she nearly stalled out, totally forgetting about that clutch. "Is he coming after us?"

"I think he was on the ramp watching for...trouble."

Maggie bit back a dark, dark word and kept driving, very slowly and to the right, so he could get around them and go find the real bad guy.

But the cruiser stayed behind them, then turned the siren on.

"Oh, for crying out loud."

"Just pull over, Maggie. We'll flirt our way out of a ticket."

Maggie fried her with a look as she eased to the side

of the road. "Right. Because we're eighteen and have boobs and not...Depends."

A minute later, a young man—okay, he might be fifty-five, but that was young to Maggie—with bulging biceps and an intimidating green sheriff's uniform ambled up to her window. Maggie refused to roll it down more than a crack.

"Evening, ma'am."

"Hello." She swallowed and looked way up at him. "Officer."

"You know what the word erratic means?"

"I do and I can spell it. What's your point?"

His dark eyes flickered with a mix of amusement and impatience. "My point is when I see someone drive like you, I think...hmmm. Erratic. What has that driver been drinking?"

"Excuse me?" Her voice rose in disbelief. "I've had water and lukewarm diet something in a can. It was disgusting and so is your insinuation."

"Can you lower your window all the way?"

She narrowed her eyes in distaste and patted the arm rest and door. Where the heck was the button?

"Ma'am?" He inched closer. "It's a crank. Right there."

"Of course. I knew that."

"New car?"

"It's not mine."

"Did you steal it?"

She sucked in a breath. "How dare you! I'm taking it

home to my friend who is dying of cancer, thank you very much. Dying! My dear friend!"

Jo Ellen put a hand on her arm. "Calm down, Maggie. Just open the window for him. You're tired and you have nothing to hide."

As she turned the blasted crank, the deputy dipped down and looked at Jo Ellen. "Who are you and what are you two ladies doing out here tonight?"

"I'm Jo Ellen." She stuck her hand out, right in front of Maggie's face like she was at a garden party making friends. He ignored it. "We drove up from South Florida, but we're staying in Destin. I'm from Ithaca. That's in New York."

"He doesn't need your life story," Maggie ground out, exhaustion and irritation going to war in her body. "Just shut up and he'll let us go."

"Ma'am." He shifted his gaze to Maggie. "I need your license and registration."

"Okay, okay. I have a license, but, oh, sweet heavens" —she whipped around to Jo Ellen—"where's all that paperwork?"

Panic crawled up Maggie's chest. This car was in Frank's name! He'd sent a picture of his driver's license, and the dealer had explained all that gobbledygook about submitting the paperwork to the DMV and gave them a temporary tag and...

Oh, no! He would think she stole this car!

Jo Ellen was elbow deep in the glovebox. "There's a bill of sale somewhere, and a temporary registration, and" —she pulled out a pack of papers that looked like a legal brief for the Supreme Court—"a lot of other stuff." Bending down, she smiled at the deputy. "Are you sure you want to go through all this?"

"License?" he said to Maggie, all niceties gone.

"All right, all right." She turned to get her handbag and pull out her wallet, producing her Georgia license and handing it to him.

He shined his flashlight on it, glanced at Maggie, then back at the license. "This expired two months ago on your...seventy-eighth birthday."

"What?"

"Ma'am, I need you to step out of the car."

"Step out...*why?*" she sputtered. "Two months? I was in Europe! I used a passport. Would you like that? You can blame my daughter, you know. I live with her, and she drives me everywhere—not that I can't drive, I certainly can—but didn't they check that in the car dealership before they let me buy this thing? What was wrong with those people?"

"Out. Of. The. Car."

She swallowed and tried to unlatch her seatbelt. Tried and tried, but Jo Ellen reached over and touched the button to free her.

"Relax," she whispered. "You didn't do anything wrong."

"Actually," the officer said, "she was swerving, driving inconsistently, and hitting eighty for the last ten miles. Also, driving with an expired license and can't produce a registration."

"I'm working on that!" Jo Ellen insisted, nervously fluttering all the papers.

"Wait. You were following me? For ten miles?"

He didn't answer, but let her open the door and step out, where she promptly swayed and nearly buckled. "Oh! This road. So uneven!"

With a harsh glare, he lifted his flashlight and shined it directly on her face. She blinked and covered her eyes. "Do you mind? As you just so kindly pointed out, I'm seventy-eight."

Jo Ellen reached over and stuck her head out the window, smiling like a pageant queen. "I found a bill of sale. Will that work? And, of course, you can call Frank, but it's late and we don't want to spoil the surprise."

When he lowered the light, she saw his metal star badge that read Deputy Sheriff Okaloosa County, and on the other side of his chest a simple name tag read Herman in block letters.

"Is that your first name or last?" Maggie asked, the words coming out fast and nervous. "I knew a Herman once. Herman Wisniewski and—"

"I'm going to ask you again. Have you had anything to drink tonight, Mrs. Lawson?"

"No, sir," she said, sucking in the thick and sticky air. "I am not an old lady hitting the sauce. I'm merely trying to get home—well, it's not really home, it's a summer house—because my grandson's girlfriend died in a car accident and he has their newborn baby and...and..." Tears of pure frustration and fear sprang. "And I *am* old, and I am not very good at highway driving but my friend has cancer and—"

He pointed to the ground and took out a phone. "Walk in a straight line, heel to toe. Please note you are being recorded."

"Oh, don't put me on one of those arrest shows. I *hate* those shows."

"Ma'am. A straight line. One foot in front of the other, please."

She swallowed and looked down at the mix of gravel and dirt and cursed herself for pridefully choosing sandals to walk around West Palm Beach so she didn't look like a tourist in big white sneakers. Now she couldn't walk like the sober woman she was.

Taking a breath, she put one heel in front of the other toe and tried to step in the darkness—he couldn't give her some light? She took two steps on the unforgiving gravel and a mosquito dive-bombed her ear.

"Oh!" She waved it away, which cost her some stability, making her flail and lose her straight line, but she didn't fall. "There. Okay? Are you happy now?"

Herman didn't look like he was ever happy.

He produced a device about the size of a walkie-talkie, but she instantly knew that thing wasn't for communication with his cop pals. He pointed to the clear plastic tube on the top. "I need you to put your mouth right there and breathe."

He might as well have asked her to run into the highway and lay down.

"Um, no." She lifted her brows. "I have no idea whose mouth has been on that."

"Oh, I do. And every one of them was over the limit. It gets wiped after every use." He held it closer. "I'm officially ordering you to take a breathalyzer, ma'am, and if you decline, you will be arrested for refusing a roadside sobriety test."

"Not taking the test cannot be against the law!"

He lifted a brow, cool as a cucumber, but she suspected his stoic patience was waning.

"Florida Statute 316.1932, also known as the implied consent law, which you agree to when you get a driver's license in any state. In addition, driving with an expired license is also a misdemeanor." He gave the box a little shake. "Breathe into it."

She recoiled, making a face. "I can't. I'll faint! I'll literally pass out on this street."

Jo Ellen leaned out the driver's side. "Officer, please. We've been on the road for eleven hours. We had fast food and bad coffee and she's just tired."

"Exactly," Maggie said. "Fatigued. Not inebriated. There's a difference."

"Florida law doesn't require drugs or alcohol for someone to be considered impaired. Exhibiting signs of extreme fatigue, impaired behavior, and reckless driving is also against the law."

Oh, good heavens. Maybe they *would* have to flirt their way out of this. She lifted her chin and attempted a smile.

"Herman. Do you really want to arrest a sweet old lady like me?"

Iceman didn't even hint at a smile. "I don't want you driving one more mile tonight, Mrs. Lawson."

"Well, I'm in the middle of nowhere, so...I'm going to have to drive eventually, right. Right?"

"I'm sorry," the officer said, clearly *not* sorry. "But I'm going to have to ask you to place your hands behind your back."

Maggie stood frozen for a full second. He could *not* be serious!

"Oh, this is rich. This is *fantastic*. This is...oh, God, I'm glad my husband isn't here to see this. He's dead, you know. I'm a widow."

He responded by twirling his finger in a circle, instructing her to turn. "With your hands behind you."

Helpless, she turned, her hands behind her, and heard the soul-stealing sound of handcuffs clicking. Hard, cold...cuffs.

"What do we do about the car, Officer Herman?" Jo Ellen asked.

"Whatever you want but Mrs. Lawson will be at Crestview substation on East James Lee Boulevard. It's about a fifteen-minute drive. This way, Mrs. Lawson."

As she stumbled away, she looked over her shoulder. "Call Frank. Call Betty. Call the Pope. But don't you *dare* call my children and do not let those kidnappers know I'm in prison! We'll never get to keep that baby!"

"Maggie, hush! You're making it worse!"

How could it be?

The officer gently guided her toward the cruiser.

She slid into the back seat of the police car, her knees cracking, her pride shattering, and her entire sense of newfound freedom crumpling like an old-school map that Jo "We'll Just Ask Oscar" Ellen refused to use.

The door slammed shut. Sirens chirped.

And Maggie started to cry.

THERE WAS, indeed, a toilet and sink in her jail cell. Just like the movies.

Although Deputy Herman had told her it was a holding room, not an actual cell, but he also told her, "This is for your own good," and nothing about this moment of hell felt good.

In addition to the toilet and sink, wafting with the nose-itching stench of bleach, there was a metal table bolted to the ground. Did they think she was going to try and steal it? Maybe throw it? She was mad enough that she might try.

And tired enough that she almost sat on the chair, dropped her head on the table, and cried herself to sleep.

She stayed standing, though, under the most unflattering and unforgiving fluorescent light and directly in front of a large surveillance camera. Who was on the other side of that camera, she wondered, and what on Earth did they think of her?

She shut her eyes and tried to recite lines from *Gone*

With the Wind, one of her favorite ways to calm down and pass time.

"'And not even a regular jail, Rhett! A horse jail!'"

But she wasn't Scarlett O'Hara in a dress Mammy had made from velvet curtains. She was Magnolia Fredericks Lawson, taken down to her last shred of humility.

Accepting that she couldn't stand one more minute, Maggie walked to the chair, perched on the edge, and folded her hands on her lap. She tried to imagine her poor husband, who'd breathed his last breath in a room very much like this one.

"Oh, Roger," she whispered, closing her eyes and remembering the young man who'd swept her off her feet with the same charm and smile as Rhett Butler. "I miss you so much."

She felt the fight go out of her, and lost the will to hold her head high, and very, very slowly let it fall to the table. Dropping her cheek on her arms for a tear-soaked pillow, she closed her eyes and fell sound asleep.

The metal clang startled her and she jumped up, wiping a shameful amount of drool from her face before turning. A different officer opened the door, stepped back, and one very spunky-looking Jo Ellen walked in.

"You're free to leave, Mrs. Lawson," the deputy said. "Everything's taken care of."

Her jaw fell. "Jo? What—"

"Oh, my darling." Jo Ellen shot forward, arms out. "Was it awful? Were you scared?" Then she drew back and pointed at the toilet. "Did you use that?"

"Don't be absurd," Maggie said, releasing the hug. "What did you do? How did you—"

"Don't ask," she said.

"Oh, no." Shame crept through her. "Eli's out there, isn't he? And Vivien. How can I possibly face them?"

"Come on," she said, sliding an arm around Maggie. "Let's get out of this place."

Unable to put up a fight, Maggie walked with her best friend, each step heavier and sadder than the ones she took to get into this particular hellhole.

"Please tell me. Eli or Vivien? Or, gracious, did I sleep so long you got Crista?"

"None of your kids are waiting out there, Maggie."

As they made their way down the short hallway toward the front office, Maggie looked around furtively, the humiliation rising like steam. "You swear to me there's no one out there?"

Jo Ellen gave her most innocent smile. "Not a soul from your family."

Maggie exhaled, heart easing—until her eyes narrowed. "Wait a minute. That look. You made up another whopper of a story, didn't you? Told them I had three months to live and wanted to check 'jail time' off my bucket list?"

Jo Ellen let out a delighted laugh. "Tempting. But no. Your real story is colorful enough, Mags. Besides, you already spilled most of it to Deputy Herman."

Maggie froze. "I did not."

"Oh, you did. You pulled out all the stops, including flirting with the guy."

Groaning, Maggie rolled her eyes. "That man could use a little sense of humor, don't you think?"

"Which is why I didn't even try any tricks," Jo Ellen said. "Just...got help."

"Help? Who?"

"Let's just say...I called in the most obvious person to know their way to a sheriff's station."

"Tessa?"

Jo Ellen gave a pretend swing at Maggie's arm. "Hey, that's my daughter you're disparaging."

"Well, we don't know any..." Maggie stopped cold. "Jo..."

"Mhmm?"

"I'm begging you, not the biker."

Before she could answer, Jo Ellen guided them around the corner and into the front lobby...where none other than Brick the bearded biker stood tall and rumpled and grinning like a man who'd just pulled off the heist of the century.

His scruffy salt-and-pepper beard looked like it had survived a wind tunnel, and his leather vest was emblazoned with enough patches to start a quilt. A helmet dangled from one hand, and his eyes—those mischievous, twinkling blue eyes—landed on Maggie like they'd been waiting all day just for her.

She froze, mouth open. "You..."

Jo Ellen gave her a little nudge. "Turns out he *did* leave his number in that helmet after all."

Brick strolled closer, his smile growing and making the creases around his eyes even deeper.

"Mags, I liked you before. But springin' you from jail?" He dipped a little closer and held her gaze. "Now, that's *my* kind of girl."

Maggie blinked, then did the only thing she could do—she laughed. One of those startled, out-of-body giggles that slipped right past her ego and straight from her soul. Because of course this ridiculous, grizzled, helmet-toting biker was the one to show up.

He grinned wider. "There's the laugh I've been dreaming of."

Still stunned, Maggie managed, "How...how did you—"

Jo Ellen leaned in. "It turns out Brick knows every deputy in Okaloosa County on a first-name basis. Brings them his homemade cheesecake on birthdays, holidays, and days that end in Y. They owed him."

And he used his cop favor for her. Maggie inched back, seeing him in a new and grateful light. "Thank you," she said softly.

"Come on, Mags." He gave a wave to the woman at the front desk. "Thanks, Mary Beth. Tell that daughter of yours to stay off Harleys."

She laughed. "I will, Brick. And thanks for the cheesecake."

Feeling like she was in a bad, bad dream, Maggie let Brick lead them through a thick glass door. A sticky Florida night greeted them with all the subtlety of a wet towel.

Maggie looked around, her chest squeezing. "Where's the car?"

"Angel drove the T-bird to Frank's house," Jo Ellen said. "He's going to park it in the driveway with a little note and we can go get our stuff tomorrow."

Maggie stared at her. "Then how are we supposed to get home?"

Randy appeared from the shadows with two shiny Harleys parked behind him.

Brick stepped forward like a magician presenting the grand finale. He held out the helmet. "Only one way, Mags. Wrap them legs around me, woman, and let's ride this hog."

Her mouth dropped open again. "You cannot be serious. I'm...I'm...I'm wearing linen pants."

He threw his head back and laughed, then put the helmet over her hair. "And I'm wearing denim dreams, baby. Come on."

She turned to Jo Ellen for backup. "Tell me we're not doing this."

"We are absolutely doing this," Jo Ellen said, adjusting the chin strap on her own helmet. "They'll have us home in forty-five minutes and we can sneak into our apartment with no one the wiser."

"Ooh, I like a woman who sneaks in past curfew."

"Will you shut up?"

Brick just laughed again, taking Maggie's hand and walking her toward the bike. She gave a fleeting, desperate look to Jo Ellen, who was laughing with Randy.

She sighed and looked up at him, barely seeing him through the thick edge of the helmet. "Thank you, Brick."

"Pleasure's mine, darlin'."

With no fight left in her, Maggie tightened the chin strap with trembling fingers, slung one leg over the bike, and settled behind Brick.

"Hold tight," he said, voice low and gravelly. "And you can scream if you want. It's kinda hot."

She smacked him in the shoulder. "Just drive, you numbskull, and do *not* do that tipping sideways thing that makes my heart stop."

He laughed. "Haven't you figured out by now that you should never challenge me, woman?"

She hadn't figured anything out.

But the engine rumbled to life like some feral beast waking from a nap, and Maggie felt her heartbeat sync to the thunder in her ears. Jo Ellen was mounted behind Randy, giving Maggie and Brick a ridiculous thumbs-up like she was some kind of biker babe.

As they peeled away from the curb, Maggie looked up at the stars. No T-bird. No jail. No family watching. Just wind, warmth, and the man in front of her who smelled faintly of leather, danger, and vanilla bean cheesecake.

The end of what had been, without a doubt, the most unforgettable adventure.

She was definitely going to miss the car, the laughs, the bad decisions, and the best time of her life.

Chapter Twenty-one

Jonah

They were coming.

Sally and Gary Danes—without their daughter Rori, Jonah was relieved to know—were en route to the Summer House to see the baby Carly had left behind.

As he waited and paced, drank a third cup of coffee and cracked every knuckle on both hands, Jonah checked the driveway repeatedly. He peeked out the window on the landing, saw nothing, then circled back through the living room feeling as though he would spontaneously combust from the stress.

Out on the deck, he could hear Dad and Kate talking softly, making cooing sounds to Atlas, who Jonah had left in his baby bouncer. When he'd walked out, his father seemed calm, but wound a little more tightly than usual. He and Kate had held hands on the sofa, which he hoped meant that their differences in how to approach this day had faded and they would be facing Carly's parents with a unified front.

Back inside, Jonah swiped his hands over the khaki shorts he'd chosen for today while exhaustion stung his eyes. He hadn't slept and, for once, he couldn't blame his son. Just raw, unfettered nerves.

His stomach was in knots, his head hurt, and he couldn't decide if the sweat on his lower back was from the Florida heat or the sheer terror of facing Gary and Sally Danes. They had to be furious that he blew out of California with their grandchild. And how could they not blame him for letting Carly run out for diapers—and into a truck? What kind of father was he?

Well, that was the question that was about to be answered as they marched their way east to cross-examine the man raising their grandson.

He popped a grape into his mouth and nearly choked when the door to the garage opened and Grandma Maggie walked in.

"Where's the welcoming committee?" she demanded, her shoulders set square for battle, her silver hair looking particularly sharp in her two-inch-long crop that accentuated her cheekbones and sky-blue eyes.

For a moment, he just stared at her, slightly disoriented. Was it because she'd been MIA for ten days or did she look...different? Younger, even. Brighter.

Had she gone to a spa or something? Jonah couldn't remember where she and Jo Ellen had said they were off to for the past week or so.

"I didn't know you'd be back in time," Jonah said.

"Of course. I was just down the road in Santa Rosa Beach."

"Really?"

She launched one of her uber-judgy brows north. "Would I lie?" she challenged.

"I don't know," he said, not really wanting to get into a verbal fencing match with this woman. He lost under the best of circumstances, and these were not ideal.

She walked toward the coffee pot, which was always hot and full in the Summer House.

"I wouldn't miss a chance to meet Atlas's maternal grandparents." She took a mug from the rack and slid him a look. "And make sure they know exactly what the 'great' in great-grandmother really means."

"Relentless, judgmental, and unwavering?" he countered.

"Don't forget possessive, bossy, and..." She added a totally out of character smile. "Fearless."

He wanted to laugh, but she was in an unusual mood and that made him even more nervous.

"Grandma," he said. "I'm begging you to not be... you."

She gave a soft hoot. "You know, if I didn't love life so much at this moment, I'd punish you for that comment, Jonah."

"You know what I mean."

She sighed. "Sadly, I do. I'll be on my best behavior, which probably isn't as good as others, but I won't ruin the party. Where is everyone? Jo Ellen said she was going on the boat with Tessa."

"Aunt Vivien went, too." He purposely didn't mention Meredith, who was upstairs in her room, secretly pregnant and certain a trip on Tessa's boat would have her blowing breakfast. "We wanted to keep this first meeting as small as possible, just my dad, Kate, me, and, of course, Atlas."

"And your grandmother." She splashed cream in her coffee just as Kate came in, holding Atlas in the bouncer, and Eli was right behind with an empty baby bottle.

"Mom?" He blinked at Maggie. "When did you get back?"

"Frank dropped us off last night and Jo and I just tiptoed into our apartment. No need to wake anyone."

Eli narrowed his eyes. "What time?"

"Oh, I don't know but we were sound asleep by ten, like good little grandmas."

"You didn't hear that rumbling engine around one?" he asked, taking the bottle to the sink. "I could have sworn it was like someone was on a hog out there."

"A *hog*?" she asked.

"It's a nickname for a Harley, Grandma," Jonah told her. "You wouldn't know."

"I certainly would not," she tsked, taking a sip. "I didn't hear a thing."

"I'm surprised," Eli said. "It was loud enough that I almost got up to see what it was, but I was too tired." He gave her a light kiss and smiled at her. "We've missed you, Mom. How was your time with the Cavallaris?"

"Peaceful and uneventful." She practically cooed the words. "Exactly what we needed. And now what we need is some ammunition against these people."

Jonah choked. "It's not a battle, and I'm serious about

reining it in. No criticisms, no digs, no demands, no judging."

"In other words, no Maggie." She tempered that with another rare smile. "Consider me declawed, Jonah."

"Thank you," he said on a sigh. "Just remember these are people in mourning. They are not the enemy. They're not here to steal Atlas."

"Now, that we don't know," Maggie muttered. "Do you want me to leave? I can hide in my apartment like a crazy Dickens character in the attic."

Dad stepped in, putting a gentle hand on his mother's shoulder. "We'd love for you to be here, Mom," he said. "You're our matriarch. We want Carly's parents to know we are a multigenerational and strong family, ready to keep Atlas safe, thriving, and surrounded by love."

Kate cleared her throat, gently placing the bouncer on the island in a safe place. "You certainly can help us assess whether this visit is just a visit—or the start of a custody claim. Do listen to their subtext. You're so good at that, Maggie."

She sliced Kate with a classic Maggie glare. "I don't know what subtext is. Why don't you just ask them?"

"Because we don't want to fight!" Jonah said, hearing his voice rise and snap. As all three of them turned and looked, he held up a hand. "Sorry. I'm just stressed out of my mind."

None of them said a word, which just made the air thicker than his broken béchamel sauce.

Before the tension could crack wide open, two car doors slammed and punctuated the moment.

Dad took Kate's hand and stepped away, closing his eyes for a second, making Jonah think he'd just sent up one of his power prayers.

"We'll go meet them," he said. "And you stay here with Atlas and Maggie." He huffed out a breath. "This is going to go well. I promise."

The two of them walked out and around to the entry-way, hand in hand in a show of solidarity that touched Jonah down to his last strand of DNA.

Surprising him, Grandma Maggie put a hand on his back and eased him closer. "Don't be afraid, Jonah. Everyone wants what's best for baby Atlas."

He gave her a quick smile, grateful for her support, then turned to get the baby out of his bouncer. He wanted to be holding his most prized possession when they came in...to take it away.

Jonah heard voices in the entryway, small talk about trips and weather, happy the introductions had been made in the driveway. He was so nervous, he might have forgotten someone's name.

He waited with Atlas in his arms as they came around the corner, his fingers fidgeting over his son's tiny bare feet sticking out of a baby-blue onesie.

"Oh!" Sally was first, looking a significant amount older than the day he'd met her. A poised and attractive professional in her fifties, Sally Danes had shadows under her eyes and had definitely lost weight. Grief had taken a toll, but her face lit up at the sight of Atlas. "There's my grandson."

"Here he is," Jonah said, feeling awkward because he

couldn't hug her, not that she'd want a hug from him. "Hello, Mrs. Danes."

She spared him a look, opening her mouth as if she wanted to say something, but just took a breath. "Jonah." She reached for Atlas. "May I?"

"Of course." He eased the baby into her arms and made sure she had a good hold before looking beyond her to Gary, a man Carly frequently described as a lovable nerd. The older man's steel-gray gaze was cold and direct, with no indication of the slightest smile.

"Welcome, Mr. Danes," he said. "Thank you for coming."

His lids closed as if he was disgusted, but his shoulders relaxed slightly as he spoke. "We appreciate the invitation, but wish we didn't have to fly across the country to see our grandson."

"I understand," Jonah said. "But you're here now and we want you to be comfortable."

"We will be in the hotel."

"You're not staying here?" Dad asked, surprised and clearly disappointed.

"We thought it best not to."

Kate smiled and tried to guide everyone to the living room. "You may change your mind when you look around," she said smoothly. "Eli is the architect for this home and before it stood so gloriously, it was a vacation house for my family and the Lawsons. Be prepared for some Destin mag..."

Her voice faded out as Sally sniffed noisily. They all turned to find her hunched over Atlas, who was kicking happily and reaching his hand up toward her face.

"He looks so much like Carly at this age," she whimpered, tears falling. "He's a carbon copy of my baby."

"Now, Sal, we made a deal." Gary walked to her, guiding her toward the sofa to sit down with comforting words. "No tears, dear. It can't change anything."

"Tears are fine and certainly expected." Maggie followed them into the room, pulling their attention. "I'm Magnolia Lawson, Atlas's great-grandmother, and if you didn't cry, I'd think something was wrong."

Surprising them all, Sally almost smiled as she looked up at Maggie. "He has a great-grandmother? Our parents are all gone, so that's nice."

"Oh, I'm not nice, as Jonah will inform you," she said, taking the chair across from them. "But I'm in love with that baby, as you soon will be."

Jonah felt the air whoosh out of him. Maggie might not be declawed, but there was something indescribably irresistible about the woman—and he needed everything he could get today.

Dad offered drinks and food, and Kate folded onto the floor in front of Sally like a teenager ready for a girl chat. Atlas continued to smile and kick, doing his best imitation of an Instagram baby.

Moment One had come and gone and no one exploded. Now if they could just get through the afternoon, Jonah might breathe again.

After a bit, Sally looked down at Atlas and started to fight tears again.

Gary hovered, his hands twitching, clearly unsure whether to comfort his wife or take the baby himself. Noticing that, Sally passed Atlas to him without a word, and Gary sat back on the couch, stiff and overwhelmed, cradling the baby like he was made of porcelain.

Maggie leaned in, smiling at him with utterly unnatural sweetness. "Where in California do you live, Gary? And what do you do?"

Small talk from a woman who despised it. Jonah made a mental note to kiss that old lady on the cheek once this was all over.

And all Maggie got from Gary was a look and a muttered, "Santa Clara. I work in tech."

For a long beat, no one spoke.

"Come help me get drinks, Jonah," Dad suggested, helping with the incredibly awkward stretch of tension.

They pulled out sodas and filled some glasses with ice as Kate talked with Sally. After a minute, they both got up and Kate put a light hand on the other woman's back, taking her out to the deck to see the Gulf view.

Jonah shared a look with his father, who watched the women leave with an undeniable look of love in his eyes.

"She's a keeper," Jonah whispered.

His dad just gave a tight smile and glanced toward Gary and the baby. "This isn't going to be easy," he said.

Jonah nodded as he heard the conversation pick up outside. "Let me check on them." He walked toward the wide-open sliders to see Kate and Sally standing side by side at the railing.

"Actually, I live in Upstate New York, in Ithaca," he heard Kate say.

"Really?" Sally turned, looking truly interested for the first time. "I went to school in Ithaca."

Kate blinked "Cornell?"

Sally nodded.

"Oh, I work at Cornell," Kate said, her smile growing. "I'm a research scientist. What did you study in college?"

"I didn't go there for undergrad, but I got a law degree there. Don't use it much, but...yes."

"Law? My father taught at the law school—Dr. Wylie."

Sally's hand slammed to her chest, eyes wide. "You're kidding? Professor Wylie is your father?"

"You knew him?"

She seemed almost speechless. "I knew and adored him. He was my favorite professor!" she gushed, then frowned. "Knew? Is he..."

Kate nodded. "We lost him less than a year ago."

"Oh, I'm sorry. I didn't see that in the alumni newsletter, but then, I don't always open it." She thought for a second, studying Kate. "He often talked about his twin daughters."

"I'm one of them," she said. "My sister, Tessa, is here, too. You'll meet her later."

As Jonah watched, he could literally feel the tension lifting, replaced by warmth, commonality, and connection.

He didn't know this great Artie Wylie fellow, but he sure wanted to thank him right now.

"Gary," Sally called, turning and coming into the house. On the way, she stopped and smiled at Jonah for the first time. "Isn't it a small world?"

"Tiny," he said, stepping aside so she could walk in.

When she did, Kate came closer, and he just reached down and hugged her. "I love you, Katherine the Great."

She smiled at his kitchen-born nickname for her. "Back at you, young man. Now, come on, let's make them comfortable."

Inside, Sally was borderline animated, sharing a story about how Dr. Wylie used Marvel characters to teach "legal boundaries and zealous advocacy"—whatever that was.

Jonah didn't care. He was just awash with gratitude.

With each compliment for her father, Kate's expression softened with pride and a touch of sorrow.

"He would have loved to hear that he made such an impression," she told Sally.

During the conversation, Jonah could see Sally visibly relax and his optimism rose.

Surely the woman who'd learned legal ethics from Saint Artie wouldn't try to abuse the law to steal her own grandchild away from his father, right?

Sally reached for the baby, who was now chewing on his own fingers, and asked, "May I feed him?"

"Of course," Jonah said. "That's his first sign of hunger. His second is...louder."

She chuckled and brushed his little cheek. "Do you cry, Muffin?" she asked in a light baby voice.

"I'll get a bottle for you," Kate said, smiling as she passed Jonah.

A few minutes later, Sally cradled Atlas with practiced ease, her eyes filled with tears again. But this time, they seemed...well, not happy, but maybe wistful and loving.

"He has her nose," she said, almost to herself. "And those little ears..."

Jonah sat on the arm of the couch, watching.

"I miss her every day," he admitted, his voice low. "She made me laugh. She made me crazy. I didn't deserve her, but I loved her."

Sally looked up at him. "I know you two had your differences, but she was certain you had a great future. She loved that you had found your path to the kitchen and being a chef."

"Still just starting," he said. "But I promise you, Mrs. Danes, I will—"

"Please, call me Sally," she said. "Or Grammie Sal. I always wanted that to be my Grandma name."

He smiled. "Grammie Sal. That's what Carly told me we would call you."

For a moment, they both sighed, holding each other's gaze. Jonah was aware of Gary watching, and maybe he was warming, too.

The conversation shifted to Jonah's studies in the culinary program, and the building of this house, and Kate talked more about her father. Eli stepped in and asked Sally about the cross around her neck, and they bonded as Christians.

Finally relaxed, Jonah barely noticed that his phone kept buzzing in his pocket. Standing up to get Gary another soda, he finally pulled it out and looked at the screen.

Meredith: *Come up. I need help. Please.*

What the...

He glanced around the room, decided not to say anything except excuse himself, and then slowly went upstairs like nothing was wrong.

But...something was wrong.

"Mer?" He knocked once before pushing her door open.

She was on the bed, rolled up, weeping. "I'm bleeding," she announced on a ragged whisper. "Jonah...I think I'm losing the baby. It hurts."

He shot toward the bed, arms out, heart freefalling. "Are you sure? Is a little blood normal?"

"It's more than a little!" she wailed. "And I want this baby!"

"I know you do, I know, Mer Bear." He stroked her hair, trying to think, trying to prioritize, trying to...not feel cursed again.

Swearing under his breath, he pushed up. "We'll get you to the ER."

"But the grandparents...the people."

"Are fine. But you're not. You can't lose this baby, Meredith."

"I think it's too late," she moaned. "I'm sorry to bother you with everything going on."

"You did the right thing," he said, though he felt like

the world was tilting off its axis again. Another person he loved, another nightmare.

Another sign that he really was cursed.

But he didn't say it. He just held her quickly, then pulled back, kissed her forehead, and said, "I'll get Dad. And Kate. And I'll come with you. Just gimme a sec."

Downstairs, the room was still full of light and easy conversation. He hated that he had to step into this with yet another tragedy. Hated it.

Taking a breath, he leaned over his father and put a hand on his shoulder. Dad looked up and Jonah didn't have to say a word.

His expression mirrored what Jonah felt. All the happiness evaporated in a heartbeat.

And the cursed darkness had returned.

Chapter Twenty-two

Eli

The air inside the hospital was clean and antiseptic, but Eli's chest was too tight to take very deep breaths. The whole place was cold, bright, and unfeeling, with a low-grade hum of fear despite the group of nurses laughing over coffee in the center station that looked out over the individual rooms surrounding the ER.

In theirs, Meredith lay on a bed with rails, pale against white sheets, one hand pressed to her belly like she could somehow hold her little embryo in place with the sheer strength of Meredith Lawson determination.

The room had two chairs, and Eli had pulled one a little closer to the bed, keeping a hand on Meredith's shoulder as he tried—and failed—to find the right words. Every once in a while, she moaned, winced, and bit her lip, clearly in pain.

Kate stood nearby, arms crossed tightly, her eyes flicking between the monitor and Meredith's face like she could understand what every beep and number meant. Maybe she could—he knew better than to underestimate her intelligence.

She'd been amazing, though, when Jonah came

downstairs, took Eli aside, and quietly delivered the news. As if she sensed a crisis, Kate joined them, her expression flickering with surprise when she learned Meredith was pregnant.

To her credit, she didn't even look sideways at Eli for not telling her this news. Instead, she instantly suggested Jonah stay with Gary and Sally, maybe take them downstairs for a tour of the nursery and a peek at the beach.

Down there, he could tell them a little of what was going on—whatever he was comfortable saying—while Kate and Eli took Meredith to the hospital.

The plan made sense and unfolded without a hitch—except Maggie was not happy and wanted to come, but they talked her out of that, insisting that she help Jonah with the guests.

Eli drove to the hospital while Kate sat in the back with Meredith, comforting her through the pain. With tears and whimpers, Meredith shared enough of her situation for Kate to fully understand why Eli might have been a little distant the last day or so.

They'd talk all about it later. Now, he had to drive, focus, and pray. Probably not in that order. Prayer first, right? But the words weren't there.

Jesus, please help Meredith was the best he could do under the circumstances.

Frustration grew as they sat in the small room for what felt like years but might have been less than half an hour.

Other than a nurse named Dena who'd set up the

monitors, offered comfort, and told them an ultrasound tech was on the way, they'd been alone.

Finally, they heard the sound of wheels and footsteps, and a woman appeared at the door with a portable apparatus he assumed was the ultrasound machine.

"Hello," she said brightly, sliding her hands under the hand sanitizer attached to the wall. "You must be Meredith. I'm Charlene, your ultrasound tech. How are you doing, hon?"

Meredith managed a pathetic smile. "Been better."

"I know, I know."

Eli stood and pulled his chair back, even though Charlene set up on the other side of the bed. "Should we stay?" he asked.

"Absolutely." She glanced at the two of them and added a kind smile. "Are you Meredith's parents?"

"I'm her father," Eli said, not sure what to say about Kate.

"And you're worried sick," Charlene added, making the awkward moment easy. "Well, let's just see what's going on here. I'm going to do a quick abdominal ultrasound," she said, wheeling the machine closer.

"Not transvaginal?" Kate said, holding her phone where he suspected she was madly searching the internet to be armed with information.

"That's ordered by a doctor after we do this first level," Charlene explained as she tapped a keyboard and adjusted a monitor.

Meredith reached her hand out and Eli instantly

went to her, taking her trembling fingers in his. "I'm sorry, Dad," she whispered.

"No, sweetheart." His voice cracked. "Don't apologize. You don't have to be sorry for anything."

"I'm going to slide this top up, honey." The nurse applied the gel to Meredith's stomach, making her flinch. Eli tightened his grip as though he could somehow transfer her discomfort to himself.

Was there a parent in the world who wouldn't trade places with a sick kid?

Kate joined him, placing her hand on his back, adding her own touch of love and sympathy.

The screen flickered to life with hazy grays and blacks, and Charlene moved the sensor slowly, methodically.

Please, God. Please let the baby be alive and okay.

He didn't realize how much he wanted that until the words formed in his head.

"Let's see what we've got here," Charlene murmured, concentrating on the screen.

Eli squinted at the shadows, but it was a blur of greys and shifting light.

Charlene moved the wand again, slower this time, scanning from one side to the other. Her brow furrowed.

"Charlene?" Kate asked. "What are you seeing?"

"Well...for about six to eight weeks... Am I right about that?"

Meredith nodded, a little fear darkening her green eyes.

"I'd expect to see something in the uterus," the

woman said. "A gestational sac, at least." She paused, adjusted the depth on the screen. "I'm not seeing that."

"What does that mean?" Meredith asked weakly. "Is it too early?"

"Sometimes dating is off," Charlene said carefully. "But...I'm also seeing quite a bit of free fluid in the pelvis."

"Fluid?" Eli asked.

Charlene nodded, eyes still on the screen. "It could be blood. It's pooling in the cul-de-sac behind the uterus." She angled the wand again. "And possibly tracking higher. The doctor needs to see this."

"Wait," Kate said, leaning in. "Are you saying this could be...internal bleeding?"

Charlene looked at her, taking her eyes off the screen. "Yes. It's possible. Meredith's blood pressure is trending low and her heart rate's up. We're on it, I promise."

Meredith turned toward Eli. "I feel dizzy. And I have to pee."

Charlene gently pulled the probe away and set it down. "I'm going to help you do that because we want you flat." She turned and grabbed something plastic, then lifted a microphone hanging around her neck. "And I'm paging the on-call OB, then I'll help Meredith relieve herself."

Eli backed up. "We'll be right outside," he murmured, placing a trembling hand on Meredith's shoulder. "We're here. Just breathe, sweetheart."

Stepping outside the room into the hushed heaviness of the ER, Eli managed a shaky breath.

Vaguely aware of an intercom page and an orderly rolling an empty gurney, Eli stepped to a window that looked out on a courtyard, his eyes burning.

"We need to pray," he said.

"We need to prepare for surgery," Kate volleyed back.

"Surgery?" he gasped, blinking at her. "What are you—"

"She has every sign of an ectopic pregnancy."

He stared at her, digging into anything he knew about obstetrics—next to nothing—for what she meant. "Is that a tubal pregnancy?"

"Exactly. The pregnancy implanted somewhere other than a uterus, usually a fallopian tube"—she lifted her phone as if referencing it—"and that tube may have ruptured and she's bleeding internally. This is life-threatening."

He felt blood drain.

"Enough Dr. Google," he said, holding up a hand. "I need to pray. For this baby, for my daughter, for her very life."

"I know you do," she said, trying to lower a strained and tense voice. "But we need to be responsible here and not get wrapped up in hospital waiting. She needs immediate attention."

"She's getting it. She also needs immediate prayer. And right now, it's all I have."

She crossed her arms and sighed, looking around as if she'd find a nurse to help her make her point.

He narrowed his eyes at her, suddenly feeling kicked in the guts. "You've shut that door so tight, Kate, I don't even know if you can hear me anymore. If I lost this grandchild and my daughter in the same breath—and you, the woman I love, still won't even look at the possibility that God is real, that He could actually work a miracle—" His voice broke. "Then what are we even doing?"

Silence fell between them like a dropped stone. Kate blinked fast, once, but didn't speak.

Eli turned away, placing both hands on the windowsill. He bowed his head, not caring if she stayed or walked away or rolled her eyes.

Footsteps echoed, pulling his attention as a tall, dark-haired woman in scrubs moved briskly toward them, white coat flapping. Eli straightened.

"Are you the doctor?"

She smiled. "Yes, I'm Dr. Sabine. I'm the attending OB and I'll be taking care of Meredith, who I assume is..."

"My daughter. The nurse is helping her go to the bathroom," Eli said. "She didn't see anything on the abdominal ultrasound."

Dr. Sabine took a step to the door. "Why don't you wait out here while we do the transvaginal ultrasound. The minute we can, we'll let you in." She added a smile. "Breathe, Mr. Lawson. And, if you're that kind of man, pray. It always helps."

As she opened the door, he looked at Kate, who wore a wry, sad smile.

"Doctor's orders," he whispered.

She just sighed, a glint of emotion in her eyes.

He believed in miracles.

She didn't.

Who would be right this time?

WHEN THE DOOR OPENED AGAIN, Charlene walked out, looking very serious. "Dr. Sabine can talk to you now," she said.

Eli took Kate's hand and walked into the room, his gaze going straight to Meredith, pale and small.

Dr. Sabine snapped off her gloves and let out a sigh. "Meredith has a suspected ectopic pregnancy. It's likely ruptured."

Eli's stomach bottomed out. "What exactly does that mean?"

"Unfortunately, this pregnancy is not viable. The embryo implanted in her fallopian tube, not the uterus, posing a potential risk to her life," the doctor continued, calm and clinical. "It's rare, but serious. There's free fluid in the abdomen—we believe that's blood. Her vitals confirm internal bleeding. We need to operate immediately."

Eli felt himself swaying. Kate steadied him with one hand, even though her own face had drained of color.

"What exactly is the surgery?" he asked, vaguely aware that the nurse and another aide had returned.

"A laparoscopic procedure, if her condition remains stable. We'll remove the pregnancy and stop the bleeding. If possible, we'll preserve the fallopian tube.

Honestly, time is of the essence if there's been a rupture."

In other words, get out of our way and let us do our job, Eli thought. He was about to do just that when Meredith whimpered, her hand flailing slightly. Eli rushed to her side and caught it in his own.

"Daddy," she whispered, "I'm scared."

"You're going to be fine," he choked out. "I'm right here. I'm not leaving."

Charlene had already started the second IV. The aide gently placed an oxygen mask over Meredith's nose and mouth.

Dr. Sabine leaned in. "We're going to take you upstairs now, okay? You're in good hands."

Everything moved in a blur after that—orders called out, Meredith being wheeled down the hallway, her hand slipping from Eli's as the stretcher turned a corner and vanished through a swinging door.

He stood frozen for a moment, then felt Kate gently taking his hand.

"Come on," she said quietly. "The aide told me where to wait for the OR."

He wrapped his arms around her, suddenly aware of how much he wouldn't want to be doing this alone. This? This was why God gave a kid two parents, and despite their differences, he couldn't be more grateful for the rock that was Kate.

A few minutes later, they were situated in the waiting area outside the OR, where they sat with three other small groups of family members. After texting Jonah and calling Vivien and his mother, Eli sat in a beige leather chair, elbows on his knees, head bowed.

Kate paced, sat, paced, checked her phone, then sat again, leaning close to Eli.

"I take it there's no relationship with the father," she said softly.

"He is...was...a mistake. A liar. A distraction for a girl who works too hard. I swear I'm going to put her on paid leave this summer."

She smiled and nodded, taking his hand with one that was surprisingly shaky. She'd scrolled the internet too much, he decided, and knew things about this procedure and situation that he didn't want to know.

All he'd seen was something about "the leading cause of maternal death in the first trimester" and he'd shut that search engine down before he took his next breath.

"She's strong," Eli said finally, voice low. "And in good hands."

Kate nodded. "Definitely. That doctor knew exactly what she was doing."

"Yeah, but I didn't mean Dr. Sabine." He slid her a wry smile. "I meant God's hands."

Kate didn't answer.

He sat back, rubbing his palms over his face while a long silence stretched between them, filled only by the distant sounds of movement behind swinging doors. Then Eli turned, grasping her hand.

"I want you to know something," he said gently. "I don't believe because it's easy. It's not. Or because it always makes sense. It doesn't. I believe because time and time again, the Lord has proven His existence to me and made me know—I mean I *know*—that He loves me, He protects me, and He has saved me. That knowledge isn't some nebulous feeling. It's concrete and tangible, and the only thing that's held me together when the world didn't."

Kate looked away. "You think that's what's happening now? God is holding you together?"

"God...and you."

"Me?" A smile pulled. "I thought...well, I didn't think I mattered much in this scenario."

He drew back, blinking. "Kate. You're steady and strong and smart and...I love you."

"Oh." The words took all the fight out of her and brought some tears to her eyes. "Eli. I love you, too."

He put his arm around her and kissed her hair, tucking her closer. "And now I'm going to pray."

"Out loud?"

"Not if you don't want me to."

She was quiet, then slowly nodded. "Yes. I want to hear you. I want to...pray with you."

He closed his eyes and dropped his head, and felt her head bow, too.

"Father God, I don't know your plan, but I know that you work for good. I know you love Meredith even more than I do, that you loved her from when you knit her in her mother's womb. I ask that you heal her, protect her body for future babies. Whatever happens—"

Kate gasped and nudged him to look toward the door.

Eli turned to see Dr. Sabine coming toward them, scrub cap still on, her expression relaxed.

"It went very well," she said as they stood to greet her.

Eli heard a grunt of relief escape his lips.

"The fallopian tube hadn't ruptured completely," she added. "We were able to resolve the ectopic pregnancy and stop the bleeding with minimal intervention."

"Oh, thank God," Kate whispered.

"She's in recovery waking from anesthesia. The good news is we did not have to remove the tube," Dr. Sabine continued, her voice warm. "She still has both fallopian tubes, and she's entirely able to conceive and carry a child in the future, though we'll monitor her next pregnancy closely. Someone will come get you when she's awake."

Eli closed his eyes and nodded, still reeling from the fact that there wouldn't be a baby, but overwhelmed with gratitude that Meredith was okay.

"We caught it just in time," Dr. Sabine added. "You got her here fast. That made the difference."

"Thank you," Kate added, her voice hoarse. "Thank you so much."

Dr. Sabine nodded and walked away, leaving the door swinging slowly behind her as Eli dropped into his seat because he wasn't sure his legs could hold him.

Kate didn't sit down right away. She stood there, arms folded, staring at the empty hallway.

Then, she sank into the seat beside Eli and let out a breath that sounded like a sob.

"Well," she said. "I think...I might've just witnessed my first answered prayer."

Eli smiled. "It's a powerful moment."

She dropped back and put her glasses on, quiet and deep in thought. Then she turned to him and took his hand. "You're a good man, Eli Lawson."

He met her gaze. "Is there a 'but' at the end of that?" he asked, feeling his body tense again. "Like, 'But I can't love someone who prays?'"

She laughed softly. "No but. You're a good man. And someone I love very much told me I'd be a fool to give up a man because he's too good."

He regarded her, affection filling his heart. "I'm not... too good. I'm not even a little good. I just live by a book that has never steered me wrong."

She nodded slowly. "I'm starting to see that."

He reached to her and folded her in an embrace. "All I ask is that you keep an open mind and heart."

She kissed his cheek. "My mind is open. And my heart? Belongs to you."

Charlene came in, walking briskly across the waiting room. "Mr. and Mrs. Lawson? You can go see Meredith now."

They shared a look and a smile and a secret. They weren't Mr. and Mrs. Lawson, but Eli knew that God answered prayers and performed miracles. Nothing was impossible, right?

Chapter Twenty-three
Maggie

Maggie had never been one to command a room—at least not with storytelling. But here she was, shattering her own personal rule against airing dirty family laundry.

A late, casual dinner on the deck ended with Maggie regaling two virtual strangers with the history of this property. She told the story of how she was able to secretly keep it as part of a plea deal for her husband, and how Artie Wylie and Roger Lawson worked hand in hand with the FBI to take down a crime ring.

Gary and Sally Danes sat rapt, listening intently and fascinated by it all.

These were the same two people Maggie had intended to intimidate right out the door. But something in her heart didn't feel intimidating today, which was probably a sign of the End Times. Or perhaps it was proof that ten days on the road and a renewed friendship with Jo Ellen really had changed Magnolia Lawson.

Meredith's brush with death didn't help, either, and like everyone else, Maggie was keeping one eye on the door, anxious for her granddaughter to be brought home from her terrible ordeal at the hospital.

During the many hours since they'd left, the couple had become quite comfortable. Tessa, Vivien, and Jo came back from the boat ride, all concerned for Meredith. And even baby Atlas had been alert and adorable all day, clearly well cared for by his doting father.

They'd had an informal dinner on the deck, and the sun had set as Maggie wrapped up her story.

"Sadly, Roger passed away from a heart attack in prison, just weeks before he would have been set free to live a safe and normal life," she concluded, getting the expected reaction of shock and sadness.

There were stunned expressions all around—Jonah, Tessa, Jo Ellen, and Vivien—but not because the story surprised them. They'd all lived through it. Surely, they were astonished that she, the great lover of secrets, had shared a big one.

"My husband made mistakes," Maggie added softly. "But in the end, he did the right thing and so did your former professor, Artie."

Sally smiled. "I'm not surprised."

"Well, I am," Jonah said on a laugh, pointing to Maggie. "Not like you to, uh, overshare, Grandma."

She shrugged and shared a look with Jo Ellen. "People change, Jonah."

"Not that much," Tessa muttered, also eyeing her suspiciously.

Wanting the subject changed, Maggie stood and picked up the dessert tray. "We should be ready for Meredith to come home."

"And we should be leaving," Sally Danes said, but

even as she spoke, she clutched little sleeping Atlas closer.

"I'd like to speak with Jonah's father before we take off," Gary said, the words sounding a little ominous.

Jonah let out a long sigh and checked his phone. "They're five minutes away."

As Maggie walked back into the house and toward the kitchen, Vivien was next to her in a heartbeat.

"Okay, who stole my mother and replaced her with a truth-spilling raconteur?" Vivien asked in a hushed tone.

"What are you talking about?" Maggie put the tray down and bit back a smile, enjoying the fact that she could still keep her grown children guessing. "You all act like I've never held a conversation in my life."

"The Queen of the Nondisclosure just told complete strangers about Dad's life. You never talk about that to anyone—not even to us!"

She lifted a shoulder, which felt lighter lately. "It's a happy ending now," she said. "And they aren't strangers— they're family through blood."

Vivien eyed her suspiciously. "You're like a different person since you got back from that stay with the Cavallaris. What did you do for the last ten days? Go into therapy?"

Maggie let out a soft laugh. If therapy was a road trip, a stick shift, and a biker named Brick? Then, yes, she had. But some secrets had to stay buried.

"It must be Jo Ellen," she said. "She brings out a different side of me."

Vivien smiled wistfully. "She always has, Mom. I like it."

Maggie liked it, too. "Oh!" She put her hand on Vivien's arm. "Is that the garage? They're home. Let's slip her upstairs without having to talk to anyone." At Vivien's look, she added, "Not to keep secrets—they know. Just to help Meredith."

"I'll take her upstairs with Tessa and Kate, and we'll get her in bed. You run interference with the guests."

Maggie nodded and turned to the door to the garage just as it opened. Kate led the way, with a pale and sickly-looking Meredith behind her, leaning into Eli.

"Meredith," Vivien cooed, rushing to her.

"I'm fine," Meredith murmured. "Just need sleep."

"Let's get you upstairs." As Vivien guided her away, Kate followed, and Tessa came in. The three of them gathered around Meredith, gently urging her toward the stairs.

As they walked away, Meredith glanced back once—her eyes locking on Maggie for a brief moment. In that instance, Maggie saw a little fear and a lot of regret.

She had to let sweet Meredith know how much she loved her. But first, she had to deal with her son, who looked like he'd been run over by a truck.

Without speaking, Eli let Maggie wrap him in what she knew was a far-too-rare hug, holding tight to this consistently strong man. They stood silent like that for a good thirty seconds until he drew back.

"They're still here?"

She nodded. "Lovely people, Eli. We talked and

talked, they walked the beach, had dinner, and got very comfortable. They are ready to leave but Gary said he wanted to chat with you if he could."

Eli grimaced. "Not sure I have much of a fight left in me."

"There won't be a fight."

They both turned at Gary's voice, seeing him with Sally standing on the other side of the island. Jonah stood behind them, holding Atlas with Jo Ellen next to him.

"We were so glad to hear your daughter is doing well," Sally said. "That must have been terrifying and sad."

Eli nodded and took a step closer. "I'm sorry to interrupt our day with you."

"No apologies necessary," Gary said, giving a tight smile. "In fact"—he turned to look at Jonah—"if anyone should be doling them out, it's us."

Jonah's eyes flickered with surprise. "You?"

"We reacted in grief and shock after Carly died," he said, putting a hand on Jonah's shoulder. "We're still grieving and will be for a long time. But, as we just told you outside, it's clear that Atlas is in a good home, well-loved and cared for."

"You're a good father," Sally said to Jonah, voice catching. "And you must let go of any thought of being cursed. You couldn't control Carly. No one could. That was why we all loved her." She gave a sad smile and looked around at each face. "This family—what we've seen here, love in the midst of trauma, support and strength...it's everything we could hope for Atlas. We won't contest anything. We don't want to fight."

Maggie felt a sigh of relief escape as she watched the exchange.

"We give you a lot of credit, Eli," Gary added. "You're clearly the leader of this unusual household, and one who'll be a wonderful influence and a terrific grandfather."

"You'll share the honor," Eli said, coming around the island with arms outstretched.

Maggie watched the two men hug, aware of her eyes filling with tears. Before she got caught getting mushy, she stepped away while the hugfest unfolded.

Vivien, Tessa, and Kate were coming down the stairs just as she reached the bottom.

"Everything okay down here?" Vivien asked.

"Yes. They're not fighting. Apparently, they love a good dysfunctional family."

Tessa snorted softly.

"Can I see Meredith?" Maggie asked Vivien.

"Yes, but Mom..." Vivien hesitated, then lowered her voice. "She's been through a lot. Emotionally and physically. Go easy. She can't be judged for what happened."

"Would you all please stop muzzling me?" Maggie asked. "I've changed. Did you not just witness me baring the soft underbelly of this family like a Lifetime movie?"

Vivien laughed. "Okay. It's just that she loves you and is, you know, afraid of you."

"She has nothing to be afraid of," Maggie said, stepping by her. "I promise you."

She made her way upstairs to Meredith's bedroom, easing the door open. Meredith lay on the bed, eyes half-closed, a bottle of water on the nightstand.

"Hello, my favorite grandchild."

Meredith moaned but it sounded like a laugh. "Don't tell Nolie."

Relieved to hear she still had her sense of humor, Maggie walked to the bed and sat on the edge. "Can I visit with you for a moment?"

"If you can stand me."

"Stop it." Maggie took her hand and folded her lovely fingers in her own wrinkled and spotted ones. "You scared me," she whispered.

It took a second, but Meredith sat up a little, wincing in pain but settling against a stack of pillows that her caretakers must have set up for her.

"I thought you'd be so disappointed in me," she said. "I hate to disappoint you."

"You hate to disappoint anyone," Maggie said. "That's what drives you."

Meredith narrowed her green eyes, her expression so like her mother—a woman Maggie had truly liked and mourned. "Well, I managed to disappoint everyone this time, including myself."

Maggie brushed her hand gently down Meredith's arm. "You set the bar too high."

"I don't think there was a bar," Meredith said. "Just a low point in my life and I tripped over it."

"Are you sad?" Maggie asked.

"I started to get excited about a baby," Meredith

admitted after a moment. "But the situation wasn't ideal, and I guess someone—or my body—knew that. I'd really rather, you know, meet Mr. Right, fall in love, do things the proper way."

"You will," Maggie assured her, her voice rich with conviction. "If you stop working so hard."

Meredith looked up, a question in her eyes.

"I mean it," Maggie said. "Take some time for you, dear one. Stay here and have a little fun. Recover, rest, and have a good long look at your life."

She blinked, obviously not expecting that advice. "But who am I if I am not...Miss Perfect, the over-achiever?"

Maggie just smiled. "Maybe it's time to find out."

Meredith looked down, her fingers twisting the hem of the blanket.

"I'm not saying give up your ambition," Maggie added. "But maybe...reframe it. Make rest part of your success. Make room for peace."

"I don't know how."

"You'll learn. I am."

"Oh, Grandma." She leaned forward, arms out. "I'm really sorry if I put you through anything today."

"All you did was remind me how much I love you." As they hugged, a low, familiar rumble echoed from outside.

Maggie stiffened with a sharp intake of breath. She felt her eyes flash as she stood to walk to the window that looked out the front.

"He wouldn't," she muttered.

"You expecting someone?" Meredith asked.

She let out a relieved grunt at the sight of a beloved candy-apple red T-bird. "It's Frank and Betty, bringing back our bags," she said, then her heart stopped.

They would march right into the house and tell everyone everything.

"I'll be back," she said, whipping around. "I need to—"

"It's fine. I want to sleep."

Maggie stole one second to lean over Meredith and kiss her head. "I love you. I don't think I've told you that often enough."

"I love you, too. But..." Her granddaughter looked up with teary eyes, then they narrowed in suspicion. "What's gotten into you?"

"Life," she whispered without hesitation.

On a chuckle, she breezed out of the room and made her way down the stairs, hearing the conversation still going in the kitchen. Jo Ellen came darting out, eyes wide.

"Frank's here!" They spoke in perfect unison, then joined hands to head outside and stop Frank and Betty before her family found out she'd been gallivanting around Florida like a teenager on spring break.

"How could you?" Betty climbed out of the sports car with rage in her eyes, bringing Jo Ellen and Maggie to a dead stop halfway down the stairs to the driveway.

"How could we what?" Jo Ellen muttered under her breath.

"I guess Betty's mad that we made her dreams come true," Maggie said, straightening her spine. "That's a little ungrateful."

"Let's find out."

Hand-in-hand, they crossed the pavers. The sun had set behind them, casting a golden light on Betty's slightly red face.

Maggie squinted at her. Was that from rage or radiation? Was this the cancer finally showing itself?

Betty didn't give them a chance to ask.

"I cannot believe the two of you went along with this cockamamie scheme," she snapped, jabbing a finger toward the T-bird. "What were you thinking?"

Jo Ellen blinked. "Um...that it was your dream car and Frank asked us to help surprise you?"

Betty turned slowly toward her husband with a glare that could have stripped wallpaper. "*My* dream car? Really, Frank?"

He looked sheepish, rubbing the back of his neck. "I thought you'd love it."

"You thought *I'd* love it?" Her voice rose an octave. "You thought a little red speed trap with no cupholders and a trunk the size of a cereal box would make me swoon? You probably thought it'd make you look so sexy I'd do more of...you know."

"Betty," Frank hissed, glancing up toward the house. "There are people—"

"Well, it didn't!" she exclaimed. "You know what

this bad decision *did* do? It made me throw my back out when you stalled three times between here and Santa Rosa Beach. You can't even drive a stick shift, Frank!"

Maggie's mouth opened, closed, and opened again. "We, uh, we thought it was what you wanted. You know, before you...uh..."

"Before I what?" Betty narrowed her eyes.

Jo Ellen shot Maggie a look that said *don't you dare.*

Maggie stammered. "Before you...had to slow down?"

Betty's hands flew to her hips. "Because I'm old?"

"No!" Maggie said quickly. "Because you're sick."

A pause. Frank's eyes widened. Betty's jaw dropped.

Jo Ellen stepped in, voice gentle. "We know you're not telling people. We saw the medications. We saw how tired you looked. We figured it was serious. Life-threatening, even."

Betty blinked. "Serious?"

Maggie nodded. "The pills, the hugging at the chemo center—"

Betty let out a choking noise that sounded like a laugh and a scoff collided mid-throat. "My *meds*? That was for a UTI!"

Maggie blinked. "Excuse me?"

"A urinary tract infection. Which I wouldn't have gotten if my husband wasn't so...you know. *Busy.*"

Frank turned crimson. "Betty."

"Well, it's true! We were trying to spice things up. He read an article in *AARP* magazine and the next thing you know, I'm pretending to be a French maid."

Jo Ellen looked like she'd seen a ghost. "Wait. Are you telling me all this drama was over a UTI?"

Betty folded her arms. "Blame him."

"But the chemo place!" Maggie choked the words. "We saw you *hugging and crying* at a cancer center!"

Betty rolled her eyes. "My friend Miriam from old-lady Pilates started chemo and asked me to go with her. I decided to bring her my Italian wedding cookies—people loved them, so I visit with a couple dozen every week. I made friends. We lost one. It got emotional. Wait. You thought I had *cancer?*"

"Well! Yes!" Maggie sputtered. "Why else would Frank order us on a covert car pickup mission to Miami?"

"Because he's ridiculous," Betty said. "And because he wanted to feel like James Bond again, I guess. Just call him Goldfinger."

Maggie glared at him. "Good grief, Frank. You're eighty-five. Doesn't the statute of limitations on sex run out at seventy-nine?"

"Apparently not," Jo muttered.

"I'm just stunned," Maggie said. "All this time we were worried sick about you."

"Well, I *was* sick," Betty said. "Just not, you know, *that* sick."

There was a long beat of silence.

Then Maggie felt a smile pull, her gaze moving from the crazy couple to the car. That car. That beautiful, liberating, fear-killing car.

"Well, I don't care," she said. "It was fun."

Betty blinked. "Driving this roller-skate with a motor

was fun? I barely fit, and Frank has absolutely no idea how to get into second gear."

"I'll teach you," Maggie said, turning to Frank. "You gotta move the gas, clutch, and shift like a choreographed dance."

"Who taught you that?" Frank asked.

"Oscar," Maggie answered, making Jo Ellen snort.

"No, no," Frank said quickly. "I'm getting rid of it. Whole thing was a bad idea."

"*Getting rid of it?*" Maggie's voice pitched higher. "You can't do that! It's the best car in the world!"

"It was...folly," he admitted.

"Folly?" She laid her hand reverently on the hood. "This car transformed me. I changed lanes without white knuckles. I learned how to shift gears and let go of fear. I stood up for myself, I got arrested, I danced with a biker named Brick—"

Betty gasped. "You *what?*"

"It's a long story," Jo Ellen said, grinning.

Maggie looked at them again, her heart full. "This car reminded me I'm not done yet. That there are still adventures to be had. It's more than a car—it's a second chance."

Frank and Betty exchanged a long look, one of those wordless, weary-but-loving glances only decades of marriage could perfect. Betty finally gave a small, reluctant nod.

Frank reached into his pocket and pulled out the keys.

"After what Roger and Artie did for us—protecting

me, making sure I didn't end up in prison for running the books—I owe you both. This is the least we can do." He dangled the keys that Maggie knew like they were her own. "The car is yours, ladies. Take good care of her."

Jo Ellen sucked in a breath. Maggie froze.

Was Frank really offering her the very thing she knew was missing in her life? And could she just accept it and the change it meant? Could she be the woman that Brick saw when he grinned at her? The woman who flew down the interstate, unburdened by fear?

Yes, she realized with a jolt. She already was that woman. And this car might not be Betty's dream, but it turned out to be Maggie's.

"Well?" Frank asked, shaking the keys.

Maggie snatched them from his hands as she and Jo squealed like teenagers and lunged to hug Frank and Betty at the same time, arms colliding in a tangled, emotional mess of laughter and joy.

"Thank you," Maggie whispered, pulling Betty into a tight embrace. "We'll take you for a joyride."

Betty touched her face, unexpected tears in her eyes. "You look like you've already been on one," she said. "I'm happy for you, Mags."

"Well, we're not just driving this thing around town," Jo Ellen announced. "We've got plans. Road trips. Adventures. Maybe a few parking lot donuts. Well, as soon as you get your license renewed."

"And we're naming her," Maggie declared, looking at Jo Ellen. Her friend just tipped her head knowingly, and they said the name in perfect unison.

"Scarlett."

Frank groaned. "You two are going to be unbearable."

"We already are," Jo Ellen said sweetly. "But now we're mobile."

Maggie flipped the keys in Jo Ellen's face with a teasing look. "I say we take Scarlett to Charleston next."

"Where Rhett was born," Jo Ellen said.

Laughing, they hugged.

"See? I paid attention to that endless movie," Jo added as a whisper in her ear.

Maggie just squeezed her friend and felt whole and excited for life. She might not have that many years left, but she was going to make every one of them count.

Chapter Twenty-four
Tessa

She was early for the house showing Lorna had scheduled, but curiosity made Tessa drive the fifteen-minute distance to Miramar Beach with a little more speed than usual. Her real estate agent had said she had a beautiful surprise—a dream property that hadn't even hit the market yet.

The "pocket listing" wasn't like anything they'd seen so far, Lorna promised, and she wanted Tessa to tour it as soon as possible.

Tessa turned off the main highway and started driving directly toward the Gulf. Each block she passed made her more certain she couldn't possibly have the right address—how could she afford to live this close to the beach?

And not any beach, she realized as she reached the very end of the side street and could see the sand, water, and sky. A public beach! One that years ago she'd helped some teenagers clean, she thought with a smile.

But even better, one that featured a rare stretch of Destin's coastline without wall-to-wall houses built to block the view—or save it for the lucky or wealthy.

She turned and followed the beach road, the Gulf

shimmering on her left like someone had tossed diamonds and sunshine from heaven. When the phone chirped that she'd "arrived," she had to double- and triple-check the address.

This *couldn't* be the right house, not for her budget. Did "pocket listing" translate to *half price?*

The house was two stories with an oddly flat roof. The blue paint on the clapboard was sun-faded and the trim was weathered and chipped, but it looked like the entire back of the house included two large decks facing the water.

And the view! It wasn't peek-a-boo Gulf glimpses or turn-your-head-the-right-way-on-Tuesday-and-maybe-catch-a-sunset. This was full-on direct ocean glory. The kind of view people paid millions for. The kind of view she didn't even dare to want or dream of affording.

"Why would Lorna bring me here?" she murmured to herself as she found the small side driveway made of crushed shells and gravel. She parked and climbed out slowly, staring at the house like it might vanish if she moved too fast.

But there it stood, on a small lot, one of three older homes that hadn't been gobbled up and razed for bigger, better, and even more expensive houses.

Likely built after Hurricane Opal, this place had character and stories in its bones. And unless Lorna had misunderstood Tessa's entire budget and brain, it was completely unattainable.

Maybe there was something inside that she wanted Tessa to see. She did say she had a surprise.

She walked up to the door, peeking through the window before knocking. The door opened to reveal Lorna, barefoot and beaming.

"Location, location, location," she sang. "Am I right?"

"I think the expression is budget, budget, budget," Tessa replied with the same tune. "Or am I in the wrong place?"

"You're in exactly the right place," Lorna said with a wink. "Come in."

The first floor was cool and quiet. A wide-open living area flowed into a modest kitchen, all in need of updating but full of potential. Beyond the French doors was a small deck with a plunge pool and a view that made Tessa stop mid-step.

"Oh, wow," she breathed. The Gulf looked close enough to kiss. "This is... I mean, I love it. But it's—"

"Let me show you the rest first," Lorna said briskly, motioning her down the hallway.

Sure, just take this kid into the candy store, hungry and penniless. "Okay," she said instead.

Two bedrooms, both with big windows and bad tile flooring with wretched old grout. A tiny office that would be adorable with the right light fixture and several coats of fresh paint. A laundry room that needed...prayer.

But that *view.* That impossible gorgeousness could be seen from every window that looked across the beach road and straight to the sand and sea.

"This is really something," Tessa said, her heart pinging against her ribs. "But...I definitely can't afford this."

Lorna didn't argue, just smiled. "The upstairs is almost an exact replica, though there's carpet, which is heinous, and no laundry, but a second bathroom. The stairs are here, behind this door."

She urged her toward a closed door in the kitchen.

"I can't look at any more," Tessa said, holding back as Lorna opened the door. "There's no way—"

"I can't afford this, Lorna." A muffled and familiar masculine voice finished her sentence, accompanied by footfalls on stairs.

Tessa froze.

Dusty stepped through the doorway, phone in one hand, a skeptical expression on his face that melted instantly into shock.

They stared at each other.

Tessa's heart stopped. Or maybe stuttered. Possibly did a full-on backflip.

"Hi," she said, because her brain had been replaced with tapioca pudding.

"Hey," he said, equally dazed.

"I...I didn't see your truck."

"She told me to park across the street in the beach lot."

They both turned to Lorna who gave a playful cringe-face. "Yeah, I, uh...did that. But doesn't it make sense?"

Absolutely nothing made sense right then, especially not the presence of a man Tessa hadn't stopped thinking about since they said goodbye. Certainly not the splash of attraction and longing and sheer happiness at the sight of him—that made zero sense.

"You're having us bid against each other?" Tessa asked, stepping back to let Dusty into the kitchen. "Because you will have multiple offers on this place."

He just looked confused and pointed toward the upstairs. "Are these...two different listings?" Dusty asked.

Lorna shook her head, looking entirely too conspiratorial and maybe a little delighted with herself.

"It's one property," she said. "Two units—upper and lower that can be lived in, rented, renovated, shared, invested, whatever. But the owner only wants to sell to a single buyer, with one contract, one bank mortgage, and a thirty-day close if possible. That's why it's not on the market yet."

They both stared at her, no doubt reciting the same questions—who, when, why, and *how much*? But they were silent, waiting for more.

"You *can* afford it," she said to both of them. "*If* you buy it together. It'll be at the high end of each of your budgets, but it's entirely doable as a co-purchase."

"A co..."

"What?"

"Just hear me out," Lorna said, holding up two hands. "I mean, you don't have to be related or married or anything like that. Just buy it together, with both names on the contract, and one loan from the bank. You can have separate living quarters—well, you'll share the laundry. But won't that make wash day more fun?"

They stayed slack-jawed and silent.

"Okay, well, it's totally possible, doable, and if you don't buy this property, you are out of your minds," Lorna finished. "I'll let you look some more, walk around, discuss. Oh, here's the price."

She held out a listing sheet and both of them stared at the upper right corner. Yes, they *could* do that...together.

Lorna pivoted and headed toward the door and slid on her sandals. "Take your time. I'm going to make some calls, and I really hope one of them can be to the listing agent, who has agreed to cut her commission if I can get an offer in today."

Today?

She walked out humming, leaving them alone and speechless.

"Well," Dusty finally said on a huffed-out breath he'd clearly been holding for a while. "You wanna see the upstairs?"

Did she?

Nervously rolling the listing sheet, she nodded. "I guess. I'm a little..."

"Yeah. I am, too," he said on a laugh. "Come on."

She followed him up the narrow stairway—yes, the disgusting carpet would have to go—which opened up to a living area much like the one below. Except the view up here was even more astounding.

Turning, she tried to take it in—both units were essentially apartments and they'd been rented hard. But the bones were spectacular and the price...

She glanced at the sheet. They were asking twice her high end. But with Dusty...

"Much the same in the back," he said. "But come and look at this. You can't get here from the lower unit."

He opened a door that was in the same place as the one in the downstairs kitchen, but this opened to concrete stairs and...sky.

As she climbed, longing clutched her throat. "This is..." She stepped onto a rooftop deck, automatically reaching for sunglasses she'd left in the car. "Bright."

"Beautiful," he said, turning to a nearly three-sixty-degree view from the water to town.

"Sunsets would be stupendous," she whispered.

"And night skies out of this world," he added.

"This is...unbelievable."

He nodded, still taking it in. "Nothing like it in Destin. At least, not for us."

Us. The word hung on the air and nearly choked her.

"C'mon," he said, ushering her to a round table with an open umbrella and two metal chairs the owner had placed up there. "Let's...discuss."

Sitting in the shade, they both laughed awkwardly, neither one knowing where to start.

"She's tricky, that Lorna," he finally said. "I gotta give her props for...orchestration."

"And an amazing house unlike anything we've seen before."

They were quiet for a long moment. She glanced at the paper, the view, then him, realizing that he hadn't taken his eyes off her.

"I've missed you," he admitted softly. "Probably more than I should."

"You're allowed to miss people. Even when you're scared."

He shrugged. "And I'm not in Vermont."

"I noticed."

"I decided not to run," he said. "But I didn't want to stay if it meant hurting you."

"And I didn't want to fall if it meant waiting around for someone who wasn't sure."

They looked at each other, the sound of a child laughing on the beach and a few cars passing the only noise besides Tessa's pounding heart.

"This house..." he began.

"It's crazy," she finished.

"But it's also..." He trailed off.

"Kind of perfect," she whispered.

He nodded. "Should we even talk about it?"

Biting her lip, she nodded.

"We wouldn't be roommates," he said. "Just... house-mates. Sharing a roof. A view. Some drywall headaches because, *oof*, this place has me wanting to haul out my tools. But we could do upstairs-downstairs two-unit living."

"Someone gets a laundry room and pool," she said, not even believing they were having this conversation.

"The other one gets this..." He gestured toward the stunning rooftop. "Would that be so bad?"

"Well, whoever got this would have to share," she said.

"And whoever got the laundry would also have to share."

After a long beat, he inched closer. "It could work, Tessa."

Her chest rose with a breath so tight it could burst her lungs. "I'd want...ground rules."

"I'd want renovations," he replied.

"I don't want free therapy," she added.

"And I don't want..."

"A relationship," she finished when he didn't.

"Not what I was going to say," he whispered. "I don't want...to miss out on something amazing because I'm healing from all I've been through."

She regarded him, swallowing hard as he took her hand and pressed both of his around it. "I'm going to say it again, Tessa. I've missed you."

"What does that mean?"

"That I can't stop thinking about you. I wake up wondering what you're doing. I want to kick myself for being a fool—which is how I think we'd both feel if we don't at least...try."

"Try...us or this house?"

He just smiled.

"What about you?" he asked. "Have you stopped thinking about me?"

"When I'm asleep."

That made him laugh but it faded as he looked into her eyes.

"Dusty..." She tried to ease back, tried to not have those dark eyes magnetically draw her closer. "I haven't changed what I want. If anything, I'm more certain. I'm not playing or cohabitating or being someone's good time."

He nodded. "I know that."

She studied him and looked around again, weirdly feeling...at home. "What if we just buy the house and each take a floor and...see what happens?"

"Yes," he said. "We can't miss out on this opportunity, Tessa. It comes along once in a lifetime, could be the best thing we ever did, and I have a really, really good feeling about it."

Once again, she didn't know if he meant the house or...them. And right then, she didn't want to.

"Should we make an offer?" she asked on a shaky whisper.

"Yes."

They both stood at the same time. He reached out his arms and she pressed her hands to her lips to keep from squealing.

"Really?" She asked.

"Really." He pulled her into him. "And we have to hug on it."

She did, melting into the embrace, but then she drew back, narrowing her eyes. "You want the laundry and pool or the rooftop deck?"

"I want the housemate, and she can pick where she lives."

"Okay," she agreed. "But you have to do my renovations before yours."

"Tessa, you drive a hard bargain."

She just laughed and slipped her hand into his, walking toward the stairs. "Let's go tell Lorna she nailed it."

At the top of the stairs, they hugged again. Standing

in the sunshine with the Gulf surf providing the background music, Tessa rested her head against Dusty's shoulder.

"I've never owned a home," she whispered.

"I've never...been so hopeful."

She closed her eyes and leaned into him because it was time to let go and try something completely new.

Yes, we promise there are more heartwarming and delightful stories in The Destin Diaries series! *The Summer We Let Go,* book five, brings change in the salt air, hope on the horizon, and more happy tears and tender moments in store for the Wylies and the Lawsons!

Want to know the minute you can preorder the next book? Sign up for our newsletters and you'll get an announcement in your email. (We only send newsletters for new releases or major announcements!)

https://www.hopeholloway.com/newsletter-signup

https://www.ceceliascott.com/newsletter-signup

Can't wait for the next book? We've got lots more to read...

Other family saga beach reads by
Hope Holloway and Cecelia Scott

Hope Holloway

Coconut Key
Shellseeker Beach
Seven Sisters

∾

Cecelia Scott

Sweeney House
Young at Heart

∾

Collaborations by Hope and Cecelia

Carolina Christmas
The Destin Diaries

∾

Visit www.hopeholloway.com and www.ceceliascott.com
for details about all of their books!

About The Authors

Hope Holloway is the author of charming, heartwarming women's fiction featuring unforgettable families and friends, and the emotional challenges they conquer. After more than twenty years in marketing, she launched a new career as an author of beach reads and feel-good fiction. A mother of two adult children, Hope and her husband of thirty years live in Florida. When not writing, she can be found walking the beach with her two rescue dogs, who beg her to include animals in every book. Visit her site at www.hopeholloway.com.

Cecelia Scott is an author of light, bright women's fiction that explores family dynamics, heartfelt romance, and the emotional challenges that women face at all ages and stages of life. Her debut series, Sweeney House, is set on the shores of Cocoa Beach, where she lived for more than twenty years. Her books capture the salt, sand, and spectacular skies of the area and reflect her firm belief that life deserves a happy ending, with enough drama and surprises to keep it interesting. Cece currently resides in north Florida with her husband and beloved kitty. Visit her site at www.ceceliascott.com

www.ingramcontent.com/pod-product-compliance
Lightning Source LLC
Chambersburg PA
CBHW051434190726
48289CB00001B/183